OWEN

THE COUNTERPUNCH SERIES
BOOK TWO

K.J. ELLIS

Owen

Published by K.J Ellis

© Copyright 2021 by K.J Ellis

All rights reserved.

This book is a work of fiction. Names, places, songs and incidents are the product of the author's imagination or are used fictitiously. Any resemblance to actual events, locales or persons, living or dead is coincidental.

Written By- K.J Ellis

Edits By - Eleanor-Lloyd-Jones at Shower Of Schmidt Editing

Formatting By – Lou Stock at LD Designs

Cover By- Eleanor-Lloyd-Jones at Shower Of Schmidt Designs

DEDICATION

For my Book Bitch Emma, plain and simple.
You fell in love with Owen from the start of this series
and he's come to life because of your help and support.
This one is for you.

ACKNOWLEDGEMENTS

First and foremost, I want to thank my son and my partner.

I've given up so much of my free time for this book that you both no doubt felt left out and for that, I'm truly sorry.

Logan, thank you for being an extremely well-behaved boy for me when Mummy was 'working' as you now call it. I promise I will make it up to you. I love you all the worldy, around the moon, the stars and back again.

Adam, I love you with all my heart, till the end of time and will continue to do so after that.

Lou Stock, for formatting Owen. Your formatting skills are second to none. You've done an amazing job; I couldn't be happier with the outcome. Thank you so much.

Eleanor, for taking every idea I threw at you and my God there were a fair few. You created exactly what I wanted with this cover. I love it. You're amazing and one hell of a talented lady. I'm looking forward to seeing what else we can create together in the future. You're a bloody star, especially for putting up with me. Not only that but your editing skills are spot on. Thank you.

My book bitch, Emma freaking Lloyd. You, girl, have been my absolute rock through this. No matter the time, day or night, you've always been there, whether it be to kick my arse, encourage me to get those words down or just to listen to my ideas. Owen's book wouldn't have been finished if it wasn't for you and you bloody well know this. The way you've supported me throughout the whole written process of this one while I've been struggling with morning sickness will not be taking for granted and it hasn't gone unnoticed. I thank you from the bottom of my heart for putting up with me, but more importantly, your friendship which has blossomed over the past two years.

My beta tarts, Nikki Young, Fiona Jones, Joy Westerfield, and Gemma Evans. Each and every one of you have helped me so much to make this book what it is today. I appreciate the time you all took out of your days to read for me. Thank you.

My ARC Team. You all know who you are. Thank you for your kind and motivating words, whether they were in a written review or in a message. It means the world to me that you enjoyed reading my book. Thank you so much.

And last but by no means least, to you, my readers. Thank you for your patience's with this book. Trying to write through morning sickness and bad days was not fun, but knowing it was for you and that you were all just as excited about Owen as me, made it more enjoyable. I hope the wait was worth it and you enjoy Owen story.

xx

PROLOGUE
OWEN

9 Years ago

"**H**ey, what you up to, Isaak?" I announce my presence as I walk through the gate of his house, entering the garage that is a makeshift gym for when he's training at home and not his dad's gym.

He looks up from the punching bag he's currently pounding away on and gives me a swift nod of his sweaty head.

"What's it look like I'm doing?" He puffs out in between throwing jabs, making the chains that attach the bag to the ceiling rattle. The look of concentration on his face and the sweat dripping off of him tells me he's been at this for a while.

"How long have you been out here for?" I ask, taking a hold of the swinging bag. He delivers one last thundering jab and sucks in a deep breath. The impact from the punch forces me to step back with the bag.

"Not long enough. I need to be on the top of my game if I wanna get anywhere with my boxing career. I need to get recognised as soon as I can. I need out of this shit hole, Owen." He grabs a towel that is off to the side of him and wipes it over his face and shoulders, getting rid of the sweat that's collected on his skin.

"Mate, the way you're going, you'll make pro in no time."

Isaak is a year older than me. I'm eighteen; he's nineteen. He's been training to become a professional boxer for as long as I've known him, which is nearly ten years. Living around the corner from each other, we've always been close and the older we've got, the more time we've spent together.

"Maybe, but I need to be the best I can be." He throws the wet towel at me, laughing when it hits me smack bang in the middle of my face.

He makes his way over to the weights bench, lays back and starts lifting. God knows what he's lifting anymore. It's always more than the last time I've seen him. Don't get me wrong, I work out in the gym with him most days, but his routine is off the charts compared to mine. I'm physically fit and toned. That's enough for me.

"Where's your dad?" Usually when Isaak is going at it hard in here, his dad is there pushing him on.

"Inside. My Uncle Benny decided to make a surprise appearance." The disgust and venom lacing his voice tells me everything I need to know. Isaak and his dad don't get on with Benny, especially since his mum left his dad for his Uncle Benny.

"You want some water bringing back out?" I ask over my shoulder, already making my way inside. I'm practically family now. I come and go from this house as if it were my own. Isaak and his father have said as much.

"Yeah, please. There's some in the fridge. They should be cold enough now."

I enter the house, navigating my way through the living room and into the kitchen. Opening the fridge, I grab two bottles of ice cold water and kick the door shut with my foot. As I'm walking back, I hear voices coming from down the hall where Gavin's office is located. It's loud enough to make me pause. Then I hear Isaak's name being mentioned, which gets my ears pricking up.

"Isaak, is my son. There is no way I'm allowing you to do this. Over my dead body, Benny," Gavin's voice bellows, making my eyes bulge out of their sockets. I've never heard him sound so menacing and threatening.

"We had a deal, Gav," Benny speaks, cool as a cucumber.

"That was before everything else that has happened—before you stole my wife from me, taking a mother away from her son. The deal is off. End of!" Gavin spits back.

I don't know why, but my feet are moving in the direction of their voices instead of running in the opposite direction.

"Isaak is off the table completely, Benny. I'll find you someone else—someone better." I get the impression he is pacing as I hear the scuff of his shoes on the carpet.

I stop dead in my tracks when I reach the door. It's ajar. I just make out Benny standing tall and Gavin slumped down in his black leather chair.

"You're telling me you know someone who is, or can be, better than Isaak?"

"Yes. Give me some time and I'll sort it out. But this is the last night, Benny. I mean it: no more."

"You have two weeks to find them and begin training them," Benny demands.

"Fuck off, Benny. I know how this shit works. I helped you start the fucking club up, don't forget."

"I'll be in touch, little brother."

Shit. Fuck.

I sprint off as fast as my numb and trembling legs will take me.

What the fuck have I just witnessed?

Isaak is off the table?

What fucking club?

Find someone else and train them?

Little did I know that the someone else would be me.

CHAPTER 1

OWEN

Present day

Risking a side glance to Devon outside the church, I see how happy she looks.

We'd been asked by Isaak and Remme to be Godparents to their beautiful boy, Logan Axel, to which we both said yes.

It had made sense for us to share a car to the church, and having her so close to me, caused my mouth to water. Never before has a woman given me the urge to undress them for a second time—once has always been enough—but with Devon, I can't seem to help myself.

But I'm a playboy. I've never had to deal with any feelings before—never thought I would need to.

Seems Devon has affected me more than I thought she possibly could.

I wait outside the church for her to get a move on, and as I take a step to see if she is ready, she spots me and smiles before making her way to me. She throws a wave over her shoulder as she parts ways with everyone else until we all meet up again at Isaak's and Remme's house where the celebrations will continue, swaying her hips in the body-hugging Cadbury-purple dress she's wearing. It shows off all her womanly curves—curves I've explored every inch off with my hands and mouth a few times before.

Like I said, this is a first for me. Only Devon has me craving for more.

I find myself having to adjust my trousers.

"You okay, Owen?" she asks as she passes me and heads to the passenger side of my Porsche 911 GT2 RS.

Does she notice the effect she's having on me? I fucking hope not. That's all I need. The thought sours my mood instantly. I've said it a thousand time before: I'm a fuck 'em and chuck 'em kinda guy.

"Yeah, good. You getting in the car or standing there all day?" I ask her with far more attitude than I intended before jumping in the car myself, not waiting for her to give me an answer.

She yanks the door open, slamming it closed again when she's seated, making me wince and grit my teeth.

My poor car is getting a right beating.

"Jesus, someone has their boxers on too fucking tight. Chill your beans," she shouts across at me while slipping the seatbelt on and clipping it in place.

I chose to ignore her, fasten my own seatbelt then put the car into drive.

The silence is short lived.

"Are we going to talk about what happened between us, Owen?" She speaks out of nowhere, making me grip the steering wheel harder, turning my knuckles white.

"There's nothing to talk about," I state, not even giving her a side glance.

"So that's it then? You fuck me more than once, as and when you wanted to with no regards to my feelings and no explanation as to why? Not only that, but I'm stupid enough to let it keep happening."

"It wasn't like that, Dev." I try to explain to her, but I just don't know how to. I'm not good with shit like this. Usually, I don't have to have this conversation with the women I fuck. This is also one of the reasons why I don't fuck women I know: it just complicates everything.

"Like what? The fact you got what you wanted from me, then as soon as you get a better offer, you just cast me aside? I know you, Owen. I know you never have sex with the same woman twice, but I thought you'd at least have some fucking respect towards them after. Towards me. But no, clearly I was wrong about you."

"Hey, you don't know a single thing about me. You see what I let you see. Nothing more; nothing less."

"Whatever. Just forget this whole conversation," she firmly states.

"Fine with me." I'm getting more and more irritated with every passing second, and I don't understand why. She just basically told me what I wanted to tell her myself. So why do I have a dull ache in the pit of my stomach that's shot up out of nowhere? I know why. It's because I'm not the one saying it. I'm on the receiving end of it for a change and I don't like it.

The rest of the car journey is spent in silence—an understated awkward silence.

Arriving outside of Isaak and Remme's place, I can't undo my seatbelt and get out of the car quick enough. Devon is faster. She is out and walking away from me without a backwards glance. Thinking nothing else about the discussion we've just had, I head towards the door, hearing the revs and roars of Saxon's car pulling up behind me. No sooner has the car stopped, Charlotte is out of it and running inside the house before me.

The front door is already open when I reach it, courtesy of Charlotte leaving it like that, and I spot Isaak so walk in his direction.

"Isaak, how's it going?" I close the door behind me and walk further inside as he pulls me in for a man hug. The door goes again immediately, any conversation with him halted for now.

"I'll get it," he shouts over his shoulder for Remme to hear.

Everyone else piles into the house and hellos and hugs are exchanged.

Remme ushers everyone into the entertainment room, and Isaak follows them. I race around them all for one of the best seats. As I get myself comfy, Isaak stands tall and proud with Remme at his side and Logan bouncing around in his chair at their feet.

Isaak whispers something in his wife's ear, and Remme says something back to him but with the hustle of everyone moving and talking, I can't make it out. They're definitely about to tell us something, that much I can tell.

"Can I have your attention, please?" Isaak calls, addressing the room and grabbing everyone's attention.

"Remme and I want to thank you all for coming, even though I know family rules have forced some of you to attend." Laughter fills the air. "But today isn't just about Logan being christened. Today we have other news to share." He places his free hand on Remme's tummy, admiration in his eyes. "My wife and I are four months pregnant with our second child."

I feel the corner of my mouth lifting up in a timid smile. Why does this not surprise me? They are like fucking rampant rabbits that pair.

I happen to glance over to where I know Devon is sitting to find her gawking at me. As quick as I am to catch her eye, she's quicker to look away again.

What was that all about?

I stand from my chair, offering my best mate and the love of his life a small congratulations. I'm pleased for them both, I really am, but that doesn't mean I'm overly fond of the lovey-dovey shit that's going on.

Not only that, I have other things on my mind—things I know will come and bite me in the arse. It's only a matter of time.

I'm making small talk with Bruce and Vinny when I spot Isaak and Saxon over by the door, talking. Trying to listen to what's being said by Bruce as well as looking at what the pair of nancies over there are talking about is hard work.

My suspicions are only amplified when they both head in the same direction and the door gets pulled closed. Looking around me, it seems I'm the only person who's noticed something is going on with those two.

I try to finish up my conversation without being rude or attracting too much attention and risk halting whatever Isaak and Sax are clearly up to. When it's appropriate to excuse myself, I head over to the door discreetly as I hear a voice I've come to dread, and that makes every inch of my skin crawl.

"Relax. I'm not here for you, Isaak. I'm here for that best mate of yours. I'm here for Owen."

I guess my time has run out and that bite in the arse has come way too soon for my liking, and typically it has to be today—unless Benny planned it this way. I wouldn't put it past him; he likes the element of surprise.

I need to sort this out before he has a chance to tell Isaak too much, and not only that, I don't want him ruining Remme's or Logan's day.

I slide myself through the door, closing it quietly behind me again.

"Benny!"

Everyone's heads crane my way and every set of eyes drill into me, all for different reasons.

"Owen, you're a hard man to get hold of." Benny's sickly, over-confident voice reaches my ears making my feet move forwards.

"Now is not the time or place, Benny," I declare through gritted teeth.

"Well, you've left me no choice in the matter have you? You've been ignoring my calls." He narrows his beady eyes on me.

"Fine, you've made your point. I'll be there tonight."

"What, I'm just supposed to believe you am I?"

I can feel Isaak and Saxon closing in on me. They still have no idea what's going on or what I've got myself into, yet, they appear to have my back, regardless.

"I'll...be...there." I emphasise each word clearly.

Benny looks from me to Isaak then to Saxon before landing on me again. "This is your last chance, Owen. Don't disappoint me." With that, he turns and drags Sandra back down the path and bundles her into the awaiting black car before jumping in himself, leaving nothing but dust in the air.

"You going tell me what the fuck that was all about?" Isaak asks from behind me.

"Like I said, now is not the time or place." I take a couple of steps back and walk away from Saxon and my best friend, Isaak.

Isaak is the guy I told everything to. Doesn't matter what it was, I just knew he'd have my back if needed but would understand nevertheless.

Once upon a time.

CHAPTER 2
DEVON

"**O**h my God, Remme. I'm so happy for you." I squeeze her in my arms for what feels like the hundredth time. In the space of twelve months, she's fallen in love, had a baby and got married and is now extending her family further after almost losing her first born—unbeknown to her at the time.

"Thank you, Devon." She beams at me once I release her from my tight grip.

Charlotte and Spencer re-join us with drinks in hand. Thank God. I need it after the altercation I had with Owen in his car. Sometimes, I wonder who's the oldest. He acts like a stubborn child half the time. I may only be turning twenty-two next weekend, but he's twenty-six. You'd think he'd behave better or at least act his age.

Charlotte hands me a fruity looking cocktail and smirks. "Sex on the beach, Dev. Remme, I'm sorry but yours is a non-alcoholic cocktail." The three of us burst with laughter at the face Rem pulls.

"Well, if you kept your legs closed or tamed the beast once in a while, you'd be able to drink," Spence jokes.

"Have you seen Isaak lately? He could get a girl pregnant with just one look, never mind how wide her legs are," Charlotte manages to get out in between laughing.

"True that," both Remme and Spence say in unison as they lift their glasses up in the air.

"I don't see it." I regret the words as soon as they leave my mouth.

"What don't you see? That man is delicious," Spencer quips.

"Spence, I am here, you know," Remme jokes, pulling a disgusted face whilst trying not to laugh again.

"Stop acting like it's news to you. You know I have a soft spot for that man."

She shrugs her shoulders agreeing with him and now all attention is shining on me.

"Spill. If Isaak isn't your type, then who is?" Charl asks quietly so no one overhears outside the circle. That's how rumours start after all.

"There's nothing to say. Isaak has always been more like a brother to me. He's just not my type," I whisper in case someone is close by.

"There's something you're hiding, Devon. I can see it in your eyes. What's up?" Remme asks, ever the mother figure.

"It's nothing really. I've kinda got myself in a situation that I didn't want to be in, and now I'm struggling with what to do about it." I find myself opening up to them. They're all at least five years older than me but they never treat me any differently, or speak to me like I'm an impetuous child. Not only that, but they won't stop until I give in and tell them in the end anyway.

"Sounds compelling," I don't miss Remme's sarcasm, and I'm suddenly taking an interest in my shiny black heels.

"I need details… For the love of all things Holy, Devon. I need more details," Spencer practically screeches at me, making my head fly back up. Both girls are looking at him with their eyes bulging.

"What? I need to get my kicks from somewhere, I'm going through a dry spell here."

Now I'm crunched over at the waist, holding my hips as stitches rock up my sides.

I find my mouth opening on its own accord, and I start to tell them about my nights with Owen. They don't need to know it's Owen I'm talking about. They'll never even put two and two together.

"I slept with this guy a few months back and again recently. It was amazing, but I'm getting the feeling he was only after one thing. Now, he's giving me the cold shoulder. I don't know what to make of it," I admit out loud. I'm confused because I don't understand why Owen makes me feel this way. It bothers me more than it should, and I'm irritated by the way he treats me, but still I went running back for seconds, regardless of how I knew he would act towards me after. I guess it was just wishful thinking that, with it being me, somehow it would be different.

"Do you like the guy?" Remme asks.

"Yes. No. Oh, I don't know."

Yes I like him a lot.

When it's just the two of us, he's a completely different person. What I am unsure of is now I've seen that side of him, I want more and I'm investing too much of myself when he clearly doesn't want the same things I do. He's a playboy: has a different woman underneath him every day of week. Okay, that is an exaggeration, but still. He's slept with a lot of women and clearly still does. I'm setting myself up for heartache and devastation with Owen, no matter which way I look at it.

"If you want my opinion, I'd give him a taste of his own medicine. You know: treat 'em mean, keep 'em keen," Charlotte says on a shrug.

"What harm could it do?" Spence adds.

"I suppose so. Anyway, I'm turning twenty two a week today. You guys wanna celebrate with me? Hit the bars or clubs, get drunk and dance the night away?" I run my eyes across each of their faces, all looking up for it.

"I can't drink; that's not fair." Remme pulls a sad face. "But I'll be there, and so will everyone else." She smiles, and we all laugh and jump up and down on the spot, full of excitement for the event to come around.

The sound of the door opening and bouncing back off the wall abruptly stuns everyone into silence. Owen stampedes his way through and flings himself back in the chair he'd been sitting in not long before.

When I get a glimpse at his handsome, clean-shaven face, his eyes have lost their usual sparkle and he looks tormented and obscenely outraged. I automatically find myself wanting to go over to him and chase all his troubles away.

Stupid, right?

"Looks like he's on one again," Remme whispers in my ear. Only myself and Remme have noticed how frequently he is acting out of character lately. It's so unlike Owen. The amount of times he had been like this at the gym when Isaak was going through this physio with Remme, was just ridiculous. We would give each other a look. Then there was the time we were both talking before she and Isaak went for the twenty-week scan when she was pregnant with Logan. That's how long he's been acting like this.

Something is clearly up with Owen and I'll give my last breath to find out exactly what that is.

CHAPTER 3
OWEN

Benny showing up here looking for me has just put everything into perspective for me.

I've been ignoring him for as long as I can, but the more I try to pull away from him and everything he's associated with, the more he pushes back and pulls me back in.

I know what he is capable of, more so than Isaak, and the fact he has the balls to turn up at Isaak's tells me everything I need to know. This is Benny's way of getting my attention: threatening the people I care about.

"You alright, Owen?" I break my stare at nothing in particular and see Devon at the side of me.

"Fine. Why wouldn't I be?" I fire back, my words coming out harsher than I intended them to.

"Sure you are. That's why the look you're sporting tells me and everyone in this room something completely different." She sits on the arm of the chair and swings her legs around, stopping just short of my knees, the soft silky smooth skin of her exposed legs now in my line of sight.

"It's nothing Devon. Just leave it," I say softly, regretting the tone I'd taken with her moments before. At the end of the day, none of this is her fault. No. It's all down to me.

The day has gone from joyful to downright fucking dreadful, and I need out of here. I need to occupy my mind with something else—with someone else.

I stand abruptly, knocking Devon's legs and making her wobble on the chair. I reach out and grab her shoulders to stop her from falling flat on her arse. "Sorry. I'm leaving. If you want a lift home, I'll be outside waiting. Five minutes then I'm gone." I head out the way I came in, passing Isaak and Remme.

"Owen?" Remme's concerned voice fills my ears.

"Hey, sorry. I've just forgotten I have something I need to sort out. Congratulations again." I spot the sad look in her eyes but choose to ignore it and instead place a quick peck on her cheek. When I pull away from her, Isaak is throwing me daggers, but I know he won't say anything in front of Remme. So I'm safe for now.

"Isaak." I nod swiftly.

"Owen." He clasps my hand in his and throws his arm over my shoulder bringing me into him. When his mouth is close to my ear he speaks for only me to hear. "This isn't over."

My shoulders sag at the thought of having to tell Isaak the whole reason his Uncle Benny has shown his face out of the blue and more importantly, why he is after me.

"I'll see you both soon," I tell them as I pull out of Isaak's brutal hold, Devon sliding up behind me.

"Owen's my ride home, so I'll catch up with you guys tomorrow, yeah?"

I don't wait around for their reply. I walk off and head for my car, thankful for some fresh air.

Once I'm seated, Devon appears, walking around the front of the car, and quickly slides into the passenger seat. Once I know she has her belt on and secured, I put the car in drive and speed off towards the gates out front of Isaak's place.

Devon doesn't speak for most of the ride back to hers, but when I reach the turn for her street, she twists her whole body my way and starts drilling me with more questions.

"So, are you ready to talk yet? Why did you act like that at Isaak and Rem's house?" I can feel her openly staring at me, waiting for me to say something.

"Will you stop? There's nothing to tell, Devon." Why won't she just drop it? Apart from Isaak, and now Saxon, she's the only other person who wants answers—answers I don't want to give her or anyone for that matter. My fingers take a death grip on the steering wheel.

"I'm trying to be a friend, Owen. I wanna help you." Her soft words break my hard shell, calming me slightly.

"I appreciate that, but the only thing that will help me right now is if I'm sinking my dic…" For a second I completely forget who I am talking to, paying more attention to what keeps running around inside my head.

"Sinking your dick in someone? Was that what you were going to say?" She's annoyed, that much I can tell, and when I pull the car up at the side of the road outside the front of her block of flats and look at her to apologise, I fall short as I really take her in and the way she's looking back at me.

There's something more to what she's asking me. What that is, I can't quite pinpoint yet.

"Well yeah. That's kinda what I do," I tell her honestly, choosing to look out the windscreen instead of straight at her.

"Owen…" What is that tone she's speaking in? Is it Want? Need? Or jealousy? And why does it make me want her?

I can't stop myself from looking back her way. "What is it, Dev?" I find myself wanting to know what she has to say about my behaviour and how I deal with my troubles.

"I'm here, Owen. Whenever you need me," She says shyly. I don't talk about my problems, especially this one. I fuck them out of my system until I can think more clearly, or until my mind is numb.

"Devon, talking isn't really my thing, but thanks for the offer." I give her my most sincere smile in the hope she can see I mean it.

"That's not what I meant. I mean, I'm here now, Owen. You don't need to go looking for a willing girl to sink your dick into."

I almost give myself whiplash as I do a I double take.

Why would she offer her body over to me like that? Why am I finding her brassness a massive fucking turn on? More importantly why am I willing to participate in whatever she is offering me?

I don't ponder over the idea for long: I know I'll somehow talk myself out of it, and right now I need exactly what she has and what she is offering.

I can't stop myself. I release the belt from around her, plucking her from the passenger seat, and have her in my lap and my mouth on hers before she can utter another word.

After what seems like forever kissing her plump lips, I realise we're still in the car. The need to be inside her is taking over me. Keeping her close to me, I reach for the handle to open the door, grab my keys from the ignition and hand them to her to hold.

I swing my legs out and tighten the grip I have on her waist as I stand.

"I can walk, you know." She chuckles adorably.

Adorably? Since when do I use that word? I mean fit, yes. Smokin' hot, most definitely.

"I know, but I like the feel of you in my arms."

Wait, what? Where the fuck did that come from?

These feelings are so foreign to me, and I don't know where they've popped up from. I push them to the back of my mind and lock that shit down in a box with a fucking massive pad lock to seal it.

Before I know it we are at her flat door.

"I need to get my key out or we will be doing this in the hall for all to see." I place her feet gently on the ground and wait for her to get the key from her little bag. Once she's fished it out, I snatch it from her grasp and unlock the door myself, eager to get her inside, naked and under me. Pulling her through the door and kicking it closed behind us. I spot her couch and drag her over to it. Taking her mouth with mine once again, I trail my palms down her sides. My lips never part from hers. Once I reach the hem of her dress, I slide my hand underneath, feeling the silky texture of her skin. My dick is like a solid steel bar, begging to be let out of my underwear.

"Turn around and bend over the back of the couch. Keep your hands in front of you and do not move them unless I tell you to," I all but growl at her. I watch her comply to my demands, and it has me smirking to myself.

Devon looks over her shoulder and gives me a playful look. My eyes zero in on her swollen lips, and I picture my cock in between them. All of sudden, I'm kneeling on the couch in front of her with my trousers and boxers around my ankles, my dick now pressing against her bottom lip like it's asking for permission to enter.

Her eyes look up at me and her tongue swipes across her lip before it connects with the head of my dick with the faintest of touches. A deep growl leaves my mouth while a small gasp leaves hers. Her lips open, wrapping me up in her hot wet mouth.

The first time I had been with her had been a quick fuck, the time after was the night of Remme and Isaak's wedding, apart from the night we both fell asleep where I'd fucked her into oblivion for the best part of four hours—not that she complained about the multiple orgasms I gave her. Her pussy had been the only hole I entered that night, but I wanted to claim every inch of her.

I didn't. I kept myself restrained.

Everything I did with her I was second guessing myself and talking myself out of it. Perhaps it's because I knew I'd see her daily at work, and she is a Godsend at work for me. Doesn't help matters that she's close with everyone I hang out with. I'm sure they'd all have something to say to her about what we've been doing, and I know for a fact I'll be seen as the bad guy.

Not that I would blame them.

Her moans vibrate against my dick and have my head snapping downwards quickly. The view alone is enough to make me want to come. Her hands move to hold the backs of my legs, I assume to keep her balance. As much as I want to scold her for disobeying me, I can't. Instead, I forcefully thrust my solidness into her throat making her gag a little from the intrusion. Saliva falls from the side of her mouth and it makes me harder. I roar out a grunt and slide myself out, letting her take in some much-needed air.

"Fuck, Devon your mouth is like heaven on earth," I say through gritted teeth.

"Owen, I know your holding back with me. I won't break. Take me, use me however you need to. Just do it."

Could I do this?

CHAPTER 4
DEVON

I'm offering myself over to Owen like a cheap whore without a care in the world. I hope he doesn't think this.

Hopefully he'll see what I'm doing is in a way of me helping him. I'm not desperate, but if this is the only way I can have a piece of him, for now, then I'll take it. If that makes me whore, then so be it.

In a way, you could say we're both getting what we want. Owen releasing his pent-up frustrations and me... Well, I get him.

"Come here," he orders with a hungry look in his eyes.

I do as I'm told and round the sofa, standing in front of him as he turns and stands himself upright.

He spins me around and pushes me down to the sofa as he gets on his knees. He grabs me under both my knees and pulls me forwards slightly, so my bum is on the edge, and ever so slowly drags his hands up under my dress again, only stopping to ask me to lift up so he can bunch it up around my waist.

"I need to taste you, Devon." He runs the tip of his tongue up my thigh at a leisurely pace, then across to my knickers before he buries his head there and inhales my scent. "Your scent drives me wild."

"Owen…" He knows what I need, yet he's taking his sweet time and treating me like glass.

He gracefully slides my knickers down my legs, past my calves and over my heels, placing them down on the floor beside him. He spreads my legs open wide, exposing all of me for him to admire.

"Damn. Already wet for me." He wastes no more time. He sweeps his tongue over my now already sensitive pussy, lapping at my juices and taking my clit into his mouth, sucking and licking my arousal like the professional he is. I can feel the burn starting to build up in the walls of my uterus and my core begins to throb as I get closer and closer to my climax. He inserts two fingers into me, thrusting them in and out repeatedly as his tongue continues to work me over the edge. I pant and moan; I'm almost there.

He drags his tongue from my butt to my clit and begins sucking rigorously, making me buck up in shock, the torturous yet delicious assault turning into pleasure. The contrast of softness with the harshness is driving me completely crazy, and he knows it because he does it again, soothing it with his tongue once more. He repeats this a couple more times and I can't hold on any longer. I grab the back of his head and fist my fingers in his hair as I push his mouth down on me harder.

"Oh God, Owen….I'm…"

He picks up the tempo of his fingers, sending me higher and higher towards my awaiting bliss.

"Let it go, Dev. Let me taste you."

And I do just that. I scream his name at the top of my lungs as his fingers work me down and his tongue collects all of my orgasm until there's nothing left to take.

My heart hammers in my chest and my eyes close of their own accord. I'm thoroughly spent and I know he's only just started.

"I'm not finished with you yet," he declares with a devilish look in his eyes, lifting me up with him as he stands to his full height, kicking off his shoes and ridding himself of his trousers and boxers that are down by his ankles.

"Good, because I want more of whatever that was. Don't hold back on me, Owen."

He carries me down the hall and into my room, kicking the door shut with his foot as he walks us over the threshold. He takes the last few steps towards my bed and unceremoniously throws me down on it.

Owen is on me the moment I stop bouncing. "I'm going to fuck you so hard, Devon. Are you ready for this?"

He is asking for permission?

Without thinking too much about what I'm agreeing to, I nod my head vigorously. "Yes, I'm ready," I say with more confidence than I feel.

"Remember, you asked for this. You do everything I say, do you understand me?" he orders, leaving no room for an argument.

"Okay," is all I can manage to get out.

The corners of his mouth tick upwards, his almost naked body flush against my dishevelled one. He manhandles me, grabbing my hips and lifting up onto his knees before flipping me over under him. He unzips my dress and pulls it down my body, shuffling down with it until he can slip it off over my still-heeled feet and taking his shirt off while he is there.

My body burns with need and I want him to take me right this second. I know he is still taking it easy with me, the warning that suggested more was to come was enough to tell me I'm right.

"Owen, please." I resort to begging but I don't even care.

"I got you Dev, I know what you want—what you need—and those heels stay on: they are sexy as fuck." He groans as he places his knees either side of my legs, grabbing my hips and pulling me up as he moves in closer. I'm totally exposed to him, and I can't find it in me to care. Right at this minute, I would agree to an orgy if he demanded it.

"Devon, I want to take you raw. I want to feel you squeeze my dick, feel you cum around me."

"How do I know you're—"

"I'm clean, Dev. I have never been bare with another woman before." He pleads with me, like he's in pain.

I think it over. "Okay," I eventually whisper with a wiggle of my hips that are still in his grasp. I feel the bed dip at my knees then the smooth end of his glorious manhood reaching my opening.

"So wet. I can see you glistening for me."

I whimper as he pushes far too softly into me. I try to push back against him, but he holds me firmly in place.

"I'm trying so hard to hold back with you, Devon, but I just can't seem to contain myself as much as I would like to. How far can I go, Devon?" he asks, and my reply is instant.

"Give me the full Owen experience."

His eyes bulge slightly, as if he's shocked that I'm asking for this. "You absolutely sure?" He's double checking, but whether it's for himself or me I don't know.

"I'm sure," I tell him, full of new found confidence.

"Not yet, but I will give you a taste. If it gets too much, just let me know and I'll stop. I don't want to taint you, Devon. You're all that's pure in my dark and twisted world."

What does he mean by that? Does he mean I'm too innocent?

I just nod in reply, not wanting him to confirm it.

Pulling out almost all the way, he thrusts harshly straight back in again, filling me to the brim.

"Put your hands behind your back and face down on the bed," he demands, and I do what he says without question, not wanting him to change his mind. His thrusts get more intense with every stroke. He takes my wrists in one hand, holding them at the bottom of my spine. I feel him getting deeper and deeper, reaching all my hidden places. My breaths are coming thick and fast. I start to feel dizzy, but I don't want it to stop.

Owen tugs on my wrists, almost dislocating my arms from their sockets, then suddenly lets them go as he pulls out of me, slapping my arse hard.

I scream out at the sting, but he rubs the sore area and leaves me with the familiar pool of desire as it runs down my thighs.

He grunts at me to turn over.

I do as I'm told without a second thought, enjoying the feel of his hands roaming all over my body.

He opens my legs for him to crawl between them and take me again, moving to where I desperately need him. My arms automatically reach for him, but he stops me in my tracks by grabbing my hands.

"Hold the bars on the headboard; don't let go."

I follow his instructions, even though I want to touch him, to feel every ridge of his toned abs.

He hovers over me, bracing himself on one arm. I want him rough and dirty. I need him to take me without abandonment.

"Owen, I need you to fuck me hard. I need you to push me past my own limits." The more he's giving me, the braver I become. No sooner are the words out of my mouth, he pushes his way back into me, so vigorously that my whole body shifts up the bed. The pain is beautiful; his thrusts don't stop. He pistons his hips forward again. The pressure grows more intense with every hit of my cervix, giving me exactly what I asked for. The tingling in my spine is a tell-tale sign that I'm close.

"Is this what you wanted, Devon? Is this hard enough for you?"

I can't speak, but a pleasurable groan slips free. My world is being turned on its axis and the Adonis causing it is Owen—the man who causes my body to light up whenever I'm near him or when he touches me.

"You're almost there. I can feel you clenching around me, Devon. Hold it until I tell you to let go."

Holy fuck, I'm not sure I can. I'm too far gone, and he isn't slowing down either: he's chasing his own climax, too.

I squeeze my eyes closed tight in the hopes it will let me hold it a little longer.

"Eyes on me. They never leave mine."

Oh, God, I'm doomed. A few more strokes into me and I hear him growling and grunting.

"Now, Dev. Come with me… Fuck." He thrusts one last time, holding himself deep in me. I swear he can feel my uterus with his twitching dick. I pull my arms down and reach for him as he flops gently on top of my chest, running my fingers through his hair as we both stay silent for a minute, enjoying the tranquillity surrounding us.

"Don't even think about going to sleep; we are far from finished."

As much as this excites me tremendously, I know I'm not going to be able to walk tomorrow—not that the thought has me pushing him away as he makes a grab for me again.

This man and his stamina.

As the sunlight outside my window turns to dark, Owen has his wicked way with me more times than I can count. The man is a bloody sex machine, that's for sure.

He finally relents and lays down beside me, and I contemplate whether or not to slide myself closer to his sweat-clad body or not. Before I decide, I feel my eyelids getting heavy and sleep takes over my senses.

The last thing I remember seeing is Owen lying on his back with his hands behind his head and his eyes closed.

Then I'm out like a light, and I know there is a smile as wide as China plastered on my face.

CHAPTER 5
OWEN

The minute I walk into the gym, the only pride and joy I have in my life, I feel at home and at ease.

It's only half five in the morning, so it doesn't open for another half hour. I've come straight here after leaving Devon's—after leaving her sated and fully satisfied. I'd woken up with her curled up in my arms, and I'd freaked out and started to panic because it felt so right.

Me being me, I left without a word or note.

I can still smell her on me, and it's causing me a permanent semi, which sends my head in a dizzy state.

Now I find myself sitting in my office—under the stairs of Remme's operation that's now up and running—in pitch black darkness, thinking the only saving grace I have is that Benny can no longer take this place from me, not now Remme owns half of it.

I don't know what the fuck has gotten into me lately, but I feel like the walls around me are starting to close in on themselves, the tightness in my chest now suffocating me, strangling me to point that I can't breathe. Being here loosens and dulls the aching feeling.

I pull out my phone from my back pocket. I have so much I need to sort out. Not knowing what the hell I can do to get myself out of this rut that I now call my life has me feeling a little on edge all of a sudden.

Just then I remember I never answered the text that Benny had sent in regards to being at the warehouse last night.

"Fuck!" The echo of my voice is loud in the dead silence. Benny will be throwing a hissy fit at me not turning up, especially since I told him I'd be there only hours before when he turned up at Isaak's looking for me. The consequences of my actions last night are far worse than they sound. I unlock my phone and sure enough I have six missed calls and two messages from him. The first text contains a lot of curse words followed by threats, the second informing me that he has managed to get hold of another fighter who's got there in time to fill in for me.

I'm sure this won't be last time I hear about it, but thankfully it hasn't been a waste of Benny's time—that should work in my favour, if only slightly.

I have no regrets about what I've done. What I still do for Benny. Not one. I'd do it all over again in a heartbeat knowing now that everything has turned out okay for Isaak. Same goes for spending the night with Devon instead of attending the warehouse.

Fuck the consequences.

That doesn't mean I want to carry on living my life this way: always on edge, anxious about what is going to happen if I don't succeed, if I somehow don't get back up again.

I need a plan, and I need to execute it right, timing it perfectly so myself and everyone I now call family comes out of this unscathed.

On top of all that, I've now gone and fucked things up with Devon. I've made our situation more complex than it was before.

The words that were coming out of my mouth and the stuff I found myself doing with her, with her body, I shouldn't have said or done. She's twenty-one, for fuck sake. Not only that but she works for me. She keeps me organised as much as she does my staff and gym.

She's now closer with the girls, so if I hurt her—which I know I will, unintentionally or not because it's what I do best—the girls will chop off my dick with a very blunt knife and have me choking on it.

My hands cup my junk and I wince, visualising the image.

Ouch.

Not a fucking chance. I'd like to keep my dick attached to my body.

Flashbacks from only a few hours ago assault my mind: Devon's mouth sucking on my dick, her pretty little addictive pussy glistening for me, then me fucking her bare back for the first time ever, and taking her repeatedly over and over, each time harder than the one before. *Bareback? What the fuck? Why did I suggest that?*

I have never gone naked with a girl before. I'm always careful no matter who it's with or what state I'm in, but with Dev, she has me in knots just as much as she has my balls in her hands (not literally) and I don't even know why. Taking Devon with nothing between us was out of this world and nothing like I could have ever imagined.

She gave me what I wanted so willingly, not once asking for anything back in return. The more time I spend with her, buried inside her, the more I find myself becoming hooked. This is going to end horribly now I've given her more of myself. More than I've ever willingly given to a woman before.

I want to explore this more, see where it could go and push her boundaries as much as my own. To see how much she wants to please me. Not that she is a true submissive but I see that she reacts to me and my commands.

A comment Remme made few months ago comes back to me, out of nowhere, like it's been pulled from the back of my mind giving me no option but let it play out.

"You know, Owen, if you found the right girl, she'd be willing to do anything to please you. She would fulfil all your wildest dreams and more. Clearly you haven't found her yet, or you'd be with her right now and not chasing the easy pussy that you surround yourself with.

"No…" I start to question myself, the events of last night and this morning with Devon. Just because she let me take her however the fuck I wanted to, doesn't mean I'm ready to settle the fuck down, least of all with her. She's too involved in my life for a start.

Then why can't I call it quits on *whatever* this is?

What does she have that keeps me going back for more?

I can have any girl I want, yet I find myself drawn to her like a moth to a flame and the way she makes me feel when she is lying beneath me. To top it off, she is now offering herself to me on a silver platter.

"Fuck!" I yell out in frustration, throwing my head in my hands. I have bigger issues to deal with right now than worrying about Devon. I need to get her out of my head and fast.

I rub deep circles into my temple, trying to soften the ache, when all of a sudden the lights flick on, causing me to squint my eyes from the blinding beams that burn my eyeballs.

I glance at my watch and see it's six am meaning I've been sitting here for half an hour and done absolutely jack shit.

I make my way out of my office and stop in my tracks when I see Devon setting up her desk and getting ready to open the gym. She's so deep in concentration that she hasn't heard me come in.

"I thought it was your day off?" I speak softly from the shadow casting over me from the stairs.

"Fucking hell, Owen. You trying to give me a heart attack?" She places her hand over her chest. "And why were you sitting in the dark?" She lifts her eyebrows up in question and confusion.

"I was thinking." I don't tell her any more than that, just make my way over to her. Her eyes assess me with every step I take.

"I don't have many days off, Owen," I sense the sarcasm before she mumbles something else about how I've never noticed it. To give her, her due, I suppose I never have.

I don't ever concentrate on the front desk as I've never actually needed to. Devon runs the front desk like a boss, I guess I really do need her in this place.

"You want a day off?" I find myself asking.

"I'd love a day off. Are you going to man the desk so I can?"

Again her sarcasm doesn't go a miss. "No, but I'll get Jemma or one of the guys to stand in for you, between their booked in training sessions," I tell her, but something tells me she's going to over complicate things.

Devon knows the rotas better than me as she's the one who does the first draft for me. She came to me one day wanted more responsibilities in work and something that would help pass the time when the gym was quiet. I hate doing the rotas, as it turns out, she loves doing them.

"All the personal trainers are fully booked up for the rest of the week. I've already checked the diary. Hence why I'm here at six o'clock in the morning. It's fine. I'll try get some time back at the weekend and see if Jemma can fill in for me," she explains with a shrug of her shoulders before turning away from me.

Is she pissed off with me about leaving her this morning?

She'd still been asleep, so I hadn't wanted to wake her.

"Are you throwing your toys out of the pram because you're working all the time or is it something else?" I don't want to be having this conversation with her, especially in work. This is why I never should have slept with her in the first place. If it's to do with the rotas, then I'll sit down with her and go through them and tweak some shifts if needs be.

"I'm not throwing anything out of a pram, Owen. If anything, you're the immature one," she throws over her shoulder at me.

"Me? It sounds like you're the one that needs to get something off your chest."

"No, not really. I'm perfectly fine. Now, if you don't mind, I have work to do... Unless you don't want the gym open today." She shoots me a questioning look, waiting for my next move.

"Fine." I swipe her keys up from off the desk in front of me and unlock the doors. As soon as they're open, a few regulars walk through, followed by a couple of personal trainers who work for me.

Without even giving her a second glance, I throw the keys back down on the desk, walk away from her and head for my office again.

I have shit I need to deal with and somewhere I need to be.

Picking up my phone, I call the number I've been ignoring for long enough and wait for the caller pick up.

CHAPTER 6
DEVON

I walk into the gym only hours after Owen has crept out of my bed after our fuck session. He'd thought I was still asleep but I'd heard him whisper, 'what the fuck' when he'd realised he'd been sleeping so close to me. He'd headed out of the door quickly, leaving me all alone with the sound of it closing again.

I hadn't been able to go back to sleep: I'd been wide awake.

Instead, I'd chosen to get up and make myself a coffee before jumping into the shower, throwing on some clothes and heading to the gym.

The whole way here, all I did was mull over the previous night's activities, thinking how it was the best sex I have ever had—not that I have slept with many men. Owen knows what he can provide for a girl; just thinking about it makes my lady parts tingle with need. He'd taken me with abandon last night, not a single doubt on his face. Just pure unhinged hunger as he'd taken what he wanted from me and my body.

I'd wanted it; I'd asked for it; and I'd fucking loved it.

I feel a smile taking over my face, but as soon as I see him hiding in the shadows, all the happiness fades into anger especially when he starts suggesting I'm throwing my toys out the pram.

He has the nerve to say I'm acting like a child when he can't even own up to the fact that he's acting like an eighteen-year-old, horny teenager and not a twenty-six year old man.

The rest of my morning doesn't go great either, and the fact that Owen disappears only half an hour after he's opened the gym hasn't gone unnoticed.

It's a good job I'm capable of running this place without him here, otherwise he'd have no business to come back to. Luckily, he doesn't have any bookings in for today and it was an office day for him. Although, if you ask me, that's besides the point. He should be here when he's on the rota to be in.

I can't wait for this weekend to roll around so I can get away from him and his brooding mood swings.

A night with the girls, and Spencer of course, is exactly what I need.

I take the opportunity of Owen being out of the gym to call Jemma and see if she's okay to work over the weekend for me, and possibly work out some shifts with her before I give Owen anymore rotas. If Jemma can't work more then I really do need to speak to him about hiring someone part time to help man the desk. I don't want the guys to lose out earning more if they have to cancel some of their personal training sessions with the clients.

I'm not one to toot my own horn, but Owen really would be lost without me in this place. I just hope he bloody well knows it. In fact, I'll make sure he's aware of it if he carries on acting the way he has lately.

Ever since Isaak won his belts back from Alex, the gym has had a huge growth in new members. Owen can't afford to keep asking one of the guys to sit on the reception desk and answer the phone. He needs every single person he can to keep up with the members on the books.

Getting on with stuff I need to do, I find Jemma's number in the phone and press the call button. She picks up after a couple of rings.

"Hi Devon, what's up? I didn't forget a shift did I?"

"No not at all, but I did wonder if you could do a shift over the weekend for me and possibly this afternoon if you have finished up at university by then?"

"Sure, is everything okay?"

"Yes, everything is fine. I'm just trying earn some time back that's all."

"Okay, cool. You know the money will come in handy."

"Great. See you soon." Hanging up the call, I remember Mum's text from the other day asking if she was going to see me before my birthday. I reply saying she would, with a promise to let her know when I had free time from work. Mum understands my need to work and be independent, but Dad hates me working here. He'd made his feelings pretty clear the day I told them I had a new job.

That's his problem not mine. I couldn't care less what he thinks: he only ever thinks about himself and what's best for him. It's not the fact of where I work, more so that he doesn't like me having any independence at all as he likes to control all the people around him. Unfortunately that includes me and my mum. I want no part in any of that if I can help it. I'm more than capable of looking after myself and providing for myself too. He will just have to deal with it.

The rest of my morning is spent making sure everything is set up for Jemma to take over from me. I'm just booking in a client when she breezes in with a bright smile on her face.

"Hey, Jem." I offer her my own smile.

"Hey, you ready to get the fuck out of here?" The girl swears like a sailor on leave, but I wouldn't have her any other way.

"I am now. Everything is set up for you. Owen is out but should be back to close up. If he hasn't returned half an hour before close, ring me and I will come back," I tell her not actually knowing if he will be back in time. He never even said bye on his way out, let alone say where he was going.

I pull up to my childhood home in a daze, swinging my car to the left of the driveway and parking it next to Mum's at the side of the house. Jumping out, I make quick work of getting back round to the front door when I notice a car I recognise parked next to Dad's.

"What the fuck?"

What is he doing here? How does he know my parents?

Opening the door, I hear mum in the kitchen.

"Hey, Mum," I say, startling her. "Sorry, I didn't mean to make you jump." It's not unusual: she's scared of her own shadow most of the time.

"What are you doing here, sweetheart?" She looks nervous, maybe even scared.

Why would she be scared though?

I look around the kitchen, trying to place what could have her so spooked. Then I hear raised voices.

My father's voice bellows through the house, though I can't quite understand what is being said. I'm desperately trying to listen, knowing that the person he is arguing with is none other than Owen.

Why is Owen here, and more importantly why is he having a slanging match with my dad?

"This isn't a good time, Devon. Maybe you should come back another day," Mum says, trying to usher me towards the door.

"Mum, what the hell is going on?" I try to stop myself from moving, but Mum is surprisingly strong when she needs to be.

"Devon, not now. Please just go while your father finishes his business meeting; I will call you later." She has pushed me right out onto the doorstep and proceeds to shut the front door in my face. I hear the lock catch behind the wood, leaving me no choice but to get in my car and leave wondering what the hell has just happened. There's so much information to digest and yet I can't.

Business meeting?

I'm rendered speechless and completely dazed at the whole situation that has just played out in front of me. I can't seem to wrap my head around it all.

First I spot Owen's car, then my mum acts like I just caught her cheating, then hearing booming voices only to be ushered quite forcefully out of my parents' house.

My head is all over the place, and I'm starting to panic. Whatever Owen is up to, it most definitely isn't healthy—nothing connected to my father is good. Everything he touches he taints and destroys.

Has Owen been lying to me this whole time? Did he know who I was when he hired me?

If he works for my father and is informing him of my whereabouts and my every move, I swear to God I'll rip him a new one.

The fact Owen doesn't know I'm on to him means I could use it to my advantage.

God, I hope I'm wrong about Owen.

CHAPTER 7
OWEN

I'm no further forward in my task of handling Benny today than I was last Sunday. It's been almost a week since I visited him and he made his demands—demands that give me no wiggle room to dismiss him. He'd finally let me leave after instructing me to be at the club on Sunday night.

Now it's Saturday, so I'm trying my best to put it at the back of mind and enjoy some downtime with Isaak, Saxon and Jason. Isaak and Saxon haven't mentioned anything about the day Benny turned up, and for that I'm grateful, even though I know I'm on borrowed time.

In my head, I'm trying to figure out just how I tell Isaak and when the right time will be.

"Right, the ride's here. Drink up. We're meeting the girls at The Hourglass," Isaak announces as he slips his phone back in the arse pocket of his jeans.

"The Hourglass? Why there?" Saxon questions with a raise of his eyebrows.

"Don't know, but that's where they are, and that's where my pregnant wife is, so I'm going. You guys coming or not?"

"Me, definitely. It's lads' night tonight, right? I could do with having a busty brunette shaking her butt cheeks in my face and on my junk." I jump up off the chair and head out of Isaak's to the mini bus Isaak's management has put together for us.

Going out with Isaak is a nightmare in itself, but he only heads to the places that can accommodate such a high-profile persona shall we say.

Such as The Hourglass.

The lads are full of energy the whole way to the club—mindless chatter about baby names or some shit. I'm not really paying attention to it all.

"Yo! Owen what's up with you, man? Girl trouble?" Saxon laughs.

"Yeah, something like that," I agree. It's not like I can tell them about the real thing on my mind. Letting them think some chick has me in knots is better for Isaak anyway. I know one day I will have to spill it, but that day isn't today. No. Tonight, I'm gonna find myself a willing pussy to pound so hard that I lose myself in oblivion.

We pull up outside the club, making our way to the bouncer on the door. I watch as Saxon and Jason greet the burly guy with a fist bump. We come here frequently, but I've never seen him before. By the way Saxon is communicating with him, I'd say he is one of his guys: he has them everywhere by the looks of things. They introduce Isaak and me and let us all in without question or without making us wait in the mile-long queue outside.

It becomes apparent as soon as we are in the main area of the club that it is in fact ladies' night tonight. That can only mean two things: one, the act tonight is female focused, and glancing over to the stage where there is a magic mike style act on and I groan; two: it's wall to wall pussy, just the way I like it.

"Well, fellas—apart from you, Isaak—looks like we have our pick of the ladies tonight." I rub my hands together and smirk.

"You can have them. Remme's the only woman I'll ever need," Isaak says proudly.

"Spoken like the whipped arse bitch you are," I say while punching him in the arm. Isaak grumbles a 'fuck you' and flips me off.

"Let's find the girls to see if they want a drink before we order," I suggest. Looking around the bar, I spot Spencer before any one of the ladies. Spencer is a nice guy, but fuck me, does he stick out like a sore thumb in amongst a room full of screaming girls. We head over to their table, and I do a double take when I get my first glimpse of Devon. Don't get me wrong, she'd looked amazing at the christening last week. Tonight, though, she looks hot as fuck in a little black number that clings to her tight little body, showing everyone her glorious figure.

Isaak instantly grabs Rem, picking her up and smothering her in kisses before putting her back down looking even more flustered than before.

I clear my throat and thoughts for long enough to ask everyone what they want to drink. Once I have their orders, I move towards the bar, Saxon and Jason following behind me to help carry the drinks back to the table.

Reeling off the order to the barman, I spin around and glance over to Saxon who is staring at me like I just whipped my dick out onto the bar.

"What?" I'm so not in the mood for this.

"I'm just wondering if you're ever gonna tell me, that's all."

Fuck my life. I should have known this would happen. Time to play dumb.

"What you talking about?" I reply while getting my wallet out and spinning back round to pay. Anything to avoid looking at the dude.

"Okay. You wanna play it that way, go right ahead."

Just when I think that's the last of it he continues.

"But know this: Isaak won't let it rest. He wants to know what his uncle wants with you—why he felt the need to rock up at the house on the day of his boy's christening. And he also wants to know if you're in trouble."

I huff out a sigh and slide my eyes back to Saxon. "Look, man, I know you guys want answers, but tonight isn't the night." I grab some of the drinks, leaving the guys behind to get the ones I can't carry without a backwards glance.

Putting the glasses on the round table in between the seats, I look up and notice Devon and Charlotte are missing. I look all around me and back over to the bar. I can't see them, but what I do spot is Saxon and Jason walking back over to us. Saxon is looking in my direction with a face like thunder. The closer he gets, the more obvious it becomes that he is actually looking over my shoulder at the stage behind me.

Wondering what's got him looking so murderous, I spin around on my heels with my beer pulled tight to my lips. When my eyes land on the stage, I almost spit my beer out all over Isaak and Remme who are unfortunately within reaching distance.

Devon and Charlotte are both sitting on chairs right in the middle of the stage, looking bashful and excited. Two of the male strippers are giving them a down right dirty strip tease. I can't take my eyes off the scene playing out in front of me. It burns my eyes to watch, but I can't turn away or close my eyes.

I must have missed the beginning of the show as the guy grinding on top of Devon's lap has already lost his shirt. He's rolling his hips in front of her face to the beat of the music, her eyes sparkling with lust and desire. Grabbing the back of her head, he thrusts his hips forward in sync with the beat, ensuring she is up close and personal with his junk. She's absolutely loving this. Me… not so much, yet I still can't drag my eyes away from them.

The male dancer runs his hands down his defined chest.

Mine is better—just saying.

As he rotates his hips, he makes a grab for her hands and spreads them out over his sweat clad abs. Her greedy fingers start a delicate journey, exploring his front before he guides them over the top of his trousers, nodding his instructions for her to remove them...and she does. She pulls them clean off his body in one swift motion.

After what feels like too fucking long of me standing watching, I go to turn around and plonk my infuriated body in the chair, but when he runs his hands down the side of her arms seductively and grabs the chair from underneath, lifting her in the air at face level, I almost lose my shit. Devon covers her embarrassment behind her hands, which is short lived when all of sudden the chair she is sitting on is dropped from underneath her, causing her to grip the top of his shoulders. When her exceptionally, stunned and eager-looking face comes back into my view, it has me adjusting my bulge.

The expression she is wearing is the same as when I'm deep inside her, riding her hard.

The male dancer has his hands all over her arse and lifts her that little bit higher, and her mouth forms an 'O'. I know what he's getting an eye full of and there's no doubt he will be able to smell her arousal—something I know smells out of this world and the fact he is doing this to something that is mine is making me want to break something.

Mine? She isn't fucking mine.

Why would I even think that?

Then a thought occurs to me.

Shit, she'd better be wearing fucking knickers under that dress.

He buries his head in between her thighs—thighs she's trying to squeeze tight around his face, as he shakes his head from left to right viciously. I can feel my patience dwindling away with each passing second that this goes on.

In a flash, he has her flipped around and starts shimmying her down his body, deliberately slowly, until she comes face to face with his boxer-covered junk, his own excitement clear for all to see. She has no choice but to wrap her arms around the back of his thighs.

Charlotte walks off the stage. Whether she's had too much or not, I don't know.

The girls and Spencer whoop and holler at Devon, telling her to do it…

Do what? What else can she do?

The guy must be saying something to her because he looks down at her and his mouth is moving. The next thing I know, she's removing his boxers quickly down his legs and then kicks them off to the side.

Oh hell no…I can't watch anymore.

I down the rest of my beer and get up forcefully, head back to the bar again and order myself another drink.

Taking a stool and dropping my arse onto it, I turn to look at what's happening on the stage because I can't stop torturing myself, so it seems, but I see Remme walking towards me before I get a chance to see what Dev and the fake Mystic Mack or whatever his name is are up to.

"You wish it were you up there, don't you?" Remme asks, bringing my focus on her now that Devon is walking off the stage wafting her hand in front of her face, smiling in complete euphoria, but it brings my blood pressure down a bit, thankfully.

"Too fucking right I do, only with a female, not a dude," I tell her with a smirk pulling at the corner of my mouth.

"That's not what I meant, and you know it, Owen." She dips her head to the side like she's studying me.

"Okay, now I'm confused. Why do women always speak in code?" I question.

"You like her, don't you?" She's not one for beating around the bush with her brashness that's for sure, and I'm not about to start spilling my guts to her about what Devon and I have really been getting up to. She'll flip her lid and start telling me that it's not good, that I'm stringing her along and will only end up hurting her in the end—all of which would be true. But like I said… I'm not about to tell her anything.

"She's a good looking girl, what's not to like about her. But that's it, Rem."

"I smell bullshit." She smirks.

"Funny, I smell nothing but sweat and baby oil." I smirk back at her.

"You know exactly what I mean, Owen." She raise's her brows at me like the action will make me confess to her.

"You're seeing things that aren't there." I need to put an end to the conversation.

"I'm not blind, Owen. You on the other hand, are blind as a fucking bat." She gives me a soft smile, a pat on the shoulder and walks off.

What the fuck does she mean by that?

This place is wreaking havoc on my already confused and complex state of mind. I need to get laid, and I need to right now.

CHAPTER 8
DEVON

Holy shit, that was the hottest thing I've ever experienced in my life. What started out as embarrassment, has made me a horny wanton woman, making me want to jump the first good looking guy I see.

"Devon, that was so fucking hot," Spence screams in my face.

"OMG, it really was. I think I left a wet patch on Isaak's lap," Remme announces as she walks back over to us, causing everyone to burst out laughing. All except Isaak. Clearly he's not impressed with her, but when she turns around to face him she sticks her tongue out. She's teasing him on purpose to get a reaction from him. One she knows she's going to get.

"Sweet cheeks, I don't need to do any of that up there. I only need to touch you and you wouldn't just be wet you'd be soaking fucking wet." He smirks up at her, his little dimples making an appearance.

"Oh, Bruiser... you know you're the only one who does it for me. So how about you take me home and show me exactly what you have in mind." she teases as she parks herself back in his lap and kisses him within an inch of his life. Not that he's complaining.

"Remme! You dirty bitch." Spencer says playfully with a pathetic tap to her arm.

"What? We're all friends and it's not like there is a prude among us." We all laugh and the lads click their beer bottles together.

I love watching them in their playfulness, even if it does cause an ache in my heart and a little jealousy to form in my stomach.

"You okay, Dev?" Charlotte places her hand on my arm, tearing my glazed stare away from the happy couple.

"Erm, yeah fine. I just need the loo. I won't be long." Giving her a soft smile, I pick my bag up from the seat and make my way to the ladies. I'm not desperate for the toilet, but I needed to clear my head somewhat and sort my no doubt flustered face out.

Just as I'm about to push the door open to the toilets, my wrist is grabbed, I'm pulled backward, lifted off the floor and carried further down the corridor.

I scream out in sheer panic which is cut short when a strong hand is placed over my mouth, silencing me. My fight or flight instincts kicking in.

My hands slap and my legs kick about as I try to defend myself against the person who's grabbed me from behind. I'm placed back on my feet, as strong hands hold my arms down by my side. I automatically want to scream but I get a whiff of aftershave that I know well from somewhere, but I can't think where. Whether or not his grip is meant to stop me from hitting out at them again, or if it's for my own safety while I regain my balance. I guess I'll never know.

When my arms are finally released, I brush my hair back out of my face and try to gather my bearings. Flicking my head from side to side I notice we're now in some kind of closet. Wondering what the hell is going on and who the fuck was man handling me the way they did, I squint my eyes trying to see in the darkness when I come face-to-face with a menacing looking Owen.

"Owen?..." I'm in complete shock. I slap his chest in annoyance for scaring me the way he did. He could have just called my name.

"Don't speak; don't say a fucking word." My eyes bulge.

I couldn't have said another word even if I wanted to because he crashes his lips on mine and pushes me up against the wall behind me. The kiss is rushed and frenzied but I kiss him back with as much hurriedness as him, showing him I'm willing without words. His hands roam over my hips, gripping them tightly as he forces his hardness against my now throbbing core.

"Can you feel what you do to me?"

I know it's not a question he wants me to answer, so I stay quiet, only letting out a weak moan when he roughly yanks the hem of my dress up and slides my knickers to the side. Without any warning, he rams two fingers inside my already slick opening.

I know this is wrong on so many levels, but I can't help the way he makes me feel. It's Owen. I know he wouldn't hurt me, at least not physically anyway.

My body feels like it's floating on air. I throw my head back in pure bliss as he starts to work me up, but when I feel my climax is within reach, he withdraws his fingers, making me look back at him. When my eyes meet his, I spot a look I've never seen before: it's animalistic and wild; it turns me on more than the act on stage did.

He places his fingers against my mouth, "Open," he demands. I part my lips slowly and use my tongue to lick around the tip of his fingers before taking them all the way into my mouth, licking and sucking them clean with no shame whatsoever. I find myself clenching my thighs together as the act has my body reacting in anticipation.

"Tastes good, doesn't it."

Again, it's not a question. I just let slip another moan as I release his fingers with a pop.

The next thing I know, his erection is at my opening, stretching me as he slides himself in deep. He doesn't wait for me to adjust to accommodate him: he picks up his tempo and gets a grip on my backside as he brings my leg up over his hip bone. My head falls forward as I moan into his cheek.

It doesn't take long for his thrusts to become frantic and uncontrolled as he nears his own euphoria. My back now hitting the wall behind me repeatedly.

"Fuck, shit and fuck," he bellows into my neck as he bites his teeth into the top of my shoulder, squeezing my arse as he empties himself inside me, spurring on my own release. We come together, our breaths coming long and loud.

He drops my leg, pulling my dress back down, puts himself back in his trousers and then he's gone.

He walks out of the closet leaving me there, alone. No backwards glance. No nothing.

What the hell was that all about?

I stick my head out around the door frame and watch Owen's retreating back as he walks the way I just came from. His hand gripping at his hair before he roughly messes it up.

My heart is beating wildly in my chest from the effects of what happened up on that stage and now the fact that Owen has just literally fucked me like a whore and I didn't do a god damn thing to stop it. I know I've not helped the situation as it takes two to tango and I didn't exactly do anything to stop him just.

I know Owen, I know he likes to be spontaneous when it comes to sex. I know I'm making excuses for him but I do understand what he needs and why he does it the way he does. He doesn't do feeling. He's already told me as much but he needs to satisfy his needs one way or another and I did give him permission to basically use me for sex instead of going looking for it.

That says more about me than it does him. But like I've said before, if it's the only way I can have a piece of Owen for now, then I'll take it.

Tears fall freely down my cheeks, and I roughly wipe them away. I get my head on straight and go to my original destination, crashing my way into the ladies. The sound of the door banging against the wall grabs the attention of a couple of girls who appear to be on a hen night and who give me a once over before resuming their chat not giving me a second thought.

I head straight for the toilet to sort myself out and when I finally get a look at myself in the mirror, I am appalled at how thoroughly fucked I look.

I fix myself up the best I can, re-applying my lip gloss and flattening my hair. It's as good as it's going to get.

I know I have to go back out there, act like nothing's wrong and try to ignore the fact that Owen had left me standing there like a wet lettuce. Ready to face the music, or not, I leave the bathroom and stagger on my heels over to the group of people I have grown rather fond of.

I could just get blind drunk and forget everything that is Owen Slater. Yeah, that's what I'll do…

So, with my game face on, I make my way straight to the bar and order two tequilas straight up and a fruity cocktail. The shots are first to be placed in front of me, and before the barman has even turned to make my other drink, both shots are gone. The burn numbing my aching heart, but not enough to stop me from feeling nothing like I wanted it to.

Guess I'll just have to keep drinking.

So what do I do? I order two more shots. The barman looks up at me and rolls his eyes.

"It's my birthday," I say in a way of explanation.

"In that case, these drinks are on me." He throws a flirty wink at me that I'm in no mood to reciprocate. I offer him a small smile instead.

"Thanks." That's all he is gonna get.

Taking my almost finished cocktail over to the table where all my friends are, hoping to avoid Owen. I have no such luck as he is sitting in my seat.

He stands to allow me to sit down but doesn't leave me much room to get by. I squeeze past, my breast rubbing over his tight shirt that hides what I know are delicious, ripped abs.

Once I'm seated, I join in with conversation with Remme, Charlotte and Spence. The whole time Owen brushes his arm or leg against mine, whether it is intentional or not, I don't know. Every time he makes some sort of connection, my heart rate picks up speed and goose bumps break out.

I wish he didn't have this much of an effect on me. He's my weakness when I'm sober; adding alcohol into the mix has my senses in overdrive.

I can't win either way.

I need another drink so I can drown in my sorrows.

CHAPTER 9

OWEN

"Who's up for birthday shots?" Dev shouts above the crowd's noise.

What the hell is she playing at?

She seems to be on a mission to have a good night, in more ways than one. Like I'm one to talk after how I've just practically violated her in a closet of a strip club.

What the fuck am *I* playing at?

It was a shitty move on my behalf and I shouldn't have treated her like that. She is a friend above all else and I'm going to ruin that friendship if I can't keep myself in check, or my dick in line regardless of what shit and pathetic idea we both seem to have agreed to without actually verbally agreeing to it.

The rest of our group all offer a 'hell yeah' in reply.

Just as I'm about to announce that I will go to the bar, Saxon pipes up. "I'll get 'em."

In next to no time, Saxon is back with a large tray filled with colourful shots and a glass of orange juice for Remme. We all take a couple of shots each from the tray. Before any of us have even blinked, Devon has downed hers and looks to be already wobbling on her feet. I take her arm and guide her back to a vacant chair, but she pulls out of my grasp sharply.

I narrow my beady eyes on her but she just ignores me. Instead she says something to Charlotte and Remme and all three make a move to the dance floor.

"Oh hell no! That's the last place I want my pregnant wife to be... on a crowded fucking dance floor," Isaak grumbles loudly as he jumps up out his chair, getting ready to pounce.

"Shut the fuck up, man, and sit your overprotective arse back in that seat and just watch her. She'll be fine." I laugh at my best friend as he throws himself back down, beer in hand.

Glancing back to the girls, I watch as Devon and Charlotte grind on each other, and my dick grows painfully hard. Devon snakes her way down Charlotte's side provocatively as her eyes land on me.

Is she doing this on purpose—purposely dancing seductively right in front of me?

When she's all the way down to the floor, her dress rises up showing the flimsy and pointless material of her underwear before she climbs back up Charl's body, swaying her hips to the beat.

She thinks she's clever. We'll see who has the last laugh. She's going to regret teasing me the way she just did.

A few songs later, my sanity is shot to pieces and the girls head back to us. Remme resumes her spot on Isaak's lap, and I can't help but wish it was me with Devon in mine.

Why do I keep thinking shit like this?

"I'll be right back," Dev states as she weaves her way past us. She is looking a little green.

My mouth moves before I can stop it. "Hey, I'm gonna get Dev home. She looks like she may throw up any second," I say looking around for her. I spot her walking back towards us with another tray of fucking shots.

Is this girl for real?

How the fuck did she get served so quick?

I glance over her shoulder and spot the bartender checking out her arse. That explains it.

"Look what I have," she sing-songs. Everyone looks at me.

Remme nods her head and mouths, "Take her home".

I nod back in agreement.

Devon lifts two more shots from the tray and downs them both one after the other, throwing her head back unsteadily. I reach her instantly before she falls flat on her arse.

"Come on you—time to head home. You've had enough." Grabbing her round the waist so she's draped over me, I carry her out of the club and into a waiting taxi—all without a single word of abuse from her. I thought she would have kicked up a stink but she doesn't fight against me when I pull her into the crook of my arm and she rests her head on my shoulder, her eyelids now growing heavy.

By the time we reach Devon's block of flats, she's out for the count. I pull some money out of my back pocket and hand the driver a twenty. I manage to get myself out the door without waking her, and leaning back in, I sweep her up into my arms and cradle her.

She automatically wraps her lax arms around my neck and rests her head against my chest as I carry her the whole way to her door.

"Shit," I curse under my breath as it dawns on me that I need to find her key. Her bag or purse—whatever girls call them—is attached to her wrist, and I can't get to it without waking her.

"Dev…wake up."

She starts to stir in my arms, her head rolling back over my arm.

"Devon, you need to wake up. I need your door key."

She opens her eyes, blinking a couple of times to clear her vision and gather her surroundings.

"Where are we, and why are you carrying me?" The frown marking her features is adorable. She wiggles in my arms, wanting me to put her on her feet, and I place her down gently without letting go in case she forgets how her legs work. She tries to slot the key into the lock but can't seem to line it up.

After a couple of attempts and many huffs later, I give up watching her struggle and take the key from her and let us in. Before I even have the door shut behind me, Dev is running—or should I say stumbling—for the bathroom, leaving the door open behind her.

I hear the echo of her emptying the contents of her stomach in the toilet bowl. Sliding in behind her, I scoop her hair up to ensure she doesn't vomit in it, and when I'm sure there's no more to come, I scoop her up and carry her to the bed. She's asleep before I slip my arms out from underneath her.

Should I strip her out of her dress?

Is that creepy when she is passed out?

It's not like I haven't seen her naked before and I don't want her to be uncomfortable or catch a chill in the night.

Thinking no more of it, I decide the best thing to do is to leave her as she is, minus her shoes and instead just pull the cover over her sleeping form.

I head to the kitchen and start looking around for what I need. Luckily I find what I'm after without to much trouble. I grab a glass, fill it with water and take it back into her with the pain killers I found.

"Devon, sit up." I try coaxing her awake but have no joy, so I try again giving her a firmer nudge this time. "Dev, you need these." Success.

She wakes enough to take my offerings but is groggy and heaving at the same time. There is no way I'm leaving her like this.

I grab the waste bin from the bathroom and place it next to her side of the bed, remove my jacket but remain fully clothed as I climb onto the bed next to her where I can keep an eye on her all night. I don't want her thinking we did anything last night. Finding me on her bed almost naked would certainly give her that impression.

Laying next to her and not touching her is pure fucking torture. I could end my misery and just go sleep on the sofa in the living room, but I can't bring myself to do that.

I only fucked her a couple of hours ago, yet as I'm replaying the way she was dancing tonight has my dick wanting another round.

God, I'm such a twat.

The last thing I remember before falling into a deep sleep, is Devon curling herself into my side and burying her head on my chest. I could move her—in fact I should—but I find myself relaxing more and more my heavy tired eyes finally give in to sleep.

CHAPTER 10
DEVON

I feel the bed moving beside me, and the sudden movement has my head spinning and banging like an orchestra playing in full swing. I feel dreadful, and can't remember much of the previous night.

I remember being on stage with the male dancer and Owen tackling me into a dark closet on my way to the toilet, but anything after that is a blur.

Oh God. I hope I didn't do something stupid or embarrass myself.

A hand skating over my hip makes me freeze and then the panic sets in.

Great, I got so intoxicated last night that I brought a random guy home.

I finally feel brave enough to take a peek and see the damage I may or may not have done. Peeling my eyelids open, I come face to face with a wide-awake Owen, and he looks devilishly refined and fresh faced. He's so Goddamn handsome it makes me nauseous, but in a really, really good way.

"Morning."

He's far too cheery for me this morning. "What are you doing here?" I ask my voice groggy from sleep.

"Coffee? Bet you need it after last night?" He's already out of bed ready to vacate the room without answering my question.

My brain catches up with me, and I remember I was extremely hot-tempered with him.

"Why, Owen?"

He stops short of the door and turns around, and I shoot daggers in his direction.

"What do you mean, why? Why did I bring you home, why did I put you to bed or why did I stay?"

By the sound of his voice, he's just as irked as me.

Does he really not know what I'm getting at? I know I didn't dream it up. I remember the feel of his hands gripping my waist, the harsh bruising kiss he gave me. I remember everything he did to me—like I always do. My blood boils at how he can so easily forget the way he manhandled me so formidably yet so intensely. "Why did you fuck me then walk away the way you did, Owen? I agreed to you fucking me whenever you wanted. I didn't agree to you fucking me then walking away from me without a backwards glance. Not even to make sure I was okay. I had nothing whatsoever. I mean, you couldn't have made me feel any less cheap if you'd stuffed a fifty pound note in my bra for services rendered," I spit at him, full of outrage.

His shoulders sag and his head drops down to the floor, but I stand my ground.

"Devon..."

"Think before you speak, Owen, because what you say next better not be a lie. You don't get to treat me like one of your one night stands who will put up with your shit." I'm really going at him now.

"That's not—"

"While we're at it, why did you fuck off from work the moment I walked through the door?" That grabs his attention, making his eyes bulge wide.

"What the fuck does that have to do with you, Devon?" He's the one raising his voice now.

I see red. I'm leaping off the bed and stalking towards him like a mad woman. He watches my every move, but I move so fast he doesn't see it coming until it's too late. My palm connects perfectly with his cheek, sending his head to the side. I try to ignore the sting in my hand.

He takes a hasty step forwards, caging my face in between his hands, then smashing our mouths together in a clash of teeth and tongues. He moves one hand to fist in my hair and tugs it to tilt my head back allowing him to slide his lips down past my jaw and onto my neck, placing wet kisses all the way down to where the material of my dress starts.

I moan because I just forget everything that is going on around me whenever he is touching me and it's spurring him on all the more.

Dropping his hands to palm my arse, he pulls me closer. I can feel how aroused he is through the fabric of his trousers.

I should be telling him no and trying to push him away from me. I know it's the right thing to do, but yet again my body responds to him like I need my next breath.

My heart wants, want it wants and there's not a damn thing I can do about it. Not where Owen is concerned.

I'm not a weak or pathetic person by any means even though my actions would suggest so.

He reaches one hand up my back unzips my dress and has my bra off in record time before he drops to his knees in front of me, his eye level with my matching bottoms to the bra that is decorating the bedroom floor along with my dress. He hooks his thumbs into the elastic waist as he draws them agonisingly slow down my legs until they are just a pool around my feet. My heart thumps wildly.

He runs his nose up my body, over every rise and dip, until we're standing eye to eye. Owen lifts me up the rest of the way with him so he's standing up to his full height again, and I wrap my legs around his hips.

"Time for breakfast," he announces before spinning me upside down in his arms. I scream playfully, but it soon turns to ecstasy when he dips his face into my soaking wet core.

"Owen. Oh... My... Ohhh."

"That's right, baby. You don't need no Mystic Mike."

Who?

It takes me a second to work out what he's on about and I chuckle quietly to myself. I think he's referring to Magic Mike. I busy myself with the zip on his trousers and roll them and his boxers down his legs far enough for him to shimmy them down and step out of before he kicks them to the side. Owen's obscenely hard length springs free almost hitting me in the face.

My greedy eyes take in the beauty of him, as my head moves of it's own accord. I open my mouth and tickle the very tip of him with my tongue, rolling it around the head of his dick.

"Fuck, Devon…" He isn't prepared for the intrusion. I lick the full length of him before I hollow my cheeks and glide all the way down until he's hitting the back of my throat. I try to relax my jaw as the need to gag overwhelms me.

"Your mouth has some astonishing skills, baby."

This spurs me on to keep going. He's huge, and I'm struggling, water now filling my eyes as they start to sting. I move my hand between us and grasp the base of him, running my fingers over his heavy balls. He grunts his approval into my pulsing heat. His tongue invades me, sucking and licking along my seam before lapping up my juices. I moan around him, the vibration in the back of my throat ricocheting down on him.

I work him up, my head bobbing up and down the best it can in this position, every now and then stopping to tease the tip of him before sinking down again.

"Fuck this, I need inside you." He expertly manoeuvres me around his body so I'm cradled in his arms, all without breaking a sweat. The blood rushes from my head to my toes, but he doesn't give my poor mind time to get it's bearing as I'm catapulted through the air, my arms and legs flinging back in utter shock. I land on the bed with a bounce, my hair all over the place and my heart pounding loudly.

"Owen, you bleeding idiot." I flap my hands out, wafting my hair out of my face. When it's splayed out behind me I can see everything that is in front of me.

Owen looks perfectly divine and mouth-wateringly good standing at the end of the bed, now completely naked. He prowls up the bed towards me. Every ripple of his torso strains, and the veins in his neck and shoulders protrude. He's magnificent.

My body tingles with need for this man—a need so incredibly strong,

I'm not sure what to do with it.

Owen dives on my nipple, clamping down with his teeth. The sensation sends a direct link to my already soaking centre, causing my arousal to dampen my thighs, my back to arch and my breasts to crush against his mouth further. I let out a tiny yelp as I glide my hands up his well-defined back, drawing my nails downward. I know I'm marking him like I own him.

He releases my tight bud with a pop, taking my mouth with a loud growl.

He enters me without warning with a thrust so hard I see stars. My legs wrap around him to take him even deeper.

"Fuck, Dev...I swear you're too good to be true," he says as he buries his face in my neck.

I lean my head forward clamping down on his shoulder. "Harder, Owen... Harder," I pant out. I know I won't be able to walk straight after, but at this point I don't care. Owen interlocks our hands and raises them above my head, pushing them down into the bed. His body lifts slightly, giving him more leverage to push harder and deeper.

The punishing pace is more than my mind can bear, but my body sings with untold pleasure, feeling what he is giving me from head to toe. He wraps my fingers around the spindles of the bed frame, and I already know I'm to leave them there and not let go. He gets to his knees without losing our connection, lifting both my legs over his shoulders, leaning forwards until I'm almost folded in half. I feel like a ball of sensations, my head swimming with need, my core screaming for more and the pit of my stomach fluttering with uncontrollable desire.

The tell-tale sign of my climax building and working its way up my whole body. We both pant so hard, our bodies coated in a layer of sweat, our pace not relenting.

"I'm...oh...come..." It's all I can manage to get out between my mewls.

"Come, Devon. I'm almost there." He thrusts relentlessly, squeezing my overly sensitive breasts at the same time. His impressive cock pulses inside me, and I know he's about to explode. One more slam of his hips and I clamp down on him, sending us both flying into orbit. A flood of our mixed heat leaks from me as we ride and grunt our way through the last embers of our desire.

"You're exquisite," he whispers in my ear, sending shivers down my neck and spine.

"Hmm, a girl could get used to this," I mumble into his shoulder. "You know what I need and you always deliver. I love that my body is so in tune with yours." The moment the words are spoken, I feel his arms tense around me.

"I need to take a shower," he says as he slides himself out of me. I feel the loss of his warmth and pull the covers over me as he leaves for the bathroom. My insecurities creep in, my heart suddenly taking a nosedive. No matter what I do or say, Owen always manages to make me feel useless—that I'm not good enough. It's always after we've had sex, and after what I can only describe as a perfect connection. We share something so special together, that feels so right and he always makes it feel wrong.

The sound of the shower offers me a lullaby, sending me into a soft slumber, which is short lived as the sound of a phone pinging invades my sated mood.

Leaning over to the bedside table, I grab the offending device without checking to see if it's mine.

The screen lights up without me unlocking it.

Benny
Warehouse 10pm sharp.
And don't even think of being a no show again. It won't
end well for you!

"What the fuck?" I whisper to myself, dropping the phone back on the side table frantically as if it's scorched my skin.

Owen attends my father's warehouse?

I'm hardly ever allowed in there, so I don't know the full ins and outs of what goes on, but I know whatever it is, it can't be good. There is a reason I don't get on with my father or tell him anything about my life. Now I find out Owen is mixed up with my dad.

Is that why he was at my parents house last week?

Is whatever is happening tonight the reason why they were arguing?

I want to question Owen again, but he will either lie to my face or distract me like he did earlier. I need to see for myself once and for all what my dad is up to and how Owen is involved. The only way I'm going to get the answers I seek, is if I go to the warehouse myself tonight and find out.

Owen strolls back into the room with my towel hanging low around his waist. Water droplets trickle down his chest across his abs, disappearing into his towel.

How can something so mundane, seem so erotic?

A small laugh makes me flick my eyes back to his.

"Like what you see?" He arches his brow.

I rise from the bed and walk towards him without saying a word, but keep our eyes connected. When I'm just inches from him, I lick my lips, then bend to catch a falling bead of water before it disappears from view. I trail my tongue up his chest, and he takes a deep breath and holds it in. Without any warning and in silent happiness, I step away from him, heading to the shower myself.

CHAPTER 11
OWEN

Seeing the unread text message on my phone after I've showered at Devon's, deflates my mood, reminding me of what I have to do for Benny tonight. I've gone from being on an almighty high to a depressed, sour-faced dickhead.

I can't face looking Devon in the eye and lying to her again about my whereabouts—she's already acting suspicious—so being the douchebag I am, I leave her a note on her pillow for her to find instead me having me waiting for her, the note telling her she needs to run the gym for a few days. No explanation as to why, but I know it'll be needed. I pull up my Uber app and order a taxi as I've left my car at home.

I don't know why it matters so much that I don't want to lie to her, but for some reason, it seems important that I don't.

I'm getting too close to her—I know I am. Devon has gotten under my skin, into my heart and I'm powerless to stop it. I'm not even sure I want to anymore.

I don't know what's in store for me when I get to Benny's rundown warehouse, but I do know I'll be in the circle, which will end with me sporting a couple of bruises and cuts on the face at least.

Taking a couple of days off work is for the best—this way the bruises will have hopefully started to fade slightly and I won't need to explain myself again.

I sit in my car having come back to my place to grab everything I need for the night's activities, not knowing where to go next. I start the engine, finding comfort in the rumble of vibrations my sporty number provides. I pull the car away from the curb and mindlessly drive away. I could go to Isaak's, but then he will be on at me about Benny showing up last week. So I head to the gym instead.

Maybe I can warm up there before I have to go to the club. Now I have a set place in mind, my journey doesn't take all that long. Before I know it, I'm parking my car in its usual spot, noticing Isaak's in the spot that Rem usually uses when she is working in the loft. I just can't catch a break today: first Devon and her curious mind then the text message; now I have to face my brother from another mother.

"What did I do to deserve this?" I huff, as I exit the car, leaving my bag on the passenger seat for later.

I do a double take when Jemma's voice bellows at me from across the reception area instead of Devon's.

"Good afternoon, Owen." She happily sings. I offer her a small lift of my chin in greeting, not trusting my own voice to sound as happy as hers.

I'm saved from coming across as the arsehole I really am, by Isaak.

"Owen, good to see you. Glad you're here. Wanna go a round or two with me?"

Isaak seems chirpy today. I wonder what put him in a good mood, then remember what he told me the last time Rem was pregnant. Her libido had been enough to make his dick fall off from overuse, which is saying something considering he used to be more of a man whore than I am—not that he'll ever admit it.

"Sure. Just give me a sec. I need to pop my phone and car keys in my office. I'll meet you in the ring," I tell him. I abandon both items on my desk, not really caring where they land, and make my way over to the ring, grabbing my own gloves on the way.

"What's up man?" Isaak asks, while he has his gloves fitted into place. He knows me too well to mistake the look on my face for anything other than what it is.

"Just have a lot on my mind, but I'm sorting it. We sparring or not?" I know my tone is coming across more aggressive than I intend but he takes it on the chin.

"Yeah, but just know I'll only let it go for so long before I eventually want some answers, Owen. You owe me that much."

He's absolutely right: he does deserve an explanation, but I'm still not ready to give him one. When I find a way out of all this then I will tell him everything he needs to know. Until then, I can't. If he knows what I got myself into back then and why, he'd want—no, need—to get involved, and I can't let him do that. He has Remme, Logan and another baby on the way; he has too much to lose. I will not let him risk everything he's worked so hard to keep.

"I will, Isaak. I promise. But the less you know, the better. For you and your family. Please just trust me." I practically beg him as I shove my hands in my gloves and wait while they're being tied.

"I do trust you. That's what I'm afraid of."

"Just give me some more time." I climb the ropes of the ring and join him. He gives a defeated head nod and drops the subject.

Knocking gloves, we begin our sparring.

By the time we've finished, we're both sweating and panting for breath. All my muscles burn, but it's what I need. Now I'm pumped up and ready to go full throttle.

When we do finally step out of the ring, I glance at the clock and breathe in a lungful of air making my chest puff out.

I've still got a little time before I need to leave and head to Benny's warehouse. So I head for the showers, grabbing a towel as I pass the rail holding the clean ones. Isaak choosing to go another round with one of the sparring lads, of which I'm thankful for. Being on my own gives me time to clear my head ready for later.

I quickly wash and re dress in clean clothes and head to my office to catch up on some things to pass the time quicker. I hate waiting around, so anything to keep my mind occupied will do me good.

Once I'm done, I head out into the gym and chat with some of the regulars and before I know it, it's almost time.

I walk over to Isaak, "I need to get going. I'll check up with you in the week, yeah?" I don't hang around for his reply. I take long strides back towards to my office, grab my phone, making a quick call for a taxi in case I'm in no fit state to drive after I've fought in the circle. Once that's done, I pocket my mobile and swipe my car keys from the desk and head on out.

As I'm about to open the main doors of the gym, Isaak stops me.

"Owen..."

I crane my neck in his direction, still in the boxing ring at the far side.

"Be careful brother."

"Always am." I nod as I slip out into the now much darker and cooler night.

The taxi pulls up as I'm locking my car after grabbing my other gym bag I take with me to Benny's.

I jump in, throwing my bag on the side of the seat next to me, and give the taxi driver the address. Leaning my head back on the headrest, I close my eyes, thinking of how I found myself here, replaying everything out in my mind as if it were only yesterday.

"Benny, I've told you this before. Isaak is off the table. He's just signed his contract to become Pro. There is no way I'm letting you fuck that up for him, just so you can make more money. You're getting too greedy, and it's gonna bite you in the arse. I can see it coming. This is going to end badly for the both of us."

I stop outside of Gavin's office at the end of the hall at the sound of Gavin talking about Isaak again. This is starting to become a habit.

What is Benny after Isaak for?

Why is he so persistent about it?

"I need a real fighter; Isaak is the full package and you know it," Benny roars.

Whatever it is they are discussing, it's not for Isaak's benefit. That much I do know, and I'm not going to sit back and let them ruin Isaak's dream over something that will not happen. I know it won't happen because I'll do everything in my power to make sure it doesn't. Isaak is my best mate, my brother and he has everything working out for him. He's on the right path and it's going to stay that way.

"Unless you can come up with a better solution, it's happening, Gavin."

"I don't know why you think you can dictate what my boy will or will not be doing."

"I think you're forgetting something, Gav... If I go down, I'll be taking you down with me. Just remember that. Isaak will be fighting for me and, what's more, you're gonna let it happen."

I can sense the smugness coming off Benny in waves, making me want to punch it straight off his face.

"Benny... Please..."

I feel a lump forming in my throat at Gavin pleading for his son. I've never had someone do that for me. My mum tries, but it's not the same as if it were a father doing it. My father... Well, he's nowhere to be seen and hasn't been since I was six years old.

I barge my way into the room, halting all conversation.

"I'll do it," I announce, even though I don't know what it is I'm agreeing to.

"Owen... No. You can't." Gavin walks around his desk, taking a firm hold of my shoulders. "How much have you heard?" he asks, staring hard at me.

"Enough to know that I can't let you both do this to Isaak," I tell him honestly.

"You shouldn't have even overheard any of this, Owen. There is no way I'm letting you get involved in this world. It's not a place you want to visit," he pleads, but it falls on deaf ears. I've already made my mind up.

"You're not letting me. I volunteer myself. This is on me. Isaak is like a brother to me. I'm doing this, and there's nothing you can do to stop me." I *swing my gaze from the only man I've ever considered as a father as tears start to build in his eyes, piercing Benny with a more unpleasant glare when he speaks again.*

"You'll do. I've seen you train with Isaak: you have potential and guts. I could use that."

I can see the pound signs twinkle in his eyes already. I knew there was a reason I'd taken an immediate dislike to this man.

"I have one condition, and I want your word or the deals off," I aim my words at Benny, the sly curl of his lip making my stomach roll.

"Name your price, Owen."

"Isaak never finds out about any of this." I make my demand and watch as Benny thinks it over.

"Okay, deal."

Taking one last look at Gavin, his sorrowful expression sitting heavy on my heart, I walked out his office as if I didn't just sign my life away to the devil.

Regardless, I know I've made the right choice.

Looking back at the inescapable day, I still believe I made the right choice.

CHAPTER 12
DEVON

I'm starting to think I made a grave mistake coming here. There are no working street lights, and it's eerily quiet.

Where the hell is Owen?

It's almost ten. The message on his phone said he needed to be here for this time and I know this is the right address. I'm about to give up and drive back home when the bright lights of a car blind me as it turns off the road and heads past me. I duck, sliding down further in my seat so I'm not spotted as the headlights flash and shine in my car. Once it's driven past, I shimmy up a little to look in my rear-view mirror, spotting a male figure jumping out of the back of a taxi and heading to the unguarded door. I only see who it is as the glow from behind the open door sheds light on him.

It's Owen.

That gets my arms and legs moving.

I open my car door, throw myself out and ever so slowly press the door closed until it clicks shut, deciding not to lock it in case the noise is too piercing and Owen or someone else hears it.

I know there's a back door around here somewhere, I briefly remember but everything looks different in the dark. I try to gather my bearings somewhat as I creep around to what I think is the back of the building. Every loud bang or clatter makes me jump, causing me to pause in my tracks and whip my head in every direction.

After what feels like an hour—when in reality it is more like a couple of minutes—I find the door I'm searching for.

Seems they don't mess around once everyone has arrived: by the sound of the racket in there, it's in full swing.

I peer my timid head around the door. Everyone's backs are to me forming a circle around a dreadful, menacing-looking cage. The hairs on my neck stand to attention at the thought of what I'm about to see. I may have never been allowed to come here, but unbeknown to my father, I'd followed him here a couple of times when I was younger, trying to find out what shady shit he was really up to. Once I'd found out the jist of his dodgy doings, I'd wanted nothing to do with it all.

I spot my dad over in the corner of the cool, dingy, dimly-lit warehouse. He passes a wad of cash to a burling, mean-looking man—the man I've seen at my parents more than once, Kyle: Dad's right hand man and lacky.

From what I can tell, it looks like all bets have been placed for the winner of the next gruelling fight. I don't envy the people who choose to fight in that cage, even if I've always wondered what makes them want to do it in the first place.

"Devon?" My father's booming voice echoes in the surroundings, making me look skittishly at him. I try to play down my feelings, not wanting him to know the real reason I'm here.

"Hey, Dad." I cautiously make my way further inside and towards my father, who's holding my stare, looking murderously dangerous.

"What are you doing here? You know this is no place for you." He knows I know this, but I'm not about to tell him I followed Owen here: that will raise too many questions that he'll demand answers to. I know how my father works: he likes to look for people's weaknesses. I can't let him see that Owen is fast becoming mine.

I start to panic as I haven't thought of what I'd say to him if he found me here. I fidget on my feet and bite my bottom lip nervously. The only thing that springs to mind is how Mum had acted the last time I saw her, so I go with that and hope it quenches his inquisitiveness.

"I wanted to get you on your own. I'm worried about Mum. She wasn't herself last time I came to visit. She literally ushered me back out the door."

"Take no notice, Dev. You know what your mum's like." He waves off my concern as if it's nothing to worry about. He knows more than he's letting on, but as this isn't the real reason for me being here, I don't push for more.

"Aahh, the main event is about to start."

I'm too busy scanning the warehouse, trying to locate Owen's whereabouts, to pay much attention to what he's saying now. All of a sudden, there's an almighty roar, and the metal on the cage rattling almost deafens me.

"You need to run along now, Devon."

I spin my head to face him again, noticing the scowl he's giving me.

"Jesus, subtle much. It's not like I don't know what the setup is here, Dad." I roll my eyes.

"I'm well aware of what you know and what you don't, but that's not what I was referring to. I don't think you'll be up to watching the next fight, that's all." The sly smirk on his face doesn't go a miss. He's up to something. I just can't work out what.

With a single nod of his head towards the cage, I follow his gaze and almost crumble to the hard cement under my feet. "Owen… No…" My words leave me breathless.

I knew he was up to something with my father, but this… Not once had it ever occurred to me, that Owen was fighting for him.

How could I have been so stupid and blind?

The amount of times Owen showed up at work with cuts and bruises covering him, or his face would be swollen. I never put two and two together, and knowing he was at my parents house a couple of days ago should have put the final piece of the puzzle together for me.

I guess I really am blindsided where Owen is concerned. I could kick myself for not seeing this nightmare happening before me.

In a daze, I miss the beginning of the fight, my whole body weighing heavy.

"Why now?" I struggle to form any words, the sight in front of me breaking me.

"You think just because you want out of this life I don't keep tabs on you, Devon? I know what you get up to and the people you care about."

Now I'm even more confused. Why is he treating me like he doesn't care about me at all?

"Why? I don't understand how you know Owen, or how you seem to think that what I do with my life has anything to do with you."

"You're my daughter, Devon. It's my job to know." He shrugs me off like what he's just said makes sense, when it doesn't whatsoever.

I whip my body around from him to face the cage. Owen is on top of the fighter, jabbing his elbow in the side of his head. His eyes are black pits of emptiness, like he's not even aware of his surroundings or what it is he's actually doing.

He looks menacing, and it's hard to watch.

"What do you have over him, Dad?" I demand to know, but it's hopeless. He wouldn't give me that information willingly.

"Owen's here of his own free will, Devon. He asked to be here."

I know my eyes show how surprised I am at his declaration. "He wouldn't… He… He…" I'm lost for words, utterly speechless. I make my way towards the cage—towards Owen—my father's laughter not making this information any easier to take.

I don't understand why Owen would be doing this.

Like a moth to a flame, I'm drawn closer to him, even though he is not who I thought he was. The person I see before me is a total stranger.

He must sense me, too.

My hands reach out connecting with the cage, the only thing blocking me from getting to him.

His head shoots up, looking directly at me, and the moment his eyes meet mine, the darkness that was in his eyes slowly disappears.

He's seen me.

I can't take this anymore.

I need to get out of here.

I turn my back on Owen and run away, past my father's seemingly happy face.

"Devon!" It's Owen's voice I hear but I don't stop.

Nothing will make me stop, not even the desperation in his tone.

CHAPTER 13
OWEN

“**D**evon!” I roar at the top of my lungs, when the dark cloud in my version begins to clear and I see her tear-streaked face briefly before she turns and runs from me.

What the fuck is she doing here?

How can she even know about this place?

There are so many questions spinning in my mind right now, that I lose focus.

I need to get out of this cage and find her.

I deliver the most powerful and violent punch I can muster, using whatever energy I have left in the tank. The other guy's nose pops, spraying my face and chest with blood. I don't stop there: bringing my fist down on the guy's face, I repeatedly hit him, raining down punch after punch. He's not fighting back, yet I still carry on my assault. I'm raging, and nothing can stop that feeling from taking over, except Devon.

The guy's out for the count.

I stand tall, my chest heaving up and down from exhilaration, my body steaming and sweat pouring off from me. I look down at my hands, the strapping around my knuckles now tainted crimson red. I seek out Benny in the crowd, waiting for the nod of his approval.

He gives it me, looking pretty fucking pleased with himself now he's just bagged himself over a hundred grand for this fight.

I stagger to the gate on the cage, my legs aching and heavy from excessive overuse. The guys who Benny is finding seem more determined to win, making me fight even harder—not for me, and not for anyone but Benny. Because I have to.

"Open the gate!" I demand of anyone with a key on the other side. No one moves, at least not quickly enough. "Open the fucking gate!" I roar, threateningly full of untold rage. My hand pounds relentlessly on the metal cage, and I grasp the slates, shaking it with all I have.

Still no one moves.

All the men look over to the man who controls almost everyone in the room—everyone except me.

"So help me, God. If someone doesn't open this gate, I'll…"

Thankfully Benny must give his permission because, finally, someone begins to open it up. As soon as the key turns in the lock, I force my way through it and push everyone who's in my way, out of it.

I grab my bag from where I left it before walking into the circle cage and run full pelt in the direction Devon had run off in.

As I reach Benny, he smirks at me as he counts some of his winnings from the previous fights and mine.

I stop the moment his eyes meet mine. There's something in the way he's looking at me that causes me to pause and falter in my steps.

"Why is Devon here looking for you, Owen?" He narrows his eyes on me.

"How the fuck should I know? It wouldn't surprise me if it were you who instigated it all. It's something you'd do, just so you can get your kicks out of other peoples misery," I say accusingly.

He tilts his head to the side, studying me with curious eyes. His hand moving again grabs my attention. "Here's your cut from the fight." He holds his hand out with what I'd say is over ten grand.

I just stare at it like it's a foreign object.

He shakes his palm, wafting the notes in my face.

"Keep it. I don't want your blood money anymore." I stare him down so he knows I mean business and then I turn to carry on in my pursuit of Devon.

"Owen…"

I stop but don't turn around.

"Stay away from my daughter. If you don't, it'll end horribly... For both of you." His threatening words leave me feeling unsettled and unsure if his threat is for me or Devon herself.

My feet move me the rest of the way, and I'm soon out the door into the chill of the night. The coldness mixed with the burning radiating inside me, a nice contradiction. I throw my head up to the heavens and take a breather.

Wait…

Did Benny just say daughter?

Devon is Benny's fucking daughter—his flesh and blood?

I'd been so focused on getting to Devon and escaping Benny's curious mind to realise what he actually said to me.

If Devon is Benny's daughter, that means she's Isaak's fucking cousin.

"Fuck, fuck, fucking fuck!" I roar in pure frustration. Not only have I gone and slept with Isaak's cousin, I've got involved with Benny's little girl—his only little girl.

Does Isaak know Devon is related to him?

That's a stupid question, of course he doesn't know. He's had nothing to do with his family for years. There's no way he could have known about Devon.

More to the point, is the only reason Devon is in all our life's because she's under the influence of her father?

I know how influencing Benny can really be, especially if he knows your weaknesses.

He now knows who is my weakness. I hate to admit it, but she is. Devon has worked her way under my skin and imprinted herself there.

I need answers, and the only person who's going to give them to me is Devon. I get my feet moving then come to an abrupt stop when I remember

I didn't drive here tonight.

I have no car.

"For fuck sake. Can this night get any worse?" I drop my gym bag to the floor and bend at the knees. Unzipping the ruck sack, I rummage around to find my phone to call another taxi. My phone lights up in the pitch black of the night.

"Going somewhere?" Her questioning voice has me rooted to the spot and my fingers pausing. I peer up from my phone and look the way her voice came from.

"Devon..."

She walks out from the shadows and stops only inches away from me. "Let me explain, ple—" The sting on my cheek catches me by surprise. I close my eyes for a brief moment and exhale long and slow before turning my heated eyes to her again.

Okay, I deserved that.

She raises her arm again, but this time I see her intentions and grab a hold of her wrist, yanking it back down to her side.

Getting up close and personal with her, I narrow my accusing eyes to her. "Was that really necessary? It seems I'm not the only one who's keeping secrets, Devon." I let go of her wrist and take a step back.

"I don't have secrets, Owen. That's something you do." Her chest bounces up and down, distracting me for what I've just learnt.

"Don't lie to me. I know who you are and what your game is!" I bellow, looking away from her as I try to gain control of my emotions.

The way she can stand there and blatantly lie to my face after everything really makes me angry.

"What game? Owen, I have no idea what you're talking about. What I do know is that you're fighting in an abandoned warehouse. Which, by the way, is illegal. How can you be so stupid?" She has the nerve to sound disappointed in me. I hate what I do, but at this moment in time there is nothing I can do about it.

"I'm not stupid, Devon. You have no idea why I do what I do." I drop my head down, the pain in my chest tightening. I hadn't wanted anyone to see me like this—to witness what I become every time I walk inside that damn metal cage.

It really is a fucking cage.

Devon is the last person I want to see me like this.

"Then tell me. Help me understand why. Please?" The plea is evident in her words.

I need to get her away from here. I can't explain myself to her outside in the dark, and not only that but she has a lot to answer for, too.

If she wants answers, then so do I.

This is going to be a long night.

"Fine, but not here. I haven't got my car, so you'll have to take me home." I'm pleasantly calm with her, but on the inside I'm mad as hell.

"Okay."

I pocket my phone and collect my bag from the ground and follow her to her car in silence.

CHAPTER 14
DEVON

The whole drive to Owen's is eerily quiet; neither one of us has spoken a word. The only movement he makes is when he frantically starts to unwrap the blood-stained tape from his hand and wipes his face, bare chest and hands roughly with a towel from his bag. Once he finishes with it, he throws it back in his gym bag. Every move he makes is robotic, like he's done the same routine so many times before he could do it in his sleep.

He's obviously inside his own head the entire time, absentmindedly watching the sleeping city as we pass it by in a daze.

I keep glancing over at him, whether he knows it or not.

He's still yet to acknowledge me.

Nothing he's been saying makes any sense. I know why I'm outraged with him, but the fact he's treating me like I'm the one who has done something wrong is baffling me. I don't have any secrets, not that I'm fully aware of anyway. Unless there's something he knows that I don't.

I pull up to his drive and switch the engine off, pulling the key out of the ignition.

"We're here," I say softly.

"Sorry, what?" He finally turns to look at me, his eyes void of… anything.

"I'd said we're here," I repeat.

"Oh, okay." He's gets out of the car, bag in hand, and walks up the path that leads to his house. He's in a world of his own. I'm not even sure he's fully aware of my presence either, which is putting me on edge even more than before.

He reaches the front door before I've even unhooked my seatbelt. I snap myself out of my funk as I jump out of my car, close the door and lock it, walking fast to catch up with him.

Once inside, he walks into the kitchen like a ghost, totally out of sorts.

"Are you going to say something?" I break the silence. It's lasted long enough.

"I have a lot to say. I'm still trying to wrap my head around it all." He places his palms down flat against on the kitchen counter, gripping it tightly and bracing his arms, making the muscles ripple in his arms and back.

"What is there to think about Owen? You have been fighting, simple, and for what, money? For kicks? Why?" I feel my anger rising to the surface again, which if you ask me, is long overdue.

"You think I wanna be doing this? You think I'd be risking everything I have for a cheap thrill and blood money for no good reason?" When he turns to face me, fury rolls off him in waves, causing me to take a step backward.

"Well, I don't fucking know," I yell back.

"You can fucking talk, Little Miss 'I can fool everyone' Secretive." The daggers he's throwing my way make me recoil. Up this close and now with lighting, I can see his face properly. He's got a cut on his bottom lip and a bruise sitting on his cheek bone.

"What are you going on about, Owen?" I'm clueless. He keeps going back to this, and I haven't the foggiest idea what he possibly means.

"You… Coming into my life, my friends' lives, pretending to be someone you're not."

"I'm not the one who's lying to them all. Do any of them even know how deep you're in with this shit?" I'm really getting started now. "You don't know my father like I do, Owen. He's... He's..." I don't get to finish.

He strides over to me, getting in my face, before I can even blink.

"I know Benny better than you fucking think, Devon. I've been Benny's pawn for years. What I didn't know was the fact that you're his fucking daughter. Tell me, did he make you do it, or did you volunteer?" He roars in my face, scaring me. I'm frozen in place at how aggressive he's being towards me. "Answer me!" I have to tilt my head back to really look at him as he's that close.

"Ask me to do what? Owen, I don't know what you're talking about." I can feel tears building, ready to slip, but I will them not to fall.

I've never seen Owen look so frightening and disconnected before. He's intimidating, and the sheer size of him should be making me run from him, but the more I stare in his eyes, the more pain and sadness I see.

"Tell me Devon. Who's your mum? What's her name?" he fires his questions.

Why would that be of any importance to him?

"San... Sandra. Why, what does she have to do with any of this?"

He slides to the floor in front of me, dropping is head in his hands, looking completely defeated.

"Fuck!" His head is downcast, now laying limply on his shoulders.

I'm even more confused than before. I've brought him home under the impression he will give me the answers to my questions, but this whole time he's been grilling me about my parents.

He definitely knows more than he's letting on, and I'm going to find out what that is.

"I don't fucking believe this." He throws his head back running his hands over his face into his hair before he starts pulling at it.

"What are you not telling me, Owen?"

"You really don't know do you?" He sarcastically laughs. "The day you walked into the gym asking for a job, you didn't know me or Isaak, or anyone for that matter did you?" He's still on his knees, but at least he's looking at me now.

"No, why would I? I was looking for a job to get away from my family's or rather my fathers reputation. It's why I changed my last name by deed poll, and then I saw the advert online." I'm still confused as to what this has to do with him fighting.

"This just keeps getting better and better." He picks himself up off the floor and moves over to the sofa, bracing his arms on the top of his legs. "What was your last name before you changed it?"

"Brookes, why?" As soon as I ask, the penny drops. Isaak's name is Brookes and it never registered before now. "Oh my God." I feel a panic attack or something coming on. I swallow it away. "Tell me everything, Owen."

"Devon, I shouldn't be the one telling you this. You should talk to Sandra." He looks tormented.

"No, I want to know what's going on, and you're going to tell me," I demand, trying to look more confident than I feel.

"Shit, Devon." He looks up at me, conflicted by what he should do or say. I'm not backing down. I need to know what he knows. I at least deserve to know the truth if it involves me.

"Fine, if Benny is your father—"

"He is."

"You going let me finish before you jump the gun?"

I keep my mouth firmly shut and nod my head.

"Sit."

I follow his order and find myself sitting down next to him. "If Benny is your father that makes Isaak your cousin, Devon."

I sit back in shock. I'm related to Isaak?

"That's not all… Now I know who your mother is... Let's just say it gets more interesting from here."

"Just spit it out, Owen. For God's sake," I yell at him.

"Sandra is Isaak's mum."

I freeze, staring straight through him.

"Devon, did you hear what I just said?"

I can't answer him, I'm not able to speak. Emotion is trapped like a tennis ball stuck in my throat.

"I...I don't understand. You're lying."

"I'm not lying."

"Why would my parents keep that from me? Mum would tell me if I had a brother."

"I don't know, Devon. Something is going on, or something has gone down in the past for them to keep you a secret."

"Does Isaak know?" Tears have broken the damn and run freely down my face.

Owen gently wipes them away. "No. Isaak's in the dark just as much as you. If he knew about you, he would have told you by now."

I lift my head and look for any sign that he's lying. He's not. He seems to be in as much pain about this as me.

"You really care about him, don't you?" I find my loose lips asking.

"Who, Isaak?"

I nod my head, his hand still grazing my face.

"He's like a brother to me."

"Where do we go from here, Owen? I mean, what do we do about all this?" I'm at a total loss here. My whole life has been a lie; everything I know has been a lie. The fact that Isaak has the same name as my father, never even occurred to me. There's plenty of people who share the same last name but are of no relation to each other.

"I don't know. I get the feeling something more is going on; I just need to find out what that is."

"Okay. What do we tell Isaak?" I'm panicking just thinking about Isaak's reaction to finding out that I'm his half sister.

"Nothing yet. I need all the facts first. What I've just told you goes no further than us. Understood?" He takes hold of my chin and gently makes me focus on him solemnly.

"Alright. As we're getting everything off our chests, you wanna tell me what's going on with you and my father now?" I press, hoping he'll open up more to me after what he's just announced.

He huffs and sighs defeatedly. "You're not going to let this lie, are you?"

I shake my head. "Fine. If you promise to keep this to yourself as well."

"I promise."

"I made a deal with Benny and Gavin—Isaak's dad—when I was eighteen. I overheard your father and Gavin having a heated discussion over Isaak. At the time, Isaak had just been signed by his promoter and management team to fight professionally. He'd fought so hard to get to that point in his career. Literally his blood, sweat and tears went into everything he did. I wasn't going to let them take that away from him. Not when I could do something to stop it."

He pauses, like he's suddenly reliving the events that unfolded that day. I stay silent and unmoving so he doesn't stop.

"Benny was telling Gavin that Isaak would be fighting for him in the circle—the cage you saw at the warehouse that I fought in."

I nod so he knows I'm listening and understanding so far.

"Anyway, Gavin was having none of it, practically begging Benny to find someone else, but Isaak was an exceptionally talented fighter, even at that age, and Benny wanted the best of best."

I can see where this is going, and I don't like it. My heart is breaking for Owen just hearing the way he speaks about Isaak, and what he was prepared to do for him.

I think I know how this story is going to end, and it only makes me fall for Owen that little bit more.

CHAPTER 15
OWEN

I don't know how she does it, but she gets me opening up to her with ease. She's sitting in a trance, taking everything I've thrown at her in her fucking stride like a little warrior.

My little warrior.

I've told her the hard part of the story, so I don't know why I'm starting to struggle telling her the end of it. I battle my way through, seeing the finish line in sight.

"Anyway, Benny got greedy. Gavin was trying to get out of Benny's grasp, but Benny threatened him, saying something about taking Gavin down with him if he was to go down. Benny was getting Isaak to fight whether or not Gavin allowed it. You getting everything so far, Devon?"

"Yes."

She doesn't say anything else but follows it up with a small smile for me to continue.

"I stormed into Gav's office and volunteered to take Isaak's place."

She sucks in a gasp, clearly shocked by my admission.

"To Benny, I was the next best thing. He'd seen me training and sparring with Isaak. I guess he saw my potential. Gavin insisted I was making a mistake, that I didn't know what I was getting myself into, but it didn't matter. I'd already made my mind up. So I signed the deal with the devil, so to speak."

"Fucking hell, Owen." The tears that slowly rolled down her cheeks before have now turned into an endless stream. "I can't believe you did that."

"I'd do it all over again, in a heartbeat. You've seen the life Isaak has now. He has a career he loves, a wife who he fucking worships. He has a family that's growing by the second. He wouldn't have any of that if Benny had sunk his money grabbing paws into him."

"Why are you still doing it? Surely my dad wouldn't try to go after Isaak now: he's in the public eye. He's not that stupid to draw attention to what his business entails?"

She's right, Benny isn't that stupid.

"Benny has ways to keep you at arm's length, yet somehow you're still within his grasp. As you know, he finds your weakness. My friends are my family. They are my weakness and he's used that to his advantage. First it was Isaak. When he couldn't use him against me, he threatened to go after my gym—the only other passion I had in my life. I couldn't let that happen. So I carried on fighting for him, trying to figure out how to get myself out and come up with a way to take him down for good. I'm still trying to figure out how. I was working on a plan. But now…" I slide my hand across the silkiness of her cheek, and she leans into it closing her eyes. "But now…I think he's found my only true weakness."

She slowly opens her beautiful green eyes, my own reflection staring back at me, making me see everything from a different perspective. She's showing me what my life would look like if I just allowed it to happen.

I realise what's been right in front of me this entire time. I've just been too blind to see it... Until now.

"What weakness is that?" She asks innocently.

"You." I simply state.

"Me?" She seems shocked or surprised by my declaration.

"Yes, you. I know you think I've only ever used you or treated you like nothing but a play toy, there just to satisfy my sexual needs, but you are my weakness, and I have been too far up my own arse to see it until now."

"Are you saying you want to try a relationship with me, not just be fuck buddies?"

I can see the hope written all over her face.

"I'm saying, I think we've always had something going on between us that's more than just fucking. I was just afraid to see it—too afraid to show you the real me. Now that I have, I want more."

"What about everything that has happened tonight? Does it not bother you that you know who I am? That I'm Isaak's sister?"

Wow, that sounds weird coming from her mouth.

"Oh shit... I've been fucking my best mates sister..." I can't stop the words flying out of my mouth. It's not like I knew that vital piece of information before hand, but Isaak will flip his fucking lid when he gets hit with all this.

"Owen, I want more with you, too, but you have been holding back on me so much, and not just about all this but how you are when we're together too. I need to understand you and what you want; I need you to explain it to me. Are you some kind of dom?"

I love how innocent she is to my way of fucking, how pure and untouched she really is.

"No, I'm not a dom, but I do like the women I'm with sexually to be somewhat submissive," I try explaining to her. I'm being honest and open about the whole thing. I'm not ashamed of what I like sexually, but I'm finding it hard to tell her what it is. Words seem to be failing me. She knows I like control, this much I have shown in our previous times together, even if I have hold back slightly. Telling her about the toys I like to play with should the mood fit might send her running, even after everything that's been said.

With Devon, I have loved the sex we've had, but I crave more. And I crave more with her. That said I haven't been with anyone else since the second time I was with her. That in itself, tells me more than I need to know. How I haven't seen it sooner is mind boggling, although I have had other things on my mind. Either that, or I've seen it coming but chose to ignore it.

"So, explain to me what it is that makes a submissive. I know very little about this world, Owen. I want to understand... For you, for us."

I can see how curious she is, and the fact she already wants to please me is a massive turn on. But I don't want her to be anymore submissive than she already is.

"There is only one way I can make you understand, baby. Let me show you." I get up from the couch, hissing in pain from the bruising on my ribs. I hold my hand out for her to take. Thankfully there is no hesitation from her.

I pull her along behind me until we get to my bedroom. I don't let go until she is perched on the end of the bed. Reluctantly, I let go and my hand loses the spark I always feel when we're connected, even if I didn't understand why it was there. I think I'm beginning to get my head around it now. I'm falling for this girl.

Undeniably Fast.

Taking the few steps needed to get to my walk in closet, I quickly locate the small trunk I have tucked away in there. Taking it into the bedroom and placing it at her feet, I take a seat on the floor next to it, ignoring the pain that screams through my body now the adrenaline has started to wear off. My feet are firmly on the floor, knees bent, hands clasped and my elbows resting on my knees.

"What is that?" She looks confused, the frown lines marring her perfect face as she leans over the bed, full of inquisitiveness.

"This is my...play box. Inside here are the things I like to use during sex, for your pleasure as much as mine." I wait for that to sink in before I show her, but she has other ideas.

She gets up from the bed and just when I think she's about to walk out, she surprises me and comes to sit in between my spread legs, now fully intrigued. She reaches forward and looks back at me, silently asking for permission to peek inside.

"You can look if you want, or I can just show you them as I use them on you?" I wrap my arms around her, and it feels...right—like it's meant to be.

This girl is perfect for me.

Her movement in my arms clears my foggy mind. Devon is on her feet and stripping her top over her head. I swallow thickly as I take in her midnight blue, silk bra. My heart rate spikes further as she lowers her hands to unfasten her skin tight jeans. I watch on in unadulterated fascination as she pushes the waistband seductively down and off her toned legs, revealing a matching thong.

"Fuck, that underwear is sinful on you, baby," I grumble as I get to my hands and knees crawling my way up her body. Running my hands up from her ankles, over her sexy calves to the backs of her creamy thighs, I pepper her stomach with tiny kisses. Taking a tight hold of her arse, I lift her up as she lets out a loud squeal before placing her back on the bed and returning to grab the box. I'm buzzing with elated anticipation at finally getting to show her the side of me I've tried to keep hidden from her.

I strip out of my shorts and boxers as fast as humanly possible, and she gasps at the sight of my body covered in the bruises that have already started to form. She runs her hands over my torso, and when she looks down she stops her roaming. I know why she's stopped, and from the look on her face she's only just noticed it. The conversation we had only moments ago kept her from taking in the sight of me, until now.

"Owen, you're hurt. We don't have to do this right now."

There is no way I'm waiting, and I'm not woefully hurt.

"Fuck that, I'm taking you right the fuck now, and as much as I love those undies, they need to come off." I open the box as she begins to take the last scraps of fabric from her body, and grab the first thing I see: a brand new set of three shiny butt plugs, all perfectly shrink wrapped for cleanliness. I can feel my pulse beating in the end of my dick just imagining her wearing them like a piece of jewellery. She's completely naked and at my mercy in the middle of the bed as I move to straddle her hips and pass her the package.

"W... Wha... Owen, I have no idea what these are." Her nerves are obvious to my ears.

"They are butt plugs. You start with the small one and work your way up the sizes to stretch you, making you ready for me to own that part of you, too." I take them from her grasp and take the smallest plug out. I hold it up to show her. "I won't take you there tonight, but I will soon. I just want you to feel the pleasure that these can give us both. You up for trying them out?" I ask, already knowing that she will. Devon wanting to please, pleases me immensely.

"I trust you, Owen."

Not giving her a chance to take it back, I lean over and grab the bottle of lube from the draw and coat the end of it.

"Get on your hands and knees, arse facing me."

Her eyes are wide, eyebrows in her hair line and her teeth worrying her bottom lip, but she promptly complies with my request.

"Deep breaths in and out and relax all your muscles. When you feel the resistance, bare down onto it. Okay?"

She nods in understanding. I place my free hand on the small of her back, holding her in place. Sliding the plug across her forbidden button, I give it a gentle but firm nudge. I can feel her gravitate backwards, silently asking for more. A small grunt fills my ears as the shiny new gem is all I can see.

"How does that feel, baby?"

I hope to God she likes it because from the view I have, it looks fucking beautiful. It's a sight I'll never get tired of seeing, but on her... it's an exceptional sight.

"Strange, but good. Now what?" She is so fucking perfect and all mine.

"Now, I'll make you feel something you've never felt or experienced before. I'm going to make you feel so fucking good, you'll be screaming for more. Lay on your back," I demand. I reach down and drive two fingers into her soaking wet pussy, my thumb pressing on her tight bundle of nerves, making her in fact scream my name like I said she would, and it sounds so fucking unbelievably good.

Keeping up the assault between her legs, I kiss her with everything I have. I don't have to hide it from her anymore, she knows the worst of me and now the best.

My dick is shouting at me, the need to be inside her becoming too much to bear, but I want to satisfy her needs first. This is not just about fucking her senseless anymore. It's about making her feel the pleasure that only I'll be giving to her from now on, whilst I take pleasure in her allowing me to fulfil the burning need in myself.

I nibble at her lips, making her moan once again.

"Owen, I need more," she pants, and I know just the thing that will tip her over the edge. But first, I need to swap the plug for the next size up. I grab the packet and make quick work of readying the next plug for her.

"I'm taking out the plug and swapping it for the next size. I want you to follow the same instructions I gave you before." I remove the small plug wiggling and gently tugging on it until it leaves her with a quiet pop. I take a second and remind her to breathe, which she does as the next size enters her. This time instead of using my fingers, I probe her entrance with my bulging head, thrusting all the way in. I hold still, balls deep, as the sensation of her being filled completely slides over my cock.

"I need you to move," she pants, and I happily start my brutal movements, filling her with every stroke. I'm not going to last long at this rate, and I can feel her getting ready to explode.

"This is going to be quick, baby. I'm sorry, but you feel too damn good wrapped around me." I growl and grunt with every sharp thrust as she matches me with her screams. I don't care if the neighbours hear me staking my claim on her because she's whole heartedly mine.

She tightens around me, milking me dry as we become a tangled knot of limbs and sheets. We both give in and come together like an explosion of fireworks erupting in a darkened sky, painting beautiful patterns for all to see.

I throw my heavy body to the side of her on the bed stretching my arm out and pulling her close. She falls asleep as soon as her head touches my chest, still with the plug in place. I reach around her and gently pull it out.

I don't know what she thought of everything I just showed her, but one thing I do know for sure: I won't be slipping out of the door undetected in the morning. No, this time I will be staying right here, with her in my arms.

CHAPTER 16
DEVON

I need the toilet, the pressure in my stomach becoming unbearable, but when I peel my eyes open, I am met with the most beautiful, sleepy form of a human being ever, I don't want to move from under his arm that is wrapped like a blanket over my hip. I wait for a little while longer.

While he's sleeping, I take the time to study his features, starting with his fine, ripped abdominals and moving to his strong, broad shoulders. The bruises are more prominent this morning—a reminder of what I found out last night—but it takes nothing away from the sight before me.

I start to feel more brave in my observation, so I gently and slowly trace the line of his neck up to his cheek with the tip of my index finger before stopping and rubbing his cheek with smooth strokes.

"You like what you see, baby?" The scratchiness of his morning voice sends pleasure waves down my spine and into my now heated core.

"Maybe. What are you going to do about it?" I say seductively as I lift my eyes from the smirk on his lips to his soul shattering eyes.

His arm that is around me pulls me closer to him, his hardened length now poking my pubic bone as he lazily draws circles on my hip. The movement makes me freeze as the pleasure at my core confuses me. Owen just laughs at me like he knows a secret.

"I can think of a few things to make you fall back in line." He shifts forwards placing a prolonged, lingering kiss on my mouth. Sliding his hand around my butt, he taps my arse cheek leaving a sting behind, the sensation sending butterflies into my stomach.

Memories of last night flood my mind.

Oh God, did I fall asleep with the butt plug still there? He must sense my slight flutter of panic, because he grins so wide that I can see all of his pearly whites, as he laughs.

"You fell asleep, so I removed it. What time is it?" He rolls away from me, the chill in the air from the loss of his body causing goose bumps to break out on my body.

Glancing over to the clock on the bedside table on my side, I see the digits.

"It's half seven." I almost start to panic at the thought of being late to open up the gym but then remember texting Jemma to see if she could cover my morning shift and arranging to relieve her just after lunch in time for her afternoon class.

"Shit. Who's opened up the gym? I hope Remme isn't standing outside waiting because she's forgotten her key again."

I chuckle at the sight of him flustered about pissing Remme off. It's cute, and in all fairness, she has got really forgetful with this pregnancy.

"Wind your neck in, Owen. I got Jemma to open up for me. You know… just in case. Plus I made some changes to this weeks rota. You weren't there to check them over so I went ahead and sent you the updated one for your records, and for the wages."

He seems to relax a little knowing I've sorted it already. "What you got planned for today then?" he asks, changing the subject to something lighter and less depressing.

"Nothing. I need to be at the gym before lunchtime to replace Jemma. You really need to sort a permanent rota out, Owen. Just hire someone or speak to Jemma to see if she can pick up any more shifts. I know she's always happy to work if she can, she wants the extra money."

"I know, I've just been side tracked lately. I'll sort it. Now get that fine behind of yours in that shower." He gives my arse a swift slap before jumping up from the bed and heading into the en suite. I hear the water running from the shower before he heads back in. I still haven't moved, and when he sees this for himself he leans his huge frame over the bed and grabs me around the waist and drags me across the bed so he can pick me up.

"Owen, put me down. I have legs." I let loose a squeal.

"You wanna walk?" He stands me on my feet with a sly smile.

What's he looking so smug about?

I get my feet working and head to the bathroom, but I soon come to a stop. "Oohhhh." I pivot on my heels.

"You were saying?"

Oh, the formidable twat.

"Nothing." I try to ignore the funny feeling in my arse and slip my naked self into the shower.

The butt plug worked wonders for me last night. I feel myself buzzing at the effect it's having on my senses. It's driving me wild thinking about it. Owen needs to rectify my current situation. After all, it's his doing.

I know he's following me: somehow, my body can sense when his is close by.

I can feel his eyes roaming down my back and no doubt looking at where his new toy had been stuck up my arse.

He thinks he's funny...

For no reason but to wind him up, I bend down and touch my toes, legs straight and arse up in the air. The growl that rolls from the back of his throat makes me shiver in delight.

"You little fucking tease." He's at my back in seconds, lining his solid erection up with me. He runs his hand delicately over my globes. "Just for me, Devon. This arse is just for me; this body is mine."

There's no room to argue with him. He's staking his claim, and quite frankly I couldn't care less.

He spins me around and stands me straight in his arms, guiding us into the shower and closing the door.

"Tell me who you belong to, Devon."

"You," I tell him breathlessly. Then his mouth is on mine and he's attacking my lips. Our tongues and teeth clash in his rushed need to claim me.

"Good girl."

This whole new taking charge with me has me more turned on than I am with my over the top, expensive vibrator I have stashed in my underwear drawers.

He's soon rubbing circles over my throbbing clitoris. He bites down on the groove of my neck, following it up with small, short kisses.

"Owen… I…I…" I'm struggling to say anything coherent. "Oh, God…"

He inserts two fingers probing me relentlessly, my body beginning to hum a tune for him. He keeps a steady rhythm, riding me to my impending release.

"You want to come, baby?"

I moan by way of response, unable to say anything.

The unexpected sound of the door bell makes me rigid and Owen mad.

"You've gotta be kidding me." He removes his fingers, the void evaporating my lust completely.

"Stay where you are." He kisses my lips again before opening the shower door and leaving me a hot puddle of wanton mess.

CHAPTER 17
OWEN

I leave Devon in the shower, pre-orgasm. I'm just as agitated as she is.

I grab a towel off the rack on my way out of the bathroom and quickly rub dry most of my body before slipping on a pair of shorts I grabbed from out my drawers.

The bell rings again, making my temper rise even more.

"I'm coming. Hold your fucking horses, will ya."

Or at least I would have been coming had I not been interrupted. If this is one of the lads, I swear to God I'll be extremely pissed.

I jog towards the door, looking through the peephole and stagger backwards a couple of steps, running my hands through my hair when I see who it is.

"Fuck." I whisper so the person on the other side of the wood doesn't hear. I contemplate whether or not to run back upstairs and keep Devon busy long enough for them to go away, or whether to open the door.

The loud knocking, has my mind made up. I will see what she wants and try to get rid of her before Devon wonders what is taking me so long.

Taking a deep breath, I pull the handle and swing the door open.

"Owen..." She seems nervous. Good, so I am—for more than one fucking reason.

"Sandra?" I'm curious. I'm not going to lie. She's never had any communication with Isaak since she left Gavin, let alone with me. Why show up now, out of the blue?

"Can I come in, please?" She's just as wary as me, that much I can tell.

I look back inside, mainly towards the stairs. "Erm, now really isn't a good time. Can I meet you this afternoon?" My nerves are shot. Devon is up the stairs, completely fucking naked, and her mum has just shown up at my door.

This isn't going to end well.

"I really need to talk to you. It's about... Devon." The mention of her name has my ears spiked and my mind made up.

"Okay, but be quick." I stand back and open the door wider so she can pass through.

"I know I have no right to be here, it's just... I didn't know who else to go to. It's not like my own son would kindly let me into his home with welcoming arms."

I see the sorrow in her eyes when I've turned to face her after closing the door.

"How did you know where I live?" I have a good idea, but I want her to confirm my suspicions.

"Benny likes to keep tabs on all his business... associates." She shrugs, embarrassed.

"Of course he does. What do you want, Sandra?" I need to move this on, quickly.

"I overheard Benny talking to someone, and..."

I tense from head to toe.

"Owen? You were taking too long, so I finished myself off." Devon giggles to herself and I feel my cheeks heating in embarrassment—or shame, I don't know which—but when my eyes meet Sandra's I know she recognises her daughter's voice. If that doesn't tell her what is going on and the reason for Devon being here, the next words from Devon's mouth does.

She descends the stairs, with a bounce in her steps. I spot her bare legs first, then work my greedy eyes up her body. Her wet locks wrapped up in a tight bun on the top of her head. I do a double take at the sight of her wearing one of my dress shirts. She looks breathtakingly sinful, and if her mum wasn't standing only a few feet away, I would have Devon flat against the wall and I'd be buried deep inside her again.

"I hope you don't mind, but I borrowed one of your shirts. And have you seen my under—" She almost stumbles when she reaches the bottom step, her eyes wide with confusion. "Mum?" She fumbles with the top couple of buttons on the shirt, trying her best to cover up her modesty. "What… Why?"

"Devon, what are you playing at?"

I think it's pretty clear what she is playing at, but I don't think now is the time for getting into details about it.

Devon comes to a stop next to me and wraps her arms around my slightly damp waist. An act of defiance towards her mum maybe. I don't know.

She straightens her spine.

"What can *we* do for you, Mum?"

I love her spunk.

"Well…I didn't know you would be here, darling. I came to talk with Owen."

Ha! Think again.

"Whatever you have to say to me, you can say in front Devon." I grip her tighter, silently letting her know that this is an end to any secrets between us. She runs her hand over my back in response.

"How much does she know?" Sandra lowers her voice like her daughter isn't even standing next to me—like she won't hear her question.

A sarcastic laugh from beside me answers her without words. Sandra doesn't so much as blink at Dev, which really gets my back up.

Then she just huffs out a sigh. "I think it's time you knew, darling."

I think this may be a mother, daughter moment and I'm still standing in nothing but a pair of shorts.

"Why don't you guys sit and talk? I'll finish my shower and get dressed."

I try to side step out of Devon's hold, but she just tightens her grip and looks up at me worriedly.

"No. I want you to come sit with us," she pleads with her eyes, as Sandra strolls past us towards the kitchen.

"How about you both go get dressed and when you're ready come back down. I have things to say to you, too, Owen." I give her a head nod and take Dev's hand in mine, walking us back to my room.

"What could she possibly want, Owen?" Devon asks me, but I'm at a total loss as well. I lean down and place a kiss to the top of her head.

"I don't know, baby, but it looks like we're going to find out. Let's get dressed and get this over with."

I throw on a pair of sweats and a clean T-shirt while Devon just puts her jeans back on, leaving my shirt in place. We head back to where her mother currently takes up space in our home.

Wait...what? Our home? No, I can't have thought that. It's way too early for saying shit like that, surely.

Right now, I don't have time to worry about something that isn't even an issue between us yet. We have an unwanted guest.

We make our way to the kitchen where three mugs of coffee and a pensive Sandra is waiting.

"So...?" Dev says, waiting for Sandra to speak.

"What's wrong? You obviously came here for a reason. How about we start there?" I suggest. Thinking it's got to be safer ground than the minefield that is Devon and Isaak's blood connection.

"I'm just going to come out and say what I came here for. I heard Benny talking on the phone with someone last night. I don't know who, but Owen, you need to be careful. Benny has been keeping his eye on you and he has something planned for you," she says with a shaky breath.

My mind goes into overdrive, trying to process that titbit of information. I knew something would arise after I was warned to stay away from Devon last night, but I didn't know what or when.

Devon is worried, her eyes now bulging out from her head as her hands begin twisting nervously in front of her.

"What does he have planned, Sandra?" I need to know what's going on so I can make my own plans and fast.

"I don't know. I wasn't in the room, and I only got snippets of his half of the conversation. There was something about finding you either at your gym or here. That's how I knew where to come." She looks truly scared, and as much as I dislike this woman for what she has done to Dev and Isaak, I can't have her in danger or harmed from all of this. "I know he said something about what you did... For Isaak all those years ago." She has more to say, I can see it her eyes, and Dev still hasn't said a fucking word.

I take her hand in mine; she grips it with all the strength she can muster. I lift it to my mouth, planting a small kiss there. Her eyes swing to me slowly, obviously still in a panic. She already knows everything, we talked it through last night but I'm guessing hearing it all from her mother's mouth, confirming what she already knew is a hard pill to swallow.

"Sandra, are you, Devon and Isaak safe?" I have to know. I know Benny is a nasty piece of work, but I also know he is ruthless with anyone who gets in the way of him getting what he wants. He was willing to take his own brother down for not complying with his demands, so I have no doubt in my mind that if Sandra or Devon were to stand up to him... I've only just got Devon; I won't lose her now.

I never did understand the reason why Sandra left Gavin for Benny. All I know is that it left Gavin devastated and heart broken and left Isaak without a mother when she stopped visiting him as a child.

Fuck, it doesn't bare thinking about.

"I don't think Benny would hurt me, not after the lengths he went through to keep me a part from Gavin. I can look after myself, but I will do—and have done—everything I can to protect both my children: Devon and Isaak. You'll just have to trust me on that."

Devon gasps. The last part of the puzzle being confirmed for her. I want to give her comfort as a single tear rolls from her glassy eyes, but my mind races with everything I need to do and what I will need to get in place. "I do worry that if Benny founds out about certain things, then Devon could be at risk. I'm so sorry. I know you're both wondering if Benny is capable of harming his own daughter, but there's things you don't yet understand. I know I need to clarify some stuff for you but I honestly don't know where to start." Sandra adds, looking from Dev to me with a worried expression on her face.

It doesn't ease the anxiety I now feel.

I need to call the only man I trust with my girl.

I need to call Saxon Evans.

CHAPTER 18
DEVON

I'm fucking floored.

Everything Owen and I spoke about last night, my mother just confirmed but it's like I'm hearing it all for the first time all over again. Only now, she's added to the cluster of issues.

She'll do anything to protect her children. That's what she said, children as in plural, more than one. I'm stunned into silence.

The way she's looking at me, with regret and remorse filling her eyes, tells me I heard her right: I have a brother. I have an Isaak.

"Isaak, is my brother?" I whisper, finding my voice, but still not believing the words I'm saying.

Owen's hand clenches mine tightly, grabbing my attention. He is away in his own head but seems aware of what's still being said, giving me the confidence to ask the questions he knows I need the answers to.

"Yes, but I need to explain it to you. You need to know the truth." She has the good sense to look guilty. I just can't find it in me to feel sorry for her. She'd deliberately kept me from knowing my brother all these years, and that fucking hurts. The pain I'm feeling in my chest, for something, someone I never knew about, is unbearable and insufferable. My own mother has caused this new and unknown pain in me. I'm angry, I'm sad but filled with joy all at the same time.

It's confusing and draining.

"You'd better start explaining it to me, because right now I'm ready to kick you out and never fucking speak to you again," I yell, not giving a shit at this point. She retreats into the chair from my harsh backlash as Owen flinches beside me.

"I think we all need to calm down. Devon, baby, let your mum speak. I think you need to hear whatever it is she has to say." Owen says with a nod of his head over in the direction of my mum.

Reluctantly, I relent and choose to give her the time of the day.

"I don't know where to start. First, I'm so sorry about the way you found out about all this. You have to believe me when I say I've wanted to tell you so many times. I knew the time was going to come soon when I overheard Benny talking on the phone, about how Devon had befriended Isaak from working at the gym. That in it's self worried Benny as you can imagine. He needed Owen back then more than he cares to admit, because of that, your father has had someone following Owen and it transpired that you were working *closely* with him. A little too close, for your father's liking. He wasn't happy in the slightest about you taking the job at the gym in the first place. If he pestered you about it, you would have started to ask questions and he wasn't ready for that. Obviously, he already knew Isaak was friends with Owen, as he's known Owen since he was a young boy." She stops to take a breather, but I'm even more confused at her ramblings.

"Mum, just stop with the unimportant details. I want to know why. Why did you keep me and Isaak in the dark?" I'm a little calmer, but on the inside, I'm full of pent up rage.

"Benny was trying to get Isaak to fight for him. Gavin was against it from the get go. Isaak had a good future ahead of him. Benny was using anything and everything to get him on side. That's when Owen stepped in. He took Isaak's place to protect him, like I did many years ago. I left my son and my husband behind... to protect them. Benny always wanted what he couldn't have, he's still the same to this day, as you're well aware of. Anyway, both Benny and Gavin wanted me for themselves when we were younger. Growing up with them two lads was a blessing just as much as it was a nightmare. Being associated with them stopped me from getting bullied at school, but the older we got the more they would fight, mainly over me. It's stupid when I think about on it, but I guess in time it all made sense. Both Gavin and Benny were very competitive as lads and when you throw money and me into the mix... Let's just say things became ugly between the brothers. In the end they both changed and both wanted different things in life. Well, all except one. Me. I chose the kind-hearted man who I knew loved me. I chose Gavin. We had Isaak, we were happy, but Benny saw it as a challenge. When his seducing me didn't work, he came to the house and straight out blackmailed me. He caught me off guard one night when Gavin was out, told me to go pack a bag and that I was leaving with him there and then. I told him it was ridiculous, that I wasn't leaving Gavin for him and that he should get out of the house." She pauses, making me tense and stop breathing with her. "That's the night I saw Benny in a completely different light. He gave me an ultimatum: I either left with him, or he was going to hurt Gavin and Isaak—make them suffer just to make me suffer but more importantly, get me to do as he wanted. Again, it comes down to Benny liking the control over people." Her tears don't stop. In fact they are free falling now, like an endless pit of misery.

"I couldn't let that happen. I left the love of my life to protect him. I left my beautiful boy to save him. I was forced to stay away from him and Gavin, only being allowed to visit on Isaak's birthday or at Christmas because I was persistent on that. He owed me that much."

Tears are now streaming down her face as well as my own. I get it now: she was forced, kidnapped and taken against her will. I want to console her, tell her I'm sorry, but I don't move. I just let her get it all out.

"Devon, I have more to say, but I don't want you to hate me for what I had to do. Please…" She begs me, her eyes pleading with me.

"I can't promise I won't be upset with whatever you have to confess, but I will try my best to understand." It's the best I can offer her.

She takes a huge breath in and let's it out with a sigh, bracing herself before she starts again.

"The days I got to spend with them both were what kept me going—kept me stronger and kept my heart beating. It was the only chance I got to see my real love. Gavin and I would spend time together while I was there. We couldn't help it: we were always drawn to one another. Then, I found out I was pregnant... with you. I was so happy. It felt like a second chance for me to be a mum again. I worked out my dates and I was terrified the dates all added up to Gavin being the father. Benny found the pregnancy test. He was so happy. It was the first time I'd seen Benny genuinely smile. Whether that was because he was finally going to be a father, or because he knew he'd have more of a hold on me. I guess I'll never know. I knew then and there that was the way it was going to be—that I would have to spend the rest of my life living a lie, telling both of my children lies. I hated myself but I knew the consequences of what would happen to us all, should the truth ever come out. That's why I stopped the visits. It broke my heart not being able to see Isaak or Gavin. If I went there, Gavin would have worked it out and he would have wanted to know his daughter. He would have wanted to be in her life, Devon. He would have sold his soul to make that happen. I couldn't let him do that. I loved him too much to see him suffer under the hands of Benny, and Benny would have taken great pleasure in watching that. Darling, I'm so sorry I lied to you. I've lied to everyone I love, purely because I love them. Benny is not your father, Gavin was… I just wished I'd told him about you before he died."

"Holy fuck!" I had not seen that coming.

Owen is in front of me in seconds, embracing me in his arms, comforting me. It feels like a massive weight is on my chest, trying to escape through my flesh. The pain in my heart builds with every breath I try to take. I vaguely feel Owens' hand rubbing large circles on my back, whilst his other hand caresses my cheek. Through my blurry vision, I can see his mouth moving, but I don't hear his voice—just white noise ringing through my ears. Static sounds fill my head. My breathing seems to come hard and fast. What's happening to me?

I close my eyes, trying to make sense of everything, but it's just blackness. *Is this what a panic attack feels like?*

Owens' voice starts to filter through. It seems so far away. It's dull and distant, but I can just make it out.

"This was information overload, Sandra. You shouldn't have come here." He's talking to my mum. I can feel myself coming back around, regaining my focus and the sound around me returning. I open my eyes and see Owen with big concerned ones, staring at me. Mum is standing close by with a glass of water, looking worried. I finally find my bearings and begin to speak.

"I think I need to be alone for a while." I get up and make my way to Owens' room. I need to lie down. I can hear the mumble of Mum and Owen as they speak for a little while longer—about what, I can't tell you. My brain has already exploded with everything that has been said. It suddenly occurs to me that I never asked if Dad, Benny, knows I'm not his daughter.

What will all this mean?

What will he do when he finds out?

He is a twisted and bitter man at the best of times, antagonising him just makes him worse. They are questions I can ask Mum when I get my head around everything.

I head to the bathroom like a zombie, needing to take care of business there first. I wash my hands and look at myself in the mirror. It's strange that I never noticed before, but now I know, it's clear I don't have any of Benny's features. I guess growing up you don't really look that close. Now I'm standing here scrutinising everything.

I feel Owen behind me before I see his reflection in the mirror. He leans against the door frame, and even in the state I'm in, my body still reacts to the closeness of his.

"How you feeling, baby?"

I don't get to answer him. He takes a few steps closer, scoops me up into his arms bridal style and carries me to the bed before placing me down lovingly. He undoes the button of my jeans and pulls them off. There is nothing sexy about the way he is stripping me of my clothes right now. He is comforting me the only way he knows how, with his body. He knows I just need to be held. He takes his own jeans off and places his phone on the bedside table before he climbs in the bed next to me.

I snuggle in close to him, my head on his chest. I need the steady rhythm of his heartbeat to soothe me and to centre me again.

It's not even dinner time, and my morning has been filled with so much drama that it could last me a lifetime. I know I need to get ready for work, but I can't find the strength to get my body working. Instead, I cry silent tears into Owen's chest.

I cry for me.

I cry for my mum.

I cry for Isaak, my brother.

Then I cry for Gavin—the father I never knew a single thing about—and then I cry harder because I know I'll never get the chance to know him. He never got the opportunity to see me or care for me or even just love me.

CHAPTER 19
OWEN

I t's been three days since the fight for Benny happened—three days since everything came out in the open with Devon and me. Not only the feelings between us, but the revelations about her whole existence. Finding out who you really are and that your whole life has been a complete lie, has to do things to a person.

She asked me for space yesterday, and I willingly gave it to her. Without question, I let her walk out of my place and have the time she clearly needs to go over things in her head. Alone and all by herself. I couldn't sleep last night: I wanted so terribly to go to her, to wrap her up in my arms—to hold her, possibly fuck her just to make her forget everything, even if just for a moment.

I eventually gave up tormenting myself and jumped into the car, not knowing where I was going or what I was doing. In the end, I found myself where I am now: at my holy grail—my sanctuary.

I sit in the middle of the boxing ring at the gym, staring at the front door, waiting. For what, I don't know. Divine intervention maybe.

Just as I'm about to give up sulking, the doors to the main entrance rattle, startling me to my feet. I peer at the clock on the wall. There's still half an hour until opening time.

Who would it be?

It's already down to me to open up today, so I know it's not one of the girls, and the guys aren't due to start their shifts just yet. I just about make out a huge figure blocking the whole door.

It's Saxon.

"Alright man, hold ya fucking horses," I shout out to him, whether or not he's heard me is debatable as Saxon's continuous banging of his fist on the glass makes the whole window panel of the door shake.

What the fuck crawled up his arse?

His relentless pounding has me picking my arse up off the canvas. I jump from the ring and swipe the keys up from the reception desk. I don't have time to open the door fully before he's swinging it my way with so much force he almost knocks me over in the process.

"Jesus, Sax. What the hell?

"What the hell? I could ask you the same thing," he bellows at me, the look in his eyes almost deadly.

"What's that supposed to mean?" I stare him down the same way he is me, only breaking eye contact when I turn and re-lock the door.

"Cut the bullshit, Owen. I know."

When I turn around to face him again, he's rubbing rough circles into his temple.

"You know what?" I don't know if it's the lack of sleep or his cryptic words, but I'm not following him.

"I know what you've been up to, where you keep disappearing off to at night, the reason you sometimes come into work with a face so banged up, you look like you've been used as somebody's personal fucking punching bag."

I swing my eyes up at his unimpressed ones.

How could he possibly know this? Has Devon spoken to him?

No, she wouldn't do that—not without raising questions about herself. So who the fuck has he being speaking to?

I have a light bulb moment, knowing exactly who has put him up to this. It makes me murderous. I'd told him to give me time and to fucking trust me, yet, he's gone behind my back and got Saxon in on it now.

My shoulders sag. "Isaak?" I'm disappointed: in Isaak, in Saxon but mostly myself.

"Yes, Isaak. He's fucking worried about you, man. Shit, so I am. Only I know why, now. What you playing at, Owen?"

I don't like the way he's looking at me—judging me. He doesn't even know the full story. I don't even know the full story myself any more.

"It's complicated, Saxon." I walk back over to the ring and perch myself on the steps that lead up to it.

"Then uncomplicate it."

If only it were that simple. It's never been that simple.

"Easier said than done. Trust me." I flick my gaze up at him as he starts to approach me. "How did you find out anyway? There is no way Isaak knows. If he did, I wouldn't be talking to you now. He'd be the one doing all the talking." This much I do know. He'd be telling me how stupid I've been. I'd see the unpleasant look of disgust followed by guilt in his eyes.

"Like I said, he was worried about you. He was right to be. He said the last time he saw you, he knew you were about to do something stupid. He rang me, I was a couple of minutes out from the gym and he asked me to follow you. I saw you getting into a taxi, so I followed you to the warehouse." He gets himself comfy on the floor in front of me, raising his knees up and resting his arms on his legs. "I didn't see everything, but I saw enough. You need to tell me what's going on."

I see determination on his face. He's not going to let this go, at least not until I've told him. Whether that's everything or not, I'm still unsure.

I dip my head limply in between my knees, not wanting to see any emotion on Saxon's face when I tell him. "It all started when I was eighteen…" I begin to tell Saxon everything—all the troubles, the stress and strains I've gone through that I've held so close to my chest, which were starting to suffocate me, squeezing me that little bit tighter, the deeper I became in all this. I tell him everything up to the point where Benny was making threats, leaving out how I came to this conclusion or where the information came from. For all Saxon knows, Benny could have made this threat face-to-face with me.

Oh, I also leave out the bit about Isaak being Devon's brother or that she's connected in some way. He must have seen her there at some point, but he doesn't question me on that.

By the time I've finished speaking, I feel like a weight has been lifted off my shoulders—not fully, but enough to allow me to breathe more freely. I've held on to this for so long, trying to deal and get myself out of it all at the same time, but I've just kept coming up empty.

"Fucking hell, Owen. How have you kept this from Isaak and for this long?" He's frustrated with me, but his voice is laced with a sadness I don't want nor need right now.

I came to terms with my decision a long time ago. I don't regret it now and I never will, no matter what happens.

"It is what, it is," I tell him truthfully, still not looking up from the floor between my legs.

"I might not understand fully, and I'm not gonna lie, some things still aren't making sense. That might have something to do with the fact you've not told me everything. You're holding back valuable information, which you obviously have your reasons for…"

I lift my head up now, cocking my head to the side in surprise and wonderment.

"You do remember what I do for a living, right?" He smirks, loosening the concerned frown lines off his face, making me chuckle with him.

"Exactly, I don't have a clue. I just know you work in security." All these years of knowing Saxon and I still don't fully understand what he does to keep a roof over his head—apart from owning his own company in offering security services. I guess I've been stuck in my own head for so long, I've not been paying much attention to my surroundings. Not in the way I should have, anyway. I've neglected my friends, my family… I've missed out on truly amazing events that have unfolded right in front of my eyes, blindly ignoring them or not really processing them in my mind enough for them to stick.

"Really? Security work? Neither you nor Isaak have a clue what it is my team and I actually do. I don't just offer babysitting as one of the jobs you know. I have connections, and I'm capable of a whole lot more. I won't bore you with the details, but what I will tell you is that I can help you." He states like it's that simple.

Can it really be that simple?

I've been trying to figure out a way to eject Benny from my life for several years and am still trying to do just that.

"How can you help me, Saxon? I'd really like to know, cause I've been racking my brains for years to accomplish just that." I throw him a sceptical look.

"Oh, ye of little faith. Trust me. I have my ways. From what you've just told me, the first objective is making sure that Benny doesn't get a whiff of any of this. The longer we can keep him in the dark about you telling anyone, the better." He stands from the floor with a new purpose, stretching out his legs. "Fuck, my arse has gone to sleep."

I leave him to rub the feeling back into his arse while I head back to the door. It's almost opening time. I pause the movement of my hand on the key hanging in the lock and look over my shoulder.

"Saxon, not a word of this to anyone, especially not to Isaak. We clear?"

"Owen, if you're asking me to lie to Isaak for you, then my answer is no. I will not lie to him. I'll hold off until I know what I'm dealing with and whilst I get things in motion. After that, you need to tell him everything, and I mean everything." He points his finger at me as he wanders over in my direction. "No more lies, Owen." He jabs his finger in my chest, accentuating his point.

"Fine." I know I'm running on borrowed time when it comes to telling Isaak, and that clock is ticking by, whether I want it to or not.

"I'll see what I can dig up on dearest Uncle Benny." He pats me on the shoulder firmly and heads out of the door as soon as I've unlocked it.

Fuck me, that was an intense conversation if I ever had one. It was worse than the one I endured with Dev and Sandra.

I just hope Saxon is as good as he's making out and comes up with something solid for me.

I'm leaving my fate in the hands of a single man, who I now call my brother, too. I really do hope he pulls through. Not just for me, but for Devon and Sandra, too.

CHAPTER 20
DEVON

I've been radio silent for the past week. I haven't seen or spoken to anyone since I left Owen's on Tuesday morning. I've had numerous missed calls from him, followed by texts, all asking if I'm okay. Then I've had the same from Remme, but for entirely different reasons.

I've ignored them all, not knowing what to say or do, but I can't keep blocking out everyone the way I have been. If I keep this up any longer, I'll drive myself insane, more than I already am.

So I pull up my big girl knickers and get ready for work.

Poor Jemma worked six days straight last week; she needs a day off. It's been a full week since I learnt my whole life has been a lie. It's long enough to dwell on the past. It's time I find the determination deep down in myself to move past all this and start living my life the way I want to and not the way people think I should. I've had information overload and my head has been truly messed up after finding out about how Owen gets through his ordeal on a day to day basis, using women as some coping mechanism, then finding out everything my mum decided to keep from me. I'm lucky I've not suffered some sort of breakdown.

I walk through the doors at the gym with my head held high and my shoulders back. I can do this.

I almost die on the spot when the first person I see is Isaak. I stagger back a couple of steps thinking I can make a swift exit again without being seen.

No such luck.

Isaak whips his head in my direction. "Well, hello there, stranger." He smiles. I know he's joking, even if it does strike a chord in me.

He really has no idea. He's in the dark about all this as much as I was.

"H...hi..." I feel awkward, so no doubt I must look like it, too.

"You alright? You look like your puppy just died." He walks the small distance between us and places a hand on my shoulder. This interaction is not unusual between Isaak and myself—we've always shared a bond together, had banter with each other. Neither of us find the other attractive in any way whatsoever. I suppose you could say we are like brother and sister but neither of us have ever really understood why.

I guess I know the answer to that now.

He deserves to know, too, but there is something making me withhold that information from him.

Would he reject me?

Will he accept the fact he's got a little sister?

God knows, but it scares the hell out of me.

"I'm fine, just unwell but I'm good now. What I miss? Anything good?" I find myself changing the subject and moving the discussion away from myself.

"Nothing that isn't normal. Owen is still a dick, Remme is still pregnant. I'm still training hard. So yeah." He shrugs.

"Same old, same old then."

Isaak looks out over the gym, and I find this the perfect opportunity to study him. The colour of his hair, the shade of his eyes and the features of his face.

All the same colouring as me. How have I not seen this before? Fucking hell, how has no one else noticed this before?

I'm forced to stop my wandering eyes when a shadow to my left grabs my attention.

Owen.

He bulldozers his way towards us, making my eyes pop. I haven't seen him for nearly a week. I've deprived my eyes of his beauty, my body of his touch and his comfort. His T-shirt clings to his chest and arms, showcasing his leanness, his hair is styled in a messy way that only he can pull off.

"Devon, can I speak to you in my office... Now," he bellows, making everyone in the gym look at me. I feel my cheeks heating in embarrassment.

"Someone's in trouble," Isaak whispers in my ear, jokingly, as he bumps his shoulder with mine.

I slap his chest playfully, making my fingers sting in the process. It's like punching a brick wall. "Shut it you. You make him worse."

Isaak stands there unfazed at my attack, whereas me... I'm shaking my hand to rid the lingering sting in my fingers.

I don't have time to say anything else as Owen practically manhandles me into his office and closes the door shut behind us.

"What the hell, Owen?" I force my arm out of his tight grasp.

"I know you asked for space, but shit, Devon it's been too long. Do you know how hard it was for me not to drive to your place and demand you speak to me. I've tried calling and texting." He looks down at me clearly worried. It's not a side everyone gets to see of him, but I see it more and more—like he is showing himself to me without any words.

"I'm sorry, I just needed time to wrap my head around everything. I'm good now. Ready to get back to work. If you'll let me, that is." I make a dash for the door ready to open it when all of sudden the air leaves my lungs with a whoosh. My body twists before my back collides with the wall and my arms are pinned up above my head.

His lips are on mine moments later in a bruising and all-consuming kiss. My hands untangle from his grip, locating the nape of his neck, pulling him gently towards me. I'm suddenly desperate to feel every inch of him against me. He must feel the same as I do as he's just as eager to feel as much of my body as he can, too.

I feel a rush of fingers skimming down my back towards my arse. I can't stop the moan that falls from my lips and into his mouth. It's like we are pouring all the passion, the anger and the rawness of the past week into each other.

"Owen... Please..." I'm rendered speechless. He makes me lose all ability to string a single sentence together.

"You missed me? Forgotten what I can do to your body, baby?" he whispers in my ear, sending a delightful shiver down my spine.

"Yes."

"Good. You going to blank me again?" He nibbles on my ear and down the side of my neck playfully.

"No." Simple answer to a simple question.

"Too fucking right you're not," he lifts me up off my feet and grinds his body into mine.

The sound of the door handle rattling echoes around the room before the wood connects with the wall.

"What the fuck did I miss?" Isaak's voice booms.

I crane my neck around to where he stands, amusement etched across his features. All of a sudden I feel ashamed that my brother just caught me with his best friend. I look at Owen then cast my eyes down, sliding my way to the floor, trying to side step away from the man who refuses to let me go.

I guess Isaak is finding out today that Owen and me are... What?

Fucking?

Dating?

Seeing each other?

Hell, I have no idea what we are at this point.

"Isaak... I... We..." What am I meant to say?

"Thanks for knocking, brother, but I'm kind of busy at the minute," Owen says as he grabs my hand and drags me around the desk. He takes a seat and places me in his lap. I guess that's enough to say what's going on, even if I am a little bit miffed off, he'd be so insensitive towards Isaak knowing what we both now know.

"Sorry, was I interrupting something?" Isaak laughs, knowing full well what he walked in on.

Would he be acting like this if he knew who I was to him—if he knew his best friend was getting too comfortable, in more ways than one, with his little sister?

"No, we were—"

"Yes, you were," Owen says, interrupting me. I swing my gaze around my back to give him a 'what the hell are you playing at' look. He just shrugs his shoulder at me.

"You roughing it these days, Devon?" I can see Isaak's joking, but I feel Owen tense under me, making me want to stay right here so he cant move and fly at Isaak.

"Dude, she's well out of your league."

I cringe on the spot. This might only be banter going back and forth between them, but I can't stop the nagging thought in the back of my head: I'm his sister. Just how out of Owen's league is he thinking? Would Owen be overstepping the mark? Will my relationship with Owen come between their friendship, their brotherhood?

Oh, God. I don't think I want Isaak to find out who I am after all.

CHAPTER 21
OWEN

"**I** should go and relieve Jemma of the reception desk she has been chained to while I was...ill," Dev says as she tries to rise out of my lap, but I don't want her to leave my arms. I like having her there. It makes me feel like I have what Isaak and Remme have. It makes me feel comfortable; that alone feels strange—a total contrast of contradiction if ever there was one.

Pulling her hips back down to me, I lean forward and kiss her cheek. Fuck Isaak being here. I don't care. I want the world to know that I have a girl who has taken me off the market—who has made me feel things I've never felt before, feelings I didn't think I ever could.

"I'll be out after I deal with the hulk here. Let Jemma know I will email her the new rota."

She looks at me like I have two heads. She doesn't know yet that I listened and finally spoke to Jemma about a more permanent role for her so Devon can get a day off every now and then.

"No problem." She is out my lap and through the door like her arse is on fire. I don't blame her: I just made us public in front of her secret brother. Shit. That is gonna take some getting used to.

"Seriously, dude. Devon is a good one, man. She isn't like your usual pump and dump, or do I have the wrong impression about her? Is she a freak in the sheets or something?"

Oh my god. He needs to stop. He can't be saying shit like that, not about her. My mind goes blank with no idea what to say to him to make him stop. My mouth moves, but no sound comes out as it dries up and I try to swallow thickly.

Thoughtlessly, words form and I'm speaking before my brain catches up. "Fuck you, Isaak. That's my girl you're talking about, and who the fuck said I was 'pumping and dumping' her?" I'm on a roll now, but I stop and take a deep breath. I have to remain calm. "I know she is a good girl, man. That's what I like about her. At first, yeah, it was just a quick fuck for both of us, but I think I wanted her from that moment, too. I have never wanted to just fuck and walk away—not with her."

Isaak is sitting slumped in the chair, his mouth agape and his brows slightly drawn together in a mix of shock and confusion I'm sure. My brother in so many ways has never seen me hung up on a girl—well not unless you count Sally Finch, my first crush in Year Six, who he teased me about immensely for back in the day. I got my revenge on the fucker, though, when I told everyone that he sucked face with the class nerd. That shit went viral around the school.

"You actually like her? As in ready to settle down like her?"

I heave out a sigh. Is it that hard to believe I want the same things as everyone else?

"Yes, Isaak, I want a real relationship with Devon, and I'm going to have it. Now, if there is nothing else, I'm busy. Do you not have training to do?" I question him, hoping he gets the hint and fucks off.

He eyes me questioningly, trying to work out if I'm bullshitting him, but I look squarely at him, one brow raised in challenge with my resolve not budging.

"It's real man. You don't have to worry: I'm not gonna hurt her." That must do the trick as he's up and out his seat.

I let out a sigh of relief.

"Then I'm happy for you guys. Don't fuck it up; she's like a little sister to me."

I cringe. If only he knew. I want to tell him, I really do, but I can't just yet.

"Yeah, that's not gonna happen," I tell him with so much honesty not even he could deny it.

I reach for the computer mouse and click it a few times making the printer come to life as Isaak leaves my office. I glance up seeing Devon's worried face staring back at me. I give her a wink to reassure her. She probably thinks I've told Isaak everything.

I collect the printed pages from the machine and head over to Dev as I need to fill her in on the new rota.

Devon's smile when I walk towards her sets me alight. I'm not sure how she has this effect on me, but I don't care anymore. If I never understand it that's fine as long as she always smiles like that at me—only for me.

I walk round the reception desk, placing the pages in front of her and slipping my free hand across her lower back, taking hold of her hip.

"What's this?" She picks up the documents and scans over them.

"I listened to what you said about always being here. I'm sorry I never noticed how hard you work before. I spoke to Jemma and offered her some more shifts around her college course, and she's agreed so that means you get your normal days off and also get that extra help." I'm hoping that I'm doing the right thing here—that this is what she wants.

"Really?" she says, smiling at me again.

"Yeah, so Jemma is going to work weekends and one full day in the week on a permanent basis, possibly picking up extra shifts when she's on break throughout the year when we have our busy periods. That way she'll be helping you out, and not having one of the guys give up their PT sessions."

Devon throws her arms up and around my neck planting her full lips to mine in a bruising crush and not caring who sees us.

I'm glad that this isn't a secret because now everyone in the gym will know to keep their eyes off her and their hands to themselves.

I part my lips and swipe my tongue across her swollen ones, waiting for her to open up to me. As soon as I feel her mouth move, I invade it. There's a clearing of throats close by, and Dev freezes.

My eyes shoot open as I see Saxon looking a little sheepish.

"Owen, I'm sorry to interrupt. I need a word." He lifts his head slightly in the direction of the office where I spot the retreating backs of Isaak and Remme as they head for the stairs.

Devon takes no notice, looking over the rota I have given her.

"Alright, I'll meet you in my office."

With a swift head nod, he leaves. I point at the paper Devon is studying. "Don't plan anything for that day: I have the same day off. You get to spend the whole day with me, baby," I inform her as I kiss her temple and walk away with a smirk, not giving her a chance to say no.

I close the door behind me to find Saxon already sitting in the seat across from mine as I lower myself into it. He looks every bit the security man he is at the moment, so I know what he wants to talk about.

"We've been following Benny, trying to get as much as we can to use against him." He lifts his foot up and places his ankle across his knee looking relaxed as he delivers this information. "He's careful, Owen. Covers his tracks well. We can't get close enough to him right now, but that doesn't mean we won't. We just need more time, and you need to act as normal as possible with Benny so he doesn't get a sniff of what you're up to. I also have someone from my team watching Sandra at all times." He shifts uncomfortably in his seat.

The hairs on the back of my neck stand on edge like I know he is going to deliver some bad news—something I won't like.

"What is it, Saxon?

"I also have Jason watching over Devon. He's one of my best men, ex army, as you know. He'll keep her safe, Owen, that I can promise you."

Okay, that isn't as bad as I thought.

"That's not all. I've found out some rather interesting facts in my search." He crosses his arms over his broad chest as his stares burn holes into me.

I swallow the golf ball in my throat. "And.."

"At first I was confused, but then I got my tech guy to fill in the blanks for me. Did you know that Devon Carter is in fact Devon Brookes?" He tilts his head and arches his eyebrow in question.

When Devon started working at the gym and she filled out all her paperwork that was filed, she did use the surname Carter. At the time I thought nothing of it, I mean, why would I?

"You understand what I'm saying here, don't you, Owen?"

I have two choices here: I can lie to him and play dumb, or I can have some respect for my mate, the guy who's helping me out and tell him the truth. I go with the latter of the two.

"Yeah, I hear you. I only found out last week myself, but Devon's name is actually Carter now, she had it changed legally by deed poll when she turned nineteen. She told me she has been trying to get out from underneath Benny trying to control every aspect of her life and his shoddy deals for a while now. As far as she's aware Benny doesn't know she has done it." I drop my head in my hands leaning my elbows on my desk.

"Fucking hell, Owen. Devon is Isaak's cousin and you didn't think to tell me?"

"It gets worse… She's actually his...his sister." I peek through a gap in my fingers as Saxon sits forward, eyes as wide as saucers.

"Excuse me?"

I throw myself back in the chair. "Yeah. Sandra paid me a visit last Monday. Confessed everything when she saw Devon was with me at mine." I began telling him everything that has happened and what had been said. The whole time he just sits in silence.

"Fuck, so he doesn't know?"

I shake my head slowly.

"Are either of you planning on telling him?"

I shrug.

"I don't like keeping secrets from him, Owen. He's one of my best mates. Now I have two fucking massive secrets I've got to keep from him."

This isn't sitting right with Saxon. I know he's not one to keep things hidden, but he can't tell Isaak just yet—not until I find my way out of the hold Benny has on me.

"I'll tell him everything, I swear, Sax, just not yet—not until we know more and what our next move will be."

Saxon rubs his hands up and down his lightly bearded face. "Fine, but I'm not liking this. If he finds out I've been holding back from him, he'll try to kill me. I know he'd murder you, especially now he knows you and Devon are an item." This does make him laugh.

"You're fucking hilarious. I'm hoping he'll be used to seeing us both together before he finds out I'm sleeping with his little sister—that I've seen her naked." Like a sledgehammer to my heart it suddenly dawns on me. "Fucking hell, he *is* going to kill me."

CHAPTER 22
DEVON

The sound of Saxon's light and carefree laugh drifts into my ears, making me look up from the computer screen. Seems the conversation he is having with Owen isn't what I thought it would be.

"Hey, Dev. How are you feeling?" I follow the sound of Remme's voice in the opposite direction as she comes to sit behind the desk with me.

"Sorry what?"

"Jemma said you were unwell last week."

"Oh yeah, sorry. I'm feeling much better now. Thanks."

She's silent for a few moments, like she's pondering on something.

"So, you and Owen, huh? I knew it all along." She laughs. "I saw it coming a mile off," she adds.

"Yeah, it just sort of happened." I smile now I can talk openly about Owen and me. "We slept together a few times and it kinda snowballed from there really." I flick my eyes from Remme's over to Owen as he talks away to Isaak and Saxon. "He's completely different with me than when he's with everyone else. I've seen the kind of man Owen really is and what he's willing to do for the people he cares about. I know he has a cheeky, take no prisoner attitude, but there is a softness to him that only I get to see." I feel my heart fill with pride at the length Owen goes to, to protect his family. The people surrounding him right now just don't know how lucky they really are.

"I think I know what you mean. When I first met Isaak, he was an obnoxious twat who just happened to have a body built like a machine, but the more time I spent with him, the more I fell in love with the person behind the fighter." She sounds like she's reminiscing her time with Isaak. I'm glad I've got to witness it. They are both so in love it's hard not to notice. The fact Remme—the girl I've become best friends with—is married to my brother, and I'm the auntie to her son Logan Axel and Tic Tac (that's what we have nicknamed Remme and Isaak's unborn child) couldn't make me any more happier.

She must spot the sadness that washes over me. "Dev, what's wrong?"

"Remme, have you wanted to tell someone something, but you're too scared to say it, not knowing how they will react?" I blurt out before I can stop myself.

"I remember when Isaak and I first got our heads out of our arses. Things started to become a lot clearer, feeling more prominent, you know? Anyway, I realised the more time I spent with him—the more we got to know each other—well I figured out I loved him. It's the scariest thought you can ever have, not knowing if what you feel is real." She smiles to herself deep in the memories.

I don't want to stop her and tell her she has it all wrong, that I'm not trying to tell her I'm in love with Owen, that I'm not there yet.

"How did you know that what you felt was real?" I ask, completely enthralled by the conversation.

Remme laughs loudly. "I think it got to the point where I had no more reasons or excuses for the way I felt. I was so consumed by him and the way he made me feel—the way he still makes me feel. It isn't like any other feeling I've ever encountered. Trust me, when you know, you know."

I don't get to finish the conversation with her as a gym member makes their way to the desk.

"I'll leave you to it." She rubs my shoulder in comfort and walks away.

I swipe the member's gym card and pass them a clean towel from the rack behind me.

I fill the rest of my shift up by going over Remme's words—the way she was talking about Isaak, how she tried to fight those feelings at first. I started thinking about how I felt towards Owen.

Am I falling in love with him?

If I am, is it too soon?

Owen has taken a while to come to terms with how he feels for me in the first place. If I hit him with the L bomb, he'll have a pissing seizure. Mindlessly, I start to clean up, grabbing dirty towels that are flung everywhere across the floor, gym equipment and the laundry bins outside the changing rooms, taking them to the laundry room to begin a wash. I move onto sorting out the recycling bins of plastic water bottles waiting to be taken to the large industrial bins out back. Then I sort through emails, sending invoices and new memberships. Before I know it, it's a few minutes to closing.

Owen catches my eye as I pick up my bag, a smile now creeping up my lips at the sight of the man. I'm wrapping my arm around his waist from behind before I realise I've even moved.

"Hey, my girlfriend won't like that I'm being manhandled by another woman." His rough voice is laced with humour.

As he turns in my arms, his hands reach up to my face and he plants a kiss to rival all kisses on my lips. He takes in the bag hanging on my shoulder with a confused look. "Where are you going?" He looks around the gym, nodding like he's just realised the time and spots Saxon in sports gear and Jason talking to him.

"I need to go see my mum. There are still some things I want answers to, and I think she is the only one who can answer them." I feel him tense then wave to Jason as he leaves.

Saxon levels Owen with a serious look. Something is going on with those two, but I don't have time for that right now. I need to get answers.

"Will I see you later? I have an out of hours client due any minute, otherwise I'd drive you," he says, his brows worrying together.

"Of course you will. I'll grab some fresh clothes on my way back and stay at your place if you want?"

Owen beams at me like I've promised him the world and delivered it to him, gift wrapped.

"Yes baby, I'd like that." He slams another kiss to my plump lips one last time before I make my way to my car. I may have lost a father I didn't know a single thing about, but I've gained Owen, and he makes me feel just as loved as I hope Gavin would have made me feel, even if we aren't *in* love yet.

My good mood continues on the drive until I'm about to pull into Mum and Benny's street where it deflates. Wow, that felt weird. Benny not dad. I've always known him as my father, but knowing what I know now it doesn't feel right to call him that anymore. At least when he's not around.

I start wondering if I've made the right discussion to come here, but I can't sit in my car any longer. I've been sitting here for over ten minutes. Benny's car isn't here, that much I can tell. So grabbing the bull by its horns I open the car door and jump out.

I knock on the door, which is weird as hell as I've never knocked on my parents door before, but I suppose everything is different now. I'm not waiting for long before my mum peers around the wood.

"Devon, sweetheart. Why are you knocking?"

I can tell it pains her already knowing why, so I don't give her an answer. "Come in." She opens the door wider, letting me past and closing it behind me.

"Sorry, I didn't call to tell you I was coming," I say, like I'm speaking to a complete stranger. I turn just in time to see the regretful look pass by my mother's face.

"Don't be silly, this will always be your home, Devon. You can come around any time."

I don't point out the fact this house hasn't been my home for years and that I haven't made a point of coming here even before I found out the secrets she's held from me and the lies she's told me.

"Sweetheart, I'm so sorry about everything. If I could change the way I dealt with everything, I would. Since the last time I spoke to you, I've been trying to think of a way around it all without getting you, Owen or anyone hurt in the process." Her hands are fidgeting in one other as she walks past me and enters the kitchen.

"What did you find?"

She turns to face me with a blank look. "Nothing. There is nothing lying around the house; he's too calculated for that."

My mouth is moving before I know what it's going to say next. "Did you check his office?"

She's shocked by my question. "Devon, no. If he caught me in there, well…all hell would break loose." She's afraid of Benny. It's written all over her face. I'm also terrified of Benny and what he's clearly capable of, so I'm not going to stand here and say otherwise.

Has he done something to her, hurt her or threatened her in any way?

The thought of him laying a finger on my mother, despite her faults, has me turning on my heels and marching down the hallway with a new found determination on my mind.

"Devon, where are you going?" I hear her voice as she follows me. She gasps in shock and horror when I stop outside of the office doors. "Devon, please stop." She grabs my arm, forcing me to turn and face her.

"Look, I know Benny is up to something, and it's not just the illegal fighting club he has. So, unless you have any better ideas about how to break free from this unbelievably tight hold he has on you, on me, on everyone else he's managed to sink his claws into, then we need to find something. I know everything we need is behind these doors, Mum." The words come out my mouth thick and fast. If I think about what I'm about to do I'll talk myself out of it, but when I see Owen's defeated face in my mind, I swing the doors open, not giving my actions a second thought.

"For the love of God, Devon. Why don't you ever do what you're told?" She follows me inside Benny's office, leaving the door open a crack.

"Just help me look will you?" I fire back at her as I move around the desk, shifting through the files sitting on top of it.

"What am I looking for?" She doesn't sound happy about any of this, but at least she's making herself useful and wanders over to the bookcase, pulling out books, searching for something.

"I don't know. Anything that looks out of place. Snooping isn't exactly one of my fortes." I can't see anything in the folders on top of the desk, so I try opening the drawers but they're locked. "Fuck."

"Devon...language. What's the matter?" She moves towards me, hastily and in a panic.

"The drawers are locked. We need a key." I stand back up and look around the office, wondering where he could possibly keep or hide one. That's if he doesn't have them on him right now. But surely he would keep a spare somewhere.

"Wait, I think I might know." She strides back across to the bookcase, looking for something. She reaches up to the top shelf, pulling down a photo frame.

I don't know why, but I find myself whispering, "What are you doing?"

"I always thought this picture looked odd in here, and I could never put my finger on why." She runs her fingers delicately and slowly across the glass cover of the picture. "This is your dad, Devon. Your real father." She strokes her index finger across his face one more time. "Benny hated his brother with every bone in his body, so why would he have a picture of them together, in here of all places? I never really questioned it until now."

I get a glance of the man standing next to Benny before she flips it over. He looks just like Isaak.

"Bingo."

Snapping myself out of my day dreaming, I see there's a key taped to the back of the frame. She carefully peels it off and passes it over to me.

"Yes. Good going, Mum." I sprint back over to the desk and insert the key into the lock. Thankful it fits. Opening the first drawer, I'm disappointed that it's just his cheque book and other unimportant files. Opening the next, I'm faced with even more devastation. I slam the door shut and yank open the last drawer, mentally crossing my fingers. I pull out a huge pile of documents, handing them over to my mother. "See if you find anything useful in these."

She takes them from me whilst I look at the rest of the papers in the drawers.

It's pointless. All there is are the deeds to the house and insurance papers. With my hands on my hips, I blow out a big puff of air before turning back to my mum. "You find anything?"

"No not really. Just some offshore accounts, which doesn't surprise me. But it's nothing useful." Her own disappointment is clear with every word she says.

"We're missing something, Mum." She neatly tucks the paper back into the folder and hands it back to me to put in the drawer again. As I shut the final wooden drawer, an idea pops into my head. I reopen the top one, removing everything out of it, and place my hand inside to feel around. I feel a gap in the base of the draw at the back. I manage to get my finger in the hole, and the draw finally comes loose. I pull it out.

"What the fuck?" Underneath the actual draw is a secret compartment. I lift out the contents. There's a black folder with a tie around the front. Untying it I flick through the pages. "Oh my God." I feel sick. This is not normal.

"What is it?" I only just hear the sound of my mothers petrified voice as it hits my ears.

I show her what's inside, pulling out pictures of everyone I have come to care for: Owen, Isaak, Remme and Logan. He's had someone following them. He knows their every move. There're documents full of things I don't have time to read. A brown piece of paper slips out and falls to my feet. My mum is quick to pick it back up.

The sharp intake of breath from her has me pausing and I glance over at her.

"Mum...what is it?" I round all the paperwork back up and throw it back in the folder, not even bothering to tie it. I put the wooden base back into the drawer and lock it back up. I've done all that and I've still not got an answer. "Mum?"

Tears she's so desperately trying to keep at bay, break free. The hand that isn't holding the paper covers her mouth but does nothing to stop the cries from coming.

"Oh, God, Devon. This is really, really bad. I don't understand how he could have known to go looking for this." It's like she's speaking in code. I don't understand what she's getting at.

"Mum, you're scaring me? What is bad?" I push for answers.

"I can't believe he went looking for this. I thought I'd covered my tracks enough to satisfy his questions. He never once asked for proof and it was never mentioned again. Oh Devon, if he knows about this, he will know everything." Mums hands really start shaking and when I look her in the eyes, it's like she's looking through me. I've never seen act like this before, but we haven't got time for this and she's just standing there like she's got all the time in the fucking world. I snatch the paper from her hands and see for myself what has gotten her so spooked. I know what it is the moment my eyes get a look at it.

My hands begin to shake and my heart thumps wildly in my chest.

This is bad.

Catastrophically fucking bad.

CHAPTER 23
OWEN

Locking the doors of the gym, I make my way over to my car as my phone chimes. Pulling it out of my pocket, I unlock it and see a message from Devon.

Baby D
Have you finished work yet? I need to speak to you, it's important. Call me when you get this. Dev x

I scroll through my contacts until I find Devon's number. I'm about to hit the call button when my phone beeps at me again.

Another message. Only this one isn't from Devon. It's Benny.

My chest expands with the huge intake of breath I inhale. I know what the message will say before I even open it, yet I open it anyway.

Benny
Warehouse 1 hour… I have a real treat for you.

Don't be late.

My whole mood deflates. All I want to do is head straight home and sink under the covers with Devon, entwine my body with hers and have my wicked way with her. Now, I have to head over there and pretend nothing is wrong and do whatever Benny says, or should I say demands.

The fact he's set this up on a Monday night and not the weekend doesn't sit well with me, but I know I haven't got a choice in the matter whatsoever, so I admit defeat.

I don't bother replying to Benny, but I need to let Devon know I won't be home for a couple of hours. I drop her a quick message apologising, that I would have to call her back when I can, as I had an issue to deal with that couldn't wait. I throw my phone on the passenger seat and start the car. I need to nip home first to change out my clothes and grab my other gym bag that I use for the sole purpose of my fights at the warehouse. I decide to risk driving after my fight tonight just so I can get back a little quicker. It's risky and stupid but the faster I get back to my girl the better. The thought of Devon brings me back to the message I sent her. I couldn't tell her I was fighting she would come to the club again and that could be dangerous for her now. This isn't just about looking out for Isaak, its about looking out for us all.

I navigate my way through a few road users and make it home in record time. I pull up to a stop in the drive and jump out my car locking it as I jog to the door. I head for a quick shower and change my clothes. I stuffed some shorts, a towel and the tape for my hands in the bag, jumping back in my car and heading to the only place that has me feeling uneasy.

I don't know what Benny has planned for tonight, but the text he sent doesn't fill me with anything but dread and trepidation. Nothing good will come out of tonight, that much I do know. For now, I have to just play along with it while Saxon hopefully finds me—and everyone that's now involved in my mess—a clean way out.

I drive in a daze, and it's not long before I pull up at the old, run down building. The far too familiar graffiti-painted bricks and boring grey concrete walls with missing brick haunt me with every step I take towards the warehouse. How it's still standing, I'll never know.

There's a strong smell of blood that lingers in the air, potent to my nose and causing me to shiver. It heightens my alerted senses, making me wonder what lies beyond the tatty, metal door for me tonight.

I yank the door open, the squeaky sound making everyone's heads turn in my direction as I begin to scan the warehouse, quickly noticing more bodies than usual.

"I was about to send out a search party." Benny's humorous voice echoes around the building.

"No need. I got your message loud and clear from the last time I was here," I grit out through tensed teeth.

"Good. You're starting to understand how this partnership works between us."

"What, you saying jump and me asking how high?" I say sarcastically.

"Yeah, pretty much." I can't wait to wipe that dirty fucking smirk off his face.

I walk further inside the warehouse and straight past him and his arse-licking chums, throwing my bag on the makeshift table just off to the left of the cage not bothering to use the room us fighters have claimed as a chill out/changing room. I strip down to my boxers and swap my clothes for a pair of loose shorts, wrapping up my hands with my blue tape.

I hear the hustle and bustle pick up from behind me, but I pay no mind as I mentally prepare myself and get my head in the place it needs to be. The quicker I take this fighter down, the faster I can get out of here and back home—back to Devon and some normality.

Once my knuckles are all taped up, I stretch out and throw a couple of quick jabs into the air to warm myself up.

"Well, well. Looks like someone forgot to take the rubbish out." The sound of the voice has my back straightening up and my body tense. I fist my taped hands up together tightly, purely to stop myself from beating the shit out of the man behind me. I turn on my heels slowly and come face to face with the fucker.

"Alexander Jenkins. Not so almighty anymore are you?" It's a rhetorical question.

"I may not be a professional boxer anymore, thanks to that mate of yours, but I'm the fucking champion here," he states. How the fuck have I never seen him here before. More to the point, why has Benny only just played this trump card with me? Why am I only just noticing Alex now?

"You've got to be kidding me?" It's all unravelling now. "You're fighting for Benny now? Fucking hell, you really have hit rock bottom." I shake my head, laughing.

"Maybe so, but what's your excuse?" He questions.

"None of your fucking business, that's what." I can feel my anger rising to the surface, the fire in my veins heating my body. This man doesn't even have to say anything and he pisses me off—all things I can use to get through the fight.

"Doesn't matter anyway. I'm still looking forward to making you bleed out." He turns and walks away. Then it dawns on me what he's said.

"Fuck sake." I mutter under my breath.

Benny has had this all planned out. How long has he had this fight up his sleeve?

Like my night couldn't get any worse, Benny decides to throw a spanner in the works. By spanner, I mean Alexander fucking Jenkins.

I enter the cage, tilting my head from side to side, loosening up the muscles as I go. Alex is already inside, jumping up and down on his toes, the whole time grinning at me.

The sound of the cage gate closing has me whipping my head round. For some reason, my whole body is on guard, like it senses more danger ahead. I'm not afraid of Alex, and I'm certainly not scared to fight him. It's the fact Benny has put this together. I'm expecting something else to follow. Benny's games have only just begun and this is his way of letting me know who calls the shots—that he's the one tightening the fucking rope around my neck, pulling it that little bit more, closing off my airways but never cutting it off completely.

"Do you know what real pain feels like, Owen?" Alex says through his grin.

"Do you?" I ask with a lift of my eyebrow. "Because you're about to." I don't wait for anything. I throw my fist forward, connecting with his jaw and sending him back a step or two. A small trickle of blood appears on his lips before he wipes it away.

"Sneaky. I'll give you that one." Seems he's in a playful mood tonight.

"We'll see." No sooner have the words left my mouth, Alex is charging towards me at full throttle, lip curled and teeth bared to all.

I know the move he's going to make before he even makes it. I helped Isaak prepare for his re-match with Alex. We both studied him closely to the point we knew his every move and where his weak spots were.

The moment he lifts his arm to land his punch, I duck and deliver a blow to his rib cage. He bends over to gather the breath he needs before standing again. I could have carried on with my assault but lets be honest, where's the fun in that?

I'm going to enjoy this fight more than I should. The fact it's Alex standing in front of me has done something to me. I want to beat him with an inch of his life for what he put Isaak through and then everything that happened to Remme. It was all his fault. He was the instigator. He hasn't fallen far enough for my liking, and if he thinks this is rock bottom, he doesn't know anything.

I'm caught off guard, thinking of all the ways I can hurt Alex in this cage. His knuckles connect with my cheekbone, knocking me to the ground. The throbbing pain starts immediately, and I pull myself up from the dirty floor only to be sent straight back down again. My feet lift up from underneath me as Alex launches himself at me, wrapping my arms around his shoulder blades and the crook of his neck as he rugby tackles me. My back hits the concrete with an almighty thump, knocking the wind out of me. My hands break away from his neck from the impact, and the only thing I can do right now until I gather some breath back, is protect my face and body the best I can with my arms.

He doesn't give me a chance to defend myself fully. His body looms over mine as his fists rain down on me, over and over again, connecting with my sides, my arms and my face. I try to cover my face and head with my hands the whole time, just in case he decides to hit me unconscious or rattle my brain around some. He gets a couple of decent punches in before I can find my way out of it.

When he pauses from sheer exhaustion I manage to swing one of my legs free and out from underneath him. I knee him in the side—once, twice, three times—giving him no choice but to move his hands down to his sides slightly. Now I have more wiggle room, I slam the heel of my palm upwards and into his chin.

His head jerks backwards giving me time to wrap my right leg around his middle, using all the power I have in my thigh and calf to roll us around so he's now underneath me.

"Looks like the table has turned, fucker." I let rip. I punch, jab, hit and strike my fists down on him, not caring where they land or how much damage or pain I'll be causing him.

Then I start to think about Devon and the life that she has lived, the lies she has been told by the people she should have been able to trust most. Then what Benny could possibly do to her just to keep us both in check.

The yelling and screaming coming from the crowd like they are getting off on seeing this unfold in front of them is sickening. The metal on the cage rattles as they bang and thump their hands against it.

I don't relent.

I carry on, and on and on, only stopping when Alex goes limp beneath my body.

I move my aching limbs, rolling onto my back beside Alex's lax and weakened beat up body. When I glance at him just lying there, hardly moving, his face beat up so bad that he's unrecognisable, I feel disgusted with myself. I'm no better than he is—no better than the men enjoying the show; no better than fucking Benny who makes his living picking miserable men from God knows where to fight for him and watch as they make the other one bleed.

I hear the distant sound of Benny's laugh, followed swiftly by a round of claps from his direction. I turn my head from Alex's still unmoving body to Benny's sadistic and unfazed features.

He's enjoying this: watching me turn into the monster he's made me—the monster I need to be, just to make it out of this and to the other side.

I take my time pulling myself up from the floor. My back, face, ribs—you name it—hurt like a bitch. Once I'm up I wrap my arm around my waist and side as best as I can. I think I've cracked a rib from my fall to the ground—no thanks to Alex. I stumble my way towards the cage's door which is still unopened.

"I don't think you're quite finished yet, Owen."

I narrow my eyes on Benny again as he gestures behind me with a nod of his head.

I turn around slowly, so as not to cause a sharp pain in my side. The spot that I'd left Alex in only moments ago is now empty.

"What the fuck?" I glance around the whole of the cage from left to right and then the next thing I know I'm up against the metal surrounding the circle and Alex is taking another swing at me.

This is going to be one long painful night.

CHAPTER 24
DEVON

"**D**evon, you need to leave. If Benny has already seen this... I... I don't know what he'll do," my mum says in a panic. She takes the key from me after the drawers are closed back up and returns it to its rightful place behind the photo frame on the top shelf.

"If he knows, why wouldn't he have said something by now?" I ask her as she quite literally drags me back out of the room, only closing the door when she's certain nothing is out of place. "You know what Benny's like: he can't hold his own water, especially when he knows it'll bring nothing but pain and misery to others or he's got something to gain from it."

I start going over all the possible outcomes of what this news could do, not only for me but for everyone else Benny could hurt with this information. I'm not entirely blind to what he does for a living. I choose to ignore it all. I'm also aware that I don't know the full ins and outs of his business, but for that I'm grateful. I don't think I'd be able to handle much more.

"I don't know, Devon, but I don't want you to be around when it all

comes to a head. You need to leave right now. He could be back any minute."
I hear the pleas in her voice, and I find myself really looking into her eyes.

I know she's lied to me about so much in my life, but the more time I've spent in this house with her tonight, the more I'm starting to understand her reasons behind it all.

She's protecting me. I can see it in her eyes, the look of determination to protect what is most precious to her, yet a sadness lingering there, too. This is what she's been doing my whole life since Benny gave her an ultimatum. No matter what happened to her, she has been willing to do whatever it takes to protect us, starting with Isaak all of those years ago.

"What about you?" I start panicking myself now. What if he does something to her.

"You don't need to worry about me, darling. I know how to handle Benny. I've been doing so for years. Now, go. I'll be in touch soon." She places a feather light kiss on my forehead before ushering me out of the door. My hands cling tightly to the folder that's pressed against my chest as if it were there to guard and shield my heart from breaking.

I look back over my shoulder towards the woman who would truly and wholeheartedly lay her own life on the line for me. She blows me an air kiss and a soft smile before disappearing inside again.

I drag my sober body the rest of the way to my car, unlocking it with my fob and jumping in. I place the folder down gently on the other seat like it might bite my hand off if I don't treat it with kindness.

It's gotten dark outside now. Clearly I've lost track of time.

"Oh, God." I fling myself around in the car to try and grab my phone from my arse pocket in a rush to see if Owen has replied or rung me back. It takes me a few seconds with my now shaky hands.

There's an unread message from him.

Owen
Going to be home late I'm so sorry.
Got an issue that needs sorting.
Will call you when I can x

That was over an hour ago. There is only one reason that comes to mind for him sending a message like that.

"Oh, God. Please no." Benny has him fighting again. I just know it.

I try to call him, even though I know he won't answer.

He doesn't, which just confirms my suspicions.

My hands are moving before my brain has time to catch up and I lift the handbrake and wheel spin out of the driveway, leaving a cloud of smoke behind me as I head in the direction of where I know Owen will be.

I don't know if it's my state of mind and the events that have happened tonight, but I'm on edge and constantly checking my mirrors.

A car is travelling behind me a few yards away.

"For God sake, Devon. You're getting paranoid," I say into the emptiness of the car. I turn on the radio to distract myself and my crazy mind from playing havoc with me, filing the quiet and eerie silence.

After driving for eight miles, the car is still following me. It's kept the same distances from my tailgate this entire time. I take the next left, steering off my original course, mainly to see if the car follows me.

It does.

I turn left again onto a narrower poorly lit road. The car behind takes the same turn. I drive a full circle, twice, just to be absolutely certain that it's following me. The car mirrors my every turn and panic sets in. My heart rate is no doubt through the roof. My breath comes in short, sharp and snappy gasps.

I apply more pressure on the accelerator.

"Think, Devon. Think." It's hopeless I haven't got a clue what to do or where to go.

I almost swerve the car off the road at the sound of my phone ringing through the bluetooth as it cuts off the music that is playing. Saxon's name appears on my dashboard. Oh, thank the heavens. I click the button on my steering wheel frantically as I take another look in my rear-view mirror, waiting for the call to connect, the car now right up my backside.

"Sax... Saxon. Are you there? Please, I need help," I scream so he can hopefully hear me.

"Devon, you need to calm down."

Why does he not seem fazed by my obvious display of distress.

"Calm down? Fucking calm down? Saxon, I'm being followed... I..." He cuts me off.

"It's Jason, Devon. Jase is behind you," he says, cool as a cucumber.

"What? How do you know?" I look from the back window to the side door as the car overtakes me.

"Is it a Black range rover?" he asks with total calmness in his voice.

"Erm... yes." I start to relax a little the more Saxon's soothing voice fills my ears.

"That's one of my vehicles, Devon. Jason is going to pull over and I want you to do the same. Can you do that for me?"

"Ye... Yes."

Just then the black rover overtakes me.

"Good. Do as Jase asks, please. No arguments. I know exactly where you were heading, and it's not happening. I'll see you soon." With that very cryptic, one sided conversation finished; he hangs up the phone.

As the indicator on the tank of a car in front signals to the left of the road. I'm in two minds whether to stop or put my foot down and carry on up the road in the hopes of losing him and getting to Owen like I'd originally planned. But something in the way Saxon was speaking to me makes me indicate and turn off the road, yanking my hand brake up sternly as Jason slides out of the car.

Throwing my own door open, I march right up to him and demand some answers.

"Why are you following me?"

"Just following orders, Devon," he says, lifting his hands up between us playfully, like he's surrendering.

"Who's doing the ordering? Saxon?"

"Yes," he states simply.

"Why would Saxon have you follow me?" I ask, pointing my fingers into my chest.

"I don't ask for details, Dev. I just do as he asks. He's the boss." He shrugs.

"I don't get it," I say more to myself, trying to work out what game

Saxon is playing. "He told me I need to do as I'm told."

"Are you going to? Or have I got to throw you over my shoulder and haul your arse in the car?" He smiles a heart-warming smile at me. He's so carefree.

"Depends. What is it you want me to do?"

"For starters, I need you to turn your car around and head in the opposite direction. No more driving in circles, just head home. It's getting late. Owen is on his way to Saxon's to sort out some stuff." He arches up one of his eyebrows.

"What did Sax mean when he said he knew where I was heading?" At the thought of Owen, I panic again in my need to get to him and tell him about what I've found. It's getting late, and the longer I stand here, the worst things could be getting for him.

I make a hasty dash back towards my car, thinking Jason will be hot on my heels, but when I reach for door handle and glance over to him, he's standing with his arms crossed over his chest and smiling at me.

"What's so funny?" I'm getting more irritated the longer it's taking me to get to Owen regardless of where he is.

"You won't find him there, Devon."

My eyes widened in shock. How does he know? How much does he know? Who else knows?

"He's not at the warehouse anymore. I've told you he's with Saxon sorting out some business. Just head home, and when I see him, I will tell him to come see you. Deal?"

I think about this for a minute before I realise he is right: if he isn't at the warehouse, there is no point in me continuing on in that direction. I might as well just go home and wait for him. I just needed to know he is okay—that he is safe. If he's at Saxon's then he is safe from Benny.

Having finally made up my mind, I jump back into my car, no more said between Jason and me. Let's face it, he'll no doubt be following me anyway.

I buckle up and watch as he climbs into his range rover. I pull off and make my way home with Jase, as predicted, hot on my heels.

As much as I want to see Owen right now, I know me going to him with my problems when he's with Saxon will only end up making matters worse for him and let onto Saxon what is really going on.

I need to be patient.

Doesn't matter how concerning the news I've just found out is.

CHAPTER 25
OWEN

I t's the longest fight of my life, or at least it feels like it is. It's a never ending circle of brutal beatings, forever backwards and forwards between Alex and myself. He goes down, I go down. He throws a punch, I throw a punch. I bleed, he bleeds.

As much as I loathe him, I can't deny it is the hardest I've had to fight in the cage of brutality.

I eventually knock Alex unconscious long enough for him to stay down. I won.

I leave Alex in an even worse state than he leaves me. I'm not going to lie and say I'm not aching because I am. In fact, I feel like I've been hit by a double decker bus, not once, not twice but half a dozen times.

I've done what needed to be done.

Benny receives an excessive amount of money from the fight, no doubt because of the fact it is Alexander Jenkins and most members bet against me, but I'd known better. I had no choice but to win the fight for Benny. I'd fight to the bitter end just so Benny wouldn't have a tighter hold on me anymore than he does now. Losing him money meant I'd be fighting for longer, and I couldn't let that happen.

I can't get out of there quick enough. I throw my T-shirt on as soon as I am out of the circle and make a move. It doesn't help matters that Benny won't let me leave this time without taking a cut of the winnings, which confuses me since I told him last time I don't want any of it. But the desperate need to get out of there outweighs everything else, so I just take the stack of money, throw it in my gym bag and leave Benny with his signature, slimy smirk in place showing me that I've pleased him—yet a-fucking-gain.

He sends me off with some parting words that leave me with chills running down my spine.

I jump in my car after throwing my bag in the boot and take a deep breath, my ribs hurting like a bitch. Driving in the state I am in isn't ideal but in my defence, I don't normally come out looking this bad.

I'm not gonna lie, Alex really did do a number on me.

I can't go home looking like this. I can't risk Devon coming around, which she might even if it has just gone midnight. I never got back to her after she messaged me, so no doubt she's put two and two together already. I start the car and roar away from the warehouse and hit the city lights.

I decide to go to the only place I can—to the only other person who knows besides Devon—and finally drive up the dirt road that leads to the hidden house, surrounded by tall trees.

I jump out as slowly and carefully as I can, holding my breath and ribs as I go. Locking the car, I make my way to the door, ringing the bell.

The light in the hallway turns on and the door swings open.

"I didn't know where else to go," I wheeze out before the door is fully open.

"Fucking hell, Owen." Saxon takes a hold of my chin, moving it left and right so he can inspect the damage. "You'd better come in." He takes a step back so I can walk over the threshold when a figure catches my eye.

"Charlotte?" I look from Charlotte who's just pulling her coat over her shoulders back to Saxon who's wearing nothing but a pair of shorts. "Am I interrupting something?" I say with a smirk, which doesn't last long as my face and lips hurt like hell as I laugh.

"No, I was just leaving." Charlotte walks past me before stopping at the side of me. "You look like shit, Owen."

I mumble at her obvious statement as she rubs my shoulder delicately. "I'll see you soon, yeah." She doesn't wait for my reply.

"I'll see Charl out. You head in," Saxon tells me over his shoulder as he turns back to the door.

I drag my feet further inside. "Sure. I'll leave you to finish eating each other's faces." I don't need to turn to see their reactions: Saxon's growl is enough to make me chuckle, the best I can in my condition.

I head into the kitchen, going straight to the fridge, and grab a bottle of water. By the time Saxon walks in, I've drunk the full bottle, ridding my mouth of any dryness.

"So…you and Charlotte. How's that working out?" I jokingly ask.

"Fuck off. That's the last thing you should be worrying about right now, Owen." He untucks one of the chairs from the table and sits himself down. "What the fuck happened?" His question hangs in the air for a few moments because he'll have a fit when he finds out it was Alex who I fought tonight, and that it was him who did this to my face.

Thankfully he hasn't seen the rest of my body, which is battered and bruised and currently growing darker and becoming increasingly tender and painful by the second. "Are you going to start talking? It's obvious where you've been. So skip that part."

"Yeah, yeah okay. So, I got the surprise of a lifetime when I got there. I already knew something was going to go down beforehand by the message he sent saying he had a treat for me. I was sceptical about it straight away, but I had to go. I didn't have a fucking choice." I begin to explain.

"Yeah, I understand that. What I don't get is why you're in this state." He gestures up to my face with his hand.

"This was my, 'treat'. Not long after I arrived, the guy who I was fighting showed up." I pause more to build up the suspense than anything else. "Alexander Jenkins was the guy that did all this," I tell him as I point my finger to my black and blue swollen face.

"Alex?" He jerks his body back in the chair, clearly shocked by this information. "I've been keeping a close eye on him. You know, just in case he reared his ugly head again. The last I heard he wasn't fighting anymore and was laying low. Too fucking low by the sounds of it." He narrows his eyes, now unhappy with his own work. "I'm sorry, Owen. I should have been on top of this. If I had known he was associated with Benny, I would have warned you before you went there again."

"Hey, it wasn't your fault, Sax. Don't beat yourself up."

He doesn't say much else on the matter, which I'm glad of. I don't want him giving himself a hard time over any of this.

"Anyway, that wasn't the worst of my night," I add.

"What else?" he asks, leaning forward in his chair and placing his elbows on the table.

"As I was leaving, Benny said something. It doesn't sit right with me." The worry or confusion must show on my face, because Saxon's own features are firm and harsh-looking.

"What did he say, Owen?" he demands with urgency.

"It's not so much what he said, it's how he said it," I state, thinking back to Benny's words, making me quiver at the uneasy feeling they left me with.

"Care to elaborate?"

"He said something about how it's amazing the lengths people go to protect the ones they love. I didn't really take any notice at first, thinking he was on about what I'd already done to protect Isaak." I start pacing in front of him as I carry on. "But the more I chew over what he said, the more I think he meant so much more than that. I know how Benny works. It's like he was warning me about something in his own fucked up way, playing his mind games. I just don't know who he's actually on about. Before, I was just doing this to keep Isaak out of Benny's grasp, but now I have so many people in my life it could be anyone next."

"You think he would hurt Devon, or any of the other girls?" he questions.

"Before I found out who Devon really was, and that she isn't Benny's daughter, I would have said no, but what if he knows just as much as we do?" I start pacing the kitchen, Saxon's wary eyes following my every move. "I don't know what to do, Saxon. I can only be in one place at a time. If he hurts any of them, I... I swear to God, I'll kill him with my bare hands." I clench my fists that hang taut at my sides, every muscle tightening with each word I speak.

"There is only one solution to all this, Owen, and you know it." He's so calm, it's starting to unnerve me. Although he's right. I know what I need to do.

"Yeah, I know. I just don't know what to tell him, or everyone else." I plonk myself down in the chair opposite him, throwing my phone down on the table.

"Might as well get it over and done with, Owen. It's time they knew, and it would be to keep them safe more than anything, mate." He locates his own phone from his shorts pocket and types out a message—at least I think that's what he's doing. He confirms my thoughts when he speaks again.

"I've just sent a group message telling everyone who needs to hear this, to get to mine as soon as possible."

"It's almost one in the morning, you think they're going to see that?" I'm not holding my breath on this.

He's typing something else out on his mobile not looking back at me. "I have my ways, don't you worry about that, Owen." He finishes typing and when he's done, he lifts his head and smirks at me.

I don't ask what he's done. I just know that every person who has come to mean something to me, become my family, will be in this room impatiently waiting for me to explain what has them out at this time in the morning.

Forty minutes tops I have to try and gather my wits about me and get ready to drop this obscene bomb shell on them all, completely fucking up their lives as much as my own.

However, I will do everything in my power to stop anything from happening to them, even if it's my last breath.

CHAPTER 26
DEVON

I get woken up by an almighty thunderous banging on my door. I bolt upright in bed and wait a few eerily silent seconds, just to see if I am imagining it. Then the bangs come again, making me jump out of my skin.

I slide out of bed slowly and as quietly as I can. I get to the door as the knocking starts up again, only now it's continuous.

"What the fuck?" I whisper to myself, as I peer through the peephole. When I see who the mad hooligan on the other side of my door is, I swing it open to find Jason with his fist raised ready to bang on the door again.

"Fucking hell Jase. What time is it and why are you trying to knock my flipping door down?" I spit out as I wipe the sleepy state of my face.

"Well, it's about time. Get dressed, you need to be as Saxon's asap," he instructs as he walks away from my door and finally drops back in his range rover. It's a good job my neighbour's door is the other side of the building. I'm sure she would have been out shouting about the noise if not.

"Just great." I slam the door harshly, getting myself dressed and somewhat half decent before I find myself sitting next to Jason in an awkward silence. I don't bother asking what's going on—he won't tell me anyway so why waste my breath—cause my sleepy head doesn't need more confusion than is necessary.

I've never been to Saxon's house before, and by the way it's hidden and sheltered underneath all the greener than green trees, I wouldn't have found it even if I wanted to.

It's then I notice a handful of cars lined up in the lengthy driveway: Isaak's, Charlotte's, Jemma's and Owen's, all in a row. Seems everyone is here. The moment I see Owen's vehicle, my heart skips a beat, as I think back to my need to see him earlier on today. I start shaking in a sheer panic, knowing deep down that everything is going to come to light within those four walls tonight.

Jason puts the Range Rover in park next to Saxon's and unbuckles his seatbelt. I'm still to make a single move.

"Dev, something wrong?" He leans over the centre of the car so he can see my face, no doubt spotting the panic beaming through.

"What? No, sorry." I shake my head and get my legs and arms moving the best I can without him seeing me struggle with my inner emotions. Once my feet hit the gravel driveway, I spot movement at the front door. It opens wide, and a man I don't recognise stands waiting to let us in.

Jase turns towards me. "I'll see you inside, Dev."

I look up in confusion as he passes the man in the doorway, giving him a quick fist bump before vanishing. As I get closer, I see who the man really is. It's a very battered and bruised Owen.

"What the fuck, Owen. What happened to you?" I've seen him come into work in some states, but this takes the fucking piss.

"I'm fine. It looks worse than it is." I know he's lying when he screws his face up as he moves to the side of the door. "Come inside. I want to speak to you before I speak to everyone else." He sounds calm, but I sense the worry. That alone scares the shit out of me.

Owen takes my hand in his while I take in his face. I can't stop myself. I step forward and wrap my arms around him tightly, and he hisses in response.

I jerk myself back away from him. "Owen how bad is it?" I ask, but not really wanting to know as I swipe the tears away.

"It's not pretty. I will explain everything. Let's just sit down in here," he says as he shuts a door behind us. I take a seat on an empty sofa and pat the cushion next to me for Owen to drop into. He does so without any hesitation, once again taking my hand in his.

"Saxon has been trying to help me. I need out from under Benny's grasp and fast. Saxon can help me do that. He has specialist knowledge and the right set of skills. He also has a team of men that can keep the people I love safe, hence why Jason was following you tonight." He pauses while I take that information in.

"Why the need to have me tailed, Owen? Am I in more danger?"

His eyebrows are raised in worry. "I'm not going to lie to you anymore, baby. I need to tell everyone that means something to me what's going on. I have to. Benny has given me no choice. I need to tell them in order to protect them." He wipes away a lone tear that rolls down my face with the pad of his thumb. "Devon, baby...I need to tell them everything. That includes everything about you."

I jump out of his grasp in absolute terror. "No, Owen. I'm not ready. Please, it's too soon. I... I... don't think I can," I struggle to say, as my chest all of a sudden feels tight.

"I wouldn't do this if I didn't think it was necessary, but please, you have to see this from a different angle. I have to do this to keep them all safe, Devon—to keep you safe. I'm sorry. I just wanted to speak to you first so you didn't think I was throwing you in at the deep end."

I understand why he needs to do this, especially telling them all about his deal with Benny, but telling Isaak I'm his sister... I know in my heart I'm not ready for it, never mind Isaak.

"I know you're scared, baby, but trust me: Isaak will only take the positive from all this, and that's the fact that he has a little sister."

I can feel my hands starting to shake. "You really think so? What if he's angry with me? I mean, I've been lying to him about this, too. It may not have been in the same context as my mum...but still. What if he hates me for doing that to him?" I'm trembling now: knees bouncing, hands shaking, whole body quivering at the thought of Isaak's reaction towards me.

I'm being completely selfish.

I'm sitting here thinking all about myself and not how Owen is feeling or what is running around his head at the thought of what everyone will think of him and the fact he's kept his secret from them this long—that he's struggled with this. Because, my god, he has. I need to do this for Owen not just for myself.

Whatever happens from here on out, I know in my heart of hearts, Owen will be there to catch me if I should fall with no regard for himself.

"Just give me a second to get my nerves under control, and then we can go tell them all," I tell him, as I take a deep breath.

Standing, I pace around the room, waiting for my panic to subside. He sits patiently waiting for me. It's always about me. He's about to release the burden that he'd caged for so many years, yet he's showing signs that's he's more worried about me, not even thinking of the consequences of what could happen to him after all this.

It's in that moment of watching him watch me cautiously that I realise I'm falling further and further in love with his man.

My nerves evaporate instantaneously.

"Okay, I'm ready."

CHAPTER 27
OWEN

I watch Devon pacing the room, shaking like a damn leaf as she tries to calm herself down.

Suddenly she stops in her tracks and looks at me in a way she's never looked at me before. It's if she's realised something. What that is I don't know, and I don't get to question it.

"Okay, I'm ready." I hear the determination in her words. "Let's get this over with before I change my mind."

"I'll be with you every step of the way, baby," I tell her as I take her hand in mine.

"Stop worrying about me. Worry about yourself and what Isaak will do to you when he finds out you've been lying to him," she tells me with a small chuckle and a soft smile.

"I was trying not to think about that. So, thanks for that. However, I'm more concerned about how he will take the fact I've been doing the horizontal tango with his baby sister." I return her infectious smile with one of my own before kissing her lips softly.

"Sorry, I tend to say all kinds of shit when I'm nervous," she tells me by her way of explanation.

"I gathered." I'm trying to hide my grin as it increases in size.

"You don't think he'll be mad at you for being with me... Do you?"

How do I tell her everything will be fine when I know he will probably punch me in the face a few times, regardless of the mess it's already in. I decide just to go with the truth.

"Are you kidding? Have you seen how incredibly protective of his flesh and blood he is?" I joke over my shoulder at her as I walk us back into the room where my friends, my family, are impatiently waiting. She hovers behind me so I have to practically tug her into the room with me so I can close the door behind us.

"You going to tell us why you've dragged us all to Saxon's house at this time in the morning? I love ya bro, but we've had to bring Logan with us, because I doubt the babysitter would have appreciated being woken up at this time of night." Isaak's irritated, but I can sense his worry lingering there, too. They didn't have to come here in the first place. None of them did, but the fact that they've all shown up means more to me than anything. I guess that's why we call ourselves a close family.

"Also, what the fuck is up with your face? Think you need to get that checked out, mate."

I hang my head in shame. "I know, I'm sorry. And no, I'm not getting checked out. The reason will all become apparent in a few minutes if you listen, I will explain." I look from him to Remme, who's currently holding a sleeping Logan in her arms.

"Let me just go and put Logan down on the sofa in one of the other rooms. I don't want him to wake if I can help it. Luckily he didn't wake when I pulled him in and out of the car." Remme stands and heads out the door, soon returning with empty arms.

Only when she takes her seat again do I continue.

"Right, I'm just going to cut to the chase because quite frankly, there is no other way of doing this." I feel Devon's hand tighten around mine. I don't know if it's her silently showing me her support, or if she's starting to freak out. I squeeze hers back in reassurance anyway.

"I've been fighting for Benny." There I've said it. No going back now.

"You fucking what?" Isaak jumps up out of the chair, instantly full of uncontrollable anger.

Remme makes a grab for his arm to stop him from charging at me. He looks down at her and in some kind of silent communication, thankfully choosing to stay where he is. That doesn't stop him whipping his head back in my direction and giving me a murderous glare, though.

"Why, Owen? You know what kind of man he is—what he is capable of." He's finding this hard to wrap his head around, that much is obvious. "Is it for the money? You know you could have come to me for that. I don't understand, Owen. I mean, I hadn't seen him in years until he knocked on my door a few weeks back…" He cringes, knowing he's just opened another can of worms.

"He was at our house? Why was he at the house, Isaak?" Remme demands, now full of rage. Rage aimed towards him.

"I didn't know it was him until I opened the fucking door. I was trying to get rid of him but…" I see him working everything out. It's coming together for him, bits at a time. "Was that why Benny turned up at mine? When he was looking for you?" He points his finger in my direction.

"Yes and no… I was already in Benny's grasp the day he showed up at yours. I had been fighting for him already, but I wanted out. I thought I could have gotten out by now. I walked away. Benny obviously didn't like that, so he came looking for me personally, knowing exactly where to find me." I begin to explain the best I can. "I never wanted to drag any of you into my mess. I thought I would be able to find my way out of his hold on me without involving you." I hang my head in shame once again. I can hear the whispers circulating around the room.

"That still doesn't explain everything, Owen. I mean, look at the state of you for crying out loud." Remme's soft voice is the only noise that breaks through everyone else mumbling.

"I'm fine; it's just bruising mostly. I know it doesn't explain much, but for this to make sense, I need to start at the beginning."

The room falls eerily quiet as I begin to tell them of how I found myself in this mess.

"I was eighteen when it all started. I came over to yours, Isaak. You were in the gym one day, and I'd gone into the house for something when I overheard Benny and your dad in his office. I know I shouldn't have been eavesdropping, and I was about to leave them to it, until I heard them mention your name."

Everyone's shocked gasps fill my ears.

"Me? Why?" Isaak sits up in the chair he's now seated in.

"They were talking about some arrangement they had going on—about Gavin's gym and Benny wanting more fighters. Everything got heated between them when Benny said he wanted you, but your dad was having none of it." I look into my best friend's eyes, the one person who has never lied to me, the guy who has my back whenever I need him to—and now I've lied to him, something I never thought I'd do. Me keeping this secret from him has been one of the hardest things for me to live with. I just hope he understands why I have done it.

The next words I'm about to say are purely for him to hear. "Benny told Gavin that he wanted you. You were one of the best fighters he'd ever seen and he wanted you for himself. Gavin tried putting a stop to the whole ordeal—said Benny had already taken so much from him that he wasn't about to hand you over to him so easily. Benny then turned nasty and started to threaten him. Something along the lines off, 'If I go down then I'll be taking you with me'. Gavin put up one hell of a fight against Benny, but I knew—and he knew—he wasn't going to win. Before I knew what I was doing, I'd barged my way into the office, abruptly halting their conversation all together." I pause, trying to gather my thoughts somewhat, I suppose getting ready for the backlash that I know is coming.

Before I can carry on, Isaak is out of this chair and coming at me.

"You stupid mother fucker." I don't need to say anymore for him to know: he knows what I did that day without me verbalising it.

I move Devon to the side of me, out of harm's way, just in time. Isaak has my back slamming into the door behind me. The moment my body hits the wood, I hiss through my teeth at the splintering pain rushing up my spine. Regardless, it goes unnoticed by Isaak.

"Fucking hell Owen, why? Why would you do that?" His anger is there in full force, but I don't fight back. I don't even try to loosen the hold he has on me to relieve some of the aching in my back. I just stare into his bulging eyes, and all I see is utter devastation shining back at me.

"I had no choice, Isaak. I couldn't stand by and watch them ruin you. You were on your way to the top, Isaak, and I wasn't going to let your Uncle Benny take that away from you. Over my dead body, I did this to protect you and to protect your career. I did it to protect your dad and in so many ways my dad too because you know that man was the closest person I could ever call as a father." I tell him honestly and surprisingly calmly.

"You made a deal with the fucking devil, Owen. Benny isn't going to let you walk away from it. At least not without a full-blown fight." He relents his hold on me but still stands tall, unmoving.

"Will someone please tell me what the hell is going on before I end up pushing this baby out far too soon!" Remme shouts out, causing us all to look at her. "You might have some understanding of what is happening, Isaak, but if you don't pull us into the loop then you'll find yourself sleeping in the spare room," she threatens, causing his shoulders sag in defeat. Remme is the only person who can tell Isaak what to do and get away with it.

"Owen basically took my place, like the stupid son of a bitch he is. That's why he has been coming to work covered in bruises." With the exception of myself, Devon, Isaak and Saxon, the rest of the room gasps disbelieving again.

All I get is a round of, 'Owen no', or, 'Owen why would you do that?', which isn't helpful in the slightest.

"Wait, so what does that have to do with the rest of us?" Charlotte speaks up, stealing the attention I'm getting.

"That's where I come into it," Saxon says, cutting his own silence.

"You knew and didn't tell me? What the fuck, Sax? Who else knows?" He looks around the room as everyone shakes their confused heads. Then his eyes land on Devon, who's taken an interest in Saxon's laminate flooring. "You told Devon before me?" He looks hurt.

"For what it's worth, I haven't known for long, and I know keeping this from you has torn Owen apart. He wanted to tell you so many times, but he didn't want you looking at him the way you are now: disappointed, angry, disloyal. He doesn't want your sympathy; he wants you to help him and possibly forgive him," Devon tells him, matching his stance. She's more like her brother than she realises. She doesn't even back down when Isaak walks towards her.

"How do you know what it is he wants? He doesn't even know that himself," he says when he comes to a stop directly in front of her.

"I don't need to know, and neither should you. It's written all over his face. If you got your head out of her arse long enough, you would fucking see that." She steps back from Isaak, panic marking her features. No doubt from her outburst that was so out of character for her. I've never seen her speak to anyone like that before. By the look on Isaak's face, I'd say he thinks the same as well.

"Excuse me?" Isaak looks taken back, yet there's a smirk creeping up the side of his mouth.

I make a move towards her, but she holds her hand up, stopping me in my tracks.

"You heard me. Doesn't matter what Owen tells you; it doesn't change the reason behind it." She retakes her place in front of Isaak, looking up at him from the height difference. "Owen did this for you, Isaak. For you." She's poked the beast. I can see Isaak's chest rising and falling with every heavy breath he takes.

"You think I don't know that, Devon? I fucking know, and because of his choices, I've been slowly losing my best friend and unable to do a God damn thing about it," he roars in her face.

"Isaak…" Remme calls his name in warning.

He'll never hurt Dev, or any woman for that matter, but Remme knows him better than anyone—even better than me and I've known him a lot longer.

"It's fine, Remme. Let Isaak 'The Bruiser' fucking Brookes have his hissy fit. Let him get it all out of his system so we can move on from this and let Saxon and Owen tell you the rest and the main reason for you all being here. And, Isaak, if you think this is a shock to your severely bruised ego, you've heard nothing yet."

I don't know where she's getting her bravery from, but it's turning me on when it shouldn't—not with a room full of people.

She goes to sit back down but he grabs her shoulder lightly to spin her back around.

"What the fuck is that supposed to mean?" he bellows.

"Nothing." She whispers, realising what she could have possible just blurted out.

"Clearly it's something, otherwise you wouldn't have said it." He lets go of her shoulder, throwing his arms out to the side of him. "So come on, you obviously know more than me. Seems all you had to do was sleep with Owen and he's poured all his secrets to you. So, enlighten me."

This isn't like Isaak at all. I get he's pissed, but he should be taking that out on me, not Devon.

"Isaak, dude. What the fuck?" I say as I get between them. "Devon, you need to hold off a little. Isaak is still trying to wrap his head around all this." Looking back at Isaak, I can tell he doesn't know what to do with himself. He's frustrated, but that doesn't excuse the way he's just spoken to her. "You need to apologise to her, Isaak."

"Me? For what?"

"You've basically just told her she's a whore. I'm not going to stand here and let that happen. I care about her and she's not just another piece of arse to me. So, apologise or me and you are done. I mean it, Isaak."

"Mate, that's not what I meant. Devon, I would never think about you. Fuck, you're like a sister to me. I'm sorry." He doesn't know how true that statement really is.

Movement at the other side of the room grabs my attention as Saxon quietly and stealthy ushers everyone but myself, Devon, Isaak, Remme and himself out of the room. I glance back to Isaak's sorrowful face to Devon's. She has tears building, and she's trying her best to hold them at bay. I know what she wants to do when she looks at me out the corner of her eye, a single tear trickling from each of her eyes.

I nod my head in understanding, letting her know I'm here to catch her if she should fall.

"That's because I *am* your sister."

CHAPTER 28
OWEN

"Come again…" Isaak stumbles back. Thankfully, Saxon and I are there to keep him up right.

"I said that's because—"

"Yeah, I heard what you said, but that's impossible, Devon. For starters, your surname is Carter. My mum surely would have told me if she'd had another child. Regardless if I spoke to her or not. He laughs awkwardly.

Neither myself or Devon say anything. I'm glad she is on the same page as me on this. We need to ease Isaak into this slowly. He notices his mistake almost instantly.

Devon goes into the whole tale of why and how she changed her name, and why I didn't pick up on who she was because of it.

"Oh, God, Benny is your father?" Isaak asks as Remme moves over on the sofa for me and Saxon to sit him down. "Wait, Benny and my mother. Jesus Christ. I never knew about you, Devon." He sinks his head into his hands as Remme begins to rub at his back in small soft circles.

"While that registers with you, I'll get the others back in tell so I can fill them in on what they need to know. That way you can all get back home to bed." Thankfully Saxon walks away, letting me have five minutes with my girl and Remme to calm Isaak.

"I'm proud of you." I whisper in her ear before placing a kiss on her forehead.

"Why? I haven't even told him the true story yet," she says, shrugging sheepishly.

"It was a start. And you had my back. Thank you."

"I'll always have your back, Owen." She smiles up at me.

"It should be the other way around, baby," I tell her. I kiss her lips quickly as Saxon comes back over after getting the others back in the room and starts telling them about the uneasy feeling I had when I left Benny at the warehouse tonight.

"We can't put anything past Benny at this moment in time, so in the meantime, while I finalise the details of a plan to help Owen out of this, I need you all to watch your backs and be extra cautious. I only have a few men spare right now. I'm spreading myself and my guys out thinner than I would like to, so I need you all on point without making this harder for them than is needed." He glances around the room, looking at us all individually. "Isaak, Remme. I'll be with you when needed, mainly with Remme and Logan when Isaak isn't with you. Jason will be taking over watching Charlotte and Devon. I have another guy—"

"Not needed. Devon isn't leaving my side. I'll keep her close to me." I know Saxon is about to deny me this, but eventually he gives in, nodding his head, knowing I won't back down.

"Fine. Jase will watch over Charlotte. I'll have my guy watch Jemma as a precaution. From what I can tell, Jemma, you aren't on Benny's radar. I wanna keep it that way, so I need you to keep as much distance from everyone else as possible. Just do what you have to do at work and then leave. I know it's unfair, but it's the only way to keep you safe."

Jemma nods nervously.

This is all my fault. I've put the people closest to me in danger, and I have no idea what lies ahead of me, or everyone in this room from here on out.

"Does everyone understand what I'm saying? The more you all corporate, the easier it will be for me and my men, which in turn will give me more time to come up with a plan to dig us all out of this mess, sooner rather than later," he adds.

Everyone nods in agreement.

"I'm so sorry I've brought you all into this mess. This is why I didn't tell any of you about it to start with. I thought if I kept you in the dark Benny wouldn't bat an eyelid at any of you." I hang my head in shame. In guilt and sheer dumbness. I should have known Benny would try this at some point to keep me in line.

Remme is the first person to speak, causing me to lift my heavy head up. "Owen, don't be so hard on yourself." She leaves Isaak's side and walks over to me. "I think you're one very brave human being. I know why you did what you did all those years ago, and I know you'd make the same decision again if you needed to. Because of what you did, I met Isaak. If that hadn't have happened, I wouldn't have that little boy who's fast asleep in the other room, or our second child growing now. I appreciate that more than you will ever know. Thank you." She wraps her arms around my neck and squeezes me tight. I bring my limp arms up and mirror her hug. She gets it. She understands why I did it. If Remme understands, I know she will help Isaak to understand, too, in time.

Remme almost leaps from my arms when Devon jumps to her feet beside us, breaking the silence with a sharp screech.

"Oh, God, I almost forgot." She runs out of the door and heads into the room I'd taken her in when she first got here before returning with something in her hands.

"Baby, what's that?" I ask as Remme removes her arms from around me.

"This is what I was trying to ring you about earlier. I went to visit my mum as I hadn't spoken to her since, well, you know."

I knew exactly what she was getting at: the day Sandra showed up at my house.

"Well, I managed to get into Benny's desk drawers. They were locked but my mum helped me out with that."

"You did what?" Isaak, Saxon and myself say in unison.

She gives us all irritated looks, telling us to quietly back off.

"Devon, that was a risky move." Saxon smiles. "But excellent work. What did you find?" he adds.

"More than I bargained for that's for sure. There were some documents that looked important, pictures and information of everyone in this room, all except Jemma, and you, Saxon." She wanders across to him, looking at him sceptically.

"I cover my tracks well, Devon. What else? Can I see the file?" Her head lowers to the folder in her arms, like she's reluctant to give it to him.

"Devon?" Sax questions, confused just like the rest of us.

"I found something else when I went through that file. It isn't good, Saxon. I don't know what to do." She's getting tearful; I can hear it in her voice.

"Babe," I join her and Saxon. "Whatever it is, we will deal with it."

"I know. It's the…the first page in there." She hands over the folder with a slight shake in her hands.

"Thank you, Devon. This might be what I've been trying to find on Benny." Saxon flips the folder open, only glancing at the first page before closing it again and standing abruptly.

"Okay, guys. It's getting late. Why don't you all head home and I'll get the ball rolling on my end. Just carry on as normal. Don't do anything out of the ordinary otherwise Benny will clock on that something is wrong. From what Devon has just shown me in this file, he has eyes everywhere. Just be careful and stay safe."

The girls are reluctant to leave at first, but eventually people start moving.

"Isaak, I need you to stay behind. There's more you need to know." Saxon say directly.

"Okay, but who's taking Remme and Logan home?"

"I'll stay with Remme and Logan. Jase can drop us all off there. That way he can keep an eye on us all until you get back, Isaak. I promise not to leave their side until you're home," Charlotte says just as she reaches us.

"How do you plan on protecting them, then?" Isaak questions jokingly with a small smile.

"I'll have you know I was top of my karate class as a teenager, I made it all the way to black belt. Jase is there as my back up." She slaps Isaak arm playfully, laughing as Isaak shouts over to her suggesting she stay the night in the spare room as she follows them all out of the door. She waves her hand in acknowledgement.

Now the others have left, it's just me, Dev, Isaak and Saxon to hash out the rest of the stuff that we've found out. I'm still in the dark about what's inside that folder as much as Isaak. Whatever it is, it has Devon more terrified than she was before.

"Okay, so it looks like the situation could take a turn for the worst. Benny knows more than he's let on, and it could go one of two ways. He'll either act on it or he won't give two shits about it. Either way it's not good, Owen." He takes a seat behind a desk in the room.

"What do you mean?" I don't know how this situation could possibly get any worse, but it is Benny we're talking about, so nothing is fully off the cards.

"Devon, are you okay for me to tell them what's in this file?" he asks her softly.

"Yeah, no more secrets." She offers him a timid smile in return.

"So, this won't come as a shock to you, Owen, as you already know most of it." Well that doesn't make me feel any fucking better. "Benny knows about Devon."

"As in what? He knows what?" I need answers.

"He knows Devon isn't his." He pulls a piece of paper out the folder and hands it to me. "That's Devon's birth certificate."

"And that's my deed poll letter confirming my name change. I have no idea how he would get hold of that. There is also a letter in there that my mother wrote to Gavin telling him about me. It also mentions how sorry she was that right now her two children could never get to know each other. You can read the letter for yourself Isaak. It may help clarify some details for you, or at least explain her reasons for what she did." Devon sighs taking a huge gulp of air into her lungs. Then speaks again while Isaak looks over the letter and another piece of paper which she handed to him.

"There is also photos in there of people I have never seen before. I found them odd as the file seems to be focused around me, Owen and Isaak." Sax nods and continues to look through the file.

Isaak looks at me and Devon and points wordlessly in confusion at the paper.

I look down and there in black and white is Devon's name and both Sandra's and Gavin's.

"Oh fuck." This really isn't good news. It's fucking bad, really fucking bad.

"Hold on, I thought you said Benny was your father?" Isaak asks, the confusion written all over his face again.

"I thought so, too, up until a week ago. My mum went to visit Owen one day and saw me there, and she cracked. She told me everything. At least I think it was everything. She told me tonight when we found the certificate that she went alone to register me so she could put my real fathers name on it. She thought by going alone Benny would have no reason to question it. I mean why would he? He thought I was his at that point. She tried to keep it all hidden, but he had reasons to go digging and that's how he found out." The nerves are back again, her voice shaking with every word she says.

"So, what does it say on there? Who's your father?"

"Isaak, we have the same parents. Gavin was my father." Tears build up in Devon's eyes before they start to run freely down her cheeks.

Isaak rips the paper from my hands and begins to read it.

"So, we're not half siblings. You're actually my sister?" he questions in a daze, not looking up from the words staring back at him. I can't tell if he's happy about this or not. I glance over to Devon, offering her my silent support, which I know she appreciates.

"Wait, how old are you, again?" he asks the question even though it's right there in front of him.

"Just turned twenty-one, why?"

I'm just as intrigued to know this myself. What's Isaak trying to work out?

"That's why she never showed up for my seventh birthday. She was trying to keep this from Dad. It's all starting to make sense now. She falls pregnant with you; makes out Benny is your father. But for what? An easier life?" The anger flashing in his eyes is enough to scare anyone and have them shaking in their boots.

"Isaak, you don't know the full story. You need to speak to your mum," I tell him.

"Speak to her? Why would I do that? I haven't spoken to her since my father's funeral," he bellows in my direction.

"She misses you, Isaak. She told me it was to keep you safe. All the secrets and lies were to keep the people she loves safe. If you have questions, then she can answer them for you. Plus, it's her story to tell, no one else's," Devon stutters out.

Isaak looks down at the paper in his hands and back up to Devon again.

"I have a little sister." No one says anything for a long time not quite sure what do to. He stares at Devon intensively before breaking the silence. "You're my sister." "You're like me in so many ways, it's scary. The fire in your eyes when you were fighting for Owen, I had that same fire in me when it came to Remme. You're a fighter, it's in your blood, just as it is mine. It's obvious to me now." His smile starts off small, and I see it growing, but all too soon, it vanishes again.

Oh, this isn't good.

His head wipes in my direction. "You're cozying up with my sister?" He shoots daggers my way.

I don't know whether to laugh or prepare for a beat down. "Erm…yeah."

"No way. Not a fucking chance. It's not happening," Isaak spits.

"What, why?" Devon has the nerve to ask. "You didn't have a problem with it before," she adds for good measure.

"What she said," I say putting my two pence worth in.

"Because she's my little sister, for God sake. Before she was a good friend, and as much as I didn't like it she is free to be with who she wants to be with. Now I know she's my sister and you broke the bro code. Siblings are off limits. Owen, I know your…bedroom habits. I was worried about you two getting together beforehand, now it's even worse." He throws his hands up, covering his eyes. "Oh fucking hell; now I have images in my head." He groans in displeasure.

I can't help myself. I ball over and howl in laughter, Devon and Saxon joining in.

"How have I broke the bro code? Neither of us knew she was your sister, and this all started before I knew she was of any relation to you, Isaak." I find myself needed to clarify myself.

"I...You... I don't know. You just did. If you weren't already busted up, I'd have done it, good and proper. You and my sister?" he adds for good measure.

"Just for the record, Isaak. Devon is different, and you know this." I give him a knowing look so he understands I'm talking about the time I last spoke to him about her in my office.

He drops his hands looking backwards and forwards between Dev and me and letting out an overly dramatic huff. "I should have said this when I first found out about the pair of you, but I'll say it now. If you hurt her, I'll beat you so fucking hard you'll be seeing stars and shitting out teeth for a week." He points his finger at my chest sternly.

"Erm, hello, boys? I am still here. As much as I appreciate the big brother riot act being given, is it really necessary?"

"Not a chance of that happening. I promise you, I'll never hurt her." I say looking Isaak in the eye then giving my girl a cheeky wink letting her know I mean it.

He gives me a firm nod of his head before taking the few steps he needs to take Devon into his arms, lifting her off the ground. "Come here, you. Yes, it was necessary. I'm your big brother it's my right to, is it not?" She lets out a girly squeal, her smile wide. Although he's looking over her shoulder, I'm getting daggers from Isaak.

Oh boy, I'm a dead man. This is all a front for Devon I'm gonna feel his wrath when he gets me alone.

"You okay about all this, then?" she asks when he finally puts her down on the floor again.

"Why wouldn't I be? You're like a little sister to me anyway. Now we just have it in writing," he says with a shrug of his shoulder. "Plus, my kids have an auntie to babysit them."

She hits him on the arm causing him to laugh.

I'm so glad everything is out in the open. Now, we can all move forward from this and hopefully find a way out. I'm not naive when it comes to my relationship with Isaak: I lied to him, kept huge secrets from him for the best part of eight years. I know he isn't going to let me off the hook that easily, but it's a start, and that's all I can ask for.

"Erm guys. I hate to break up the family reunion, but there is something you should know." We all stop and wait for Saxon to elaborate.

"The photos of the other people in this file, are people I know. They are the police. They are undercover police, and this woman here is the chief inspector. Clearly they aren't that under fucking cover if Benny knows about them. Fuck!"

"Holy shit." I mutter, while Devon stands with her mouth agape.

"I will deal with this. I doubt the police even know that Benny is on to them. I'll let you guys know what I find out." Saxon adds, not at all impressed by what he's seen.

Now, I just hope Saxon can pull through and come up with a plan.

CHAPTER 29
DEVON

It's been a couple of weeks since Owen called everyone around to Saxon's house, two weeks since Isaak found out I was his biological sister, and two weeks since I stepped foot into my parents' house.

I've rung my mum since. She told me everything was fine, that Benny hasn't noticed the file missing or said anything to her, but I have a feeling in my gut that she's not being truthful with me. After all, the information and photographs inside the file were not something he'd easily misplace. This is worrying and when I mention it to Owen, he gets Saxon right on it.

Saxon came and told us that the police have been watching Benny for a while and Owen had been seen in connection with him. Saxon being the legend he, managed to cut a deal with his cop friend, Jessica. Owen still wasn't out the woods yet, but Jess wanted to use the only in she would get when it came to Benny. Owen was now her way in. He's become somewhat of an informant for them. Saxon said this is the best outcome for Owen at this point.

I've spent every day since then at Owen's place, not returning to my apartment unless it is for clothes or to collect my mail. Every time I go, Owen is with me the whole time, never leaving my side.

To say the past five and a half weeks I've spent with Owen have been eventful would be an understatement. You couldn't write this shit in a month of Sundays, that's for sure, but it is what it is, and we just need to move forwards the best we can. We've tried to act as normal as possible in our day-to-day routine, just in case Benny has his men watching us, and now we know this to be true.

I walk into the gym on my day off. I'm here for a purpose: I need something from Owen.

I don't often ask people for help, but the truth is, I need this more than ever.

It's almost the end of the day, so the gym is quiet. A couple of regulars are grafting away on equipment that clunks and clangs, and I hear the women's over-the-top laughter before I see them. A blonde is on the treadmill while a brunette flirts and makes doe eyes at Owen, who looks like he's enjoying the attention far more than he should be.

I can't help the pang of jealousy that flows through my veins, making them hot beneath my skin. It's funny, with everything that's going on right now the one thing that is making my blood boil is the thought of Owen and those two gym bunnies.

Is that what he likes: two girls at once?

I never usually interrupt a personal training session, but watching those girls fall over themselves to get his attention has me riled. I make my way over to the treadmill and the two girls spot my movements. They halt their workout, causing Owen to follow their line of sight. He turns his whole body before he starts walking towards me, his face beaming with a huge smile. The two bunnies look like I just rained on their parade.

"Hey beautiful lady," he says reaching out for me, pulling me closer and attacking my lips with his. "Not that I don't want you here or anything, but what you doing here on your day off?"

"I wanted to ask you a favour, but I see you're busy with Barbie and her bestie over there, so it can wait." I tilt my head in their direction and make sure I say it loud enough for them to hear me. It hits the mark, as they now look embarrassed by their behaviour.

"Don't do that, Dev: green doesn't suit you. The colour of my handprint on your backside will, though." He wiggles his eyebrows suggestively and I can't ignore the heat that makes its way to my legs as they turn to jelly. Just the thought of Owen laying his hands on me like that makes me horny as fuck.

The door at the main entrance closes with a slam, bringing me back to my senses.

"How about you go make sure there are no stragglers left in the changing rooms, I'll finish up with my clients and then you can ask me that favour while you help me clean and lock up." Owen spins on his heels, telling the gym bunnies that their session is done for the day and if they didn't want to get locked in then they should hurry and get their stuff.

Making a beeline for the laundry bins that are scattered around, I collect them and put the towels on a wash so they're ready to dry in the morning, take the dry ones out the dryer folding them and taking them out to the reception area and place them on the shelf.

When I turn around, there's only Owen left in the gym area. He must have sent the other couple of trainers home early as they had no clients and nothing else to do.

I watch as he picks up the discarded weights off the floor, his back is to me. I just watch for a minute, with fascination at how the muscles in his back stick out slightly and stretch with every movement he makes; how cute his arse is when he bends to pick up the weights; and how lifting that weight makes the muscles in his forearms tense up, a ripple effect rolling up to his bicep. My mouth waters, and I can't stand it any longer. My body aches for his touch.

As he makes his way over to the ring area, I double check the door is locked up and make my way over to him. By the time I get to him, he's in the ring, having just swept it. I climb into the ring and Owen looks up at me, confused by my actions.

"What are you doing, Dev?"

"I couldn't wait any longer to kiss you. You looked so damn delicious from over there." I want more than that from him, but that can wait. First, I need that favour.

"Owen, that favour I mentioned."

He nods his head for me to go on.

"Well, I kinda want you to teach me self-defence." He teaches some classes here every once in a while, taking it in turns with Isaak. They only starting them a few months ago after Remme was pushed down the stairs by a psycho. It's probably more Isaak's thing, but I'm not initially comfortable asking him for help with this.

"Okay, but why?" He looks confused again, and I can't stop the tears from falling as I think about my answer. It's the one thing I never thought I would be saying.

"My father"—I roll my now swollen eyes and Owen's hands take a hold of both my cheeks in comforting support, allowing me to continue on—"I mean Benny, is a dangerous man. I guess on some level I always knew that about him. He was always protecting me, you know. I never once thought I would need to protect myself from him, though. I can handle myself alright in a cat fight at the bar, but against Benny and his merry men, I don't think so." I look up into Owen's worried eyes as I explain my need to do this. I can see the understanding.

"Fine, I'll teach you. Not because I think you will need it, but because I want to give you some peace of mind. Then I'm hoping that tormented, haunted look in your eyes will vanish."

Since we are already in the ring, we get to work immediately.

He quickly tapes and gloves me up and picks up the sparring pads I have seen him use a million times before with my brother, so they need no explanation.

Owen calls out the moves he wants me to do, shouting for me to punch harder. At first, my targets are still, but he soon starts moving around, changing the pads to different heights, still shouting at me.

All goes well, I think, until I miss the pad, sending me off balance and causing me to punch him in the stomach. Owen pretends to go down like I've KO'd him. I can't stop the laughter bursting from me as I flop to the canvas next to him in an exhausted heap, pulling the gloves off.

"You did good, baby," he says, rolling his toned body over my sweaty one.

"You think so?" I hadn't been expecting miracles in a day.

"Yeah, I do. It must run in the family. You have that fighter in you that Isaak does."

I lean up and place a peck on his lips. "I like this look on you, Dev: the hot, sweaty, gym bunny look." Owens hand that rests on my hip finds its way up my side and over my breast as he kneads it in his palm over the tiny sports bra I have on under my hoodie. He pulls down the lycra to reveal the tight nub of my sensitive nipple. He takes it in his mouth at the same time his hips start to rock into me, making me wish for less clothing.

"Let's go home, Owen. I need you." I'm so desperate to get out of here so I can have him, I'm already trying to shuffle out from under him.

"I need you, too, but I can't wait that long to have you. I want you right here, right now." He leans up to sit on his knees and looks lustfully down at me, reaching forward, stripping me of my gym leggings and taking my underwear and trainers with them in quick succession. He helps me to all fours in front of him before swiftly spanking my arse hard, sending pleasurable shockwaves between my legs before rubbing the area gently.

I grunt out a slight scream. "Again," is all I can manage.

Another two spanks, followed by the softness of his palm soothingly the stings, come one after the other. I feel him shuffling closer to me, and I brace myself, holding onto the corner padding of the ring as I wait for the next blow to what I am sure is now my bright red backside. But it doesn't come.

Glancing over my shoulder, I watch as Owen is up on his knees staring at my arse and my very wet pussy. He blinks fast and shakes his head like he's pulling himself from a daydream as he grabs a hold of my hips instead. His darkened eyes flicker up to mine and keeps me captive in his web as he slams straight into me.

"Owen," I start but don't finish.

"Christ, you're so damn wet for me, baby. You like it when I spank you." Thankfully it's not a question: I don't think I could answer even if I wanted to.

He never stops or slows his pace, just continuous, deep and satisfying penetration, Owen grunting and me mewling at just how good it feels—how good *he* feels.

As he leans over me, he wraps an arm around me finding the button between my legs, pushing on it causing a symphony of sensations to start in my tummy, making their way lower. It's not long until I hear Owen's breathing speed up and his movements become more erratic. He's getting close, and I'm fast catching up to him. His fingers start moving in a small circular motion, faster and harder, my screams getting louder and louder the closer I am to exploding around him.

Owen's free hand grips my arse cheek, his fingertips bruising the flesh, not that I care. I love each mark he leaves on my skin like a claim.

Two more soul crushing thrusts are all it takes for every muscle in my body to clench, my pussy holding on so tightly to Owen's dick as I let go with a scream of his name.

He pushes into me so deeply, and I feel him empty inside of me.

Cool air glides across my back as he lets go of his breath. Both of us breath frantically as he pulls himself free and rolls out of the ring, pulling his shorts back up. He reaches for my hand and my clothing, pulling me under the bottom rope, but instead of placing me on the ground he lifts me bridal style.

"I think we need to shower, do round two in there and get cleaned up, don't you?" he asks before kissing me with so much passion, I don't want to lose this feeling.

Not now, not ever.

CHAPTER 30
OWEN

I can feel the warm softness of Devon's arm as it sits pretty across my chest, something I never thought I'd enjoy—not any time soon anyway—but I really fucking do.

I flutter open my eyes fully and turn my head in the direction of the naked goodness lying sound asleep next to me. Her blonde locks are spread out over the pillow behind her, the bed sheet snaked around her hips, her breasts peeking out, taunting me.

I can't help myself, and turn my body slowly towards hers. I level my mouth with one of her nipples and release a soft blow of air, watching with pure satisfaction as her nipple tightens into a hard pebble before my eyes.

When I hear a small moan leave her lips, I make my move, wrapping my mouth around her now hardened bud. I pull it gently between my teeth before releasing it again and swipe my tongue over her hypersensitive area.

"A girl could get used to this kind of wake-up call."

I can tell she's smiling through her words by the sound of her voice.

"My dick could, too," I tell her, laughing as I thrust my hips against her thighs.

"Way to ruin the moment, Owen."

I know she's only joking as she giggles and makes a play to leave the bed.

I reach up and grab her waist, pulling her back to me again. "Don't leave me to deal with this all by myself. Help a guy out." I nod at my groin and solidness when she turns to face me.

"Do you plan to stay in bed all day?" She looks at me from under her long lashes in question.

"Well, I see no reason to leave this room for anything other than bathroom breaks and fuel to keep us going." I wiggle my eyebrows at her suggestively, knowing she won't go for it.

"Not a chance, babe. You promised me some one-on-one time if you remember."

I think back to when I may have made said promise, but for the life in me I can't remember. My face must show my confusion because she is looking at me with a death stare—one that could have me buried six feet under in five seconds flat.

"You don't remember, do you? When we were leaving the gym last night. I asked you whilst you were rushing me out of the door to get home."

I'm still clueless. Reaching a hand up and scratching the back of my head, I try my best to think back on what she is banging on about.

"Baby, I'm sorry, but I was rushing you out that building with only one thing on my mind," I mutter, laughing to try to lighten the mood a little. She swats her hand to my chest, amusement shining in her eyes.

"You said you'd teach me a bit more today." Devon gets up off the bed and grabs herself some fresh gym clothes.

It looks like we're not staying under the covers then.

Grabbing a pair of boxers and gym shorts, I dress quickly. "Meet me downstairs," I shout towards her in the bathroom. I don't mind teaching her, but we will be doing it in the comfort of our home today.

Our home.

I keep doing this sort of thing, saying the odd slip of the tongue stuff and to be honest it doesn't feel bad either. I'm not breaking out in a cold sweat,

I'm not on the verge of hyperventilating, and I haven't passed the fuck out. I realise that's what I now want, and I want it with her. I want it with Devon. With my mind made up, I head to get the coffee machine on the go.

I walk past a mirror and I catch myself grinning like a Cheshire cat.

"What're you grinning at, weirdo?" I hear from behind me.

I turn around and grab her quickly by the hips, lifting her up to me, pinning her to the wall with my lips on hers so fast she can't even squeal at the element of surprise. I kiss her with everything I have in me.

"Move in with me," I blurt out softly.

The look of shock on her face is so blank, I don't know if it's a good surprise or not. I don't get much chance to push her for an answer, though, as there is a knock on the door.

"You better get that." Devon nods her head to the door as the knocks turn to thumps of impatience.

"Hold ya fucking horses, I'm coming," I huff out, already annoyed that I have been interrupted in the first place. "Don't ya know it's a Sunday, for fucks sake—"

I'm cut off as Benny pushes past me with murder in his eyes as soon as I have the lock undone.

"Where the fuck is she?" he spits, just as Dev walks towards us.

"Where's who?" Devon questions, already sensing something is wrong.

"Sandra. Where is she?" The venom in his voice hasn't gone unnoticed.

"I don't know what you're talking about; she isn't here that's for sure," I tell him, wanting to get him out of my house sooner rather than later. Benny walks further into my home, eyeballing the kitchen and the hallway, then proceeds to shout up the stairs for Sandra.

"Benny she isn't here. What's going on?" Devon shouts at him, forcing his head to snap back around so fast at the sound of his name leaving her lips instead of 'dad'.

His mouth opens then closes a few times before he seems to shake himself a little then speaks again. "She is missing. She left for her early morning jog and hasn't come back."

And he assumed she would come here…

"Have you tried calling her?" Devon asks taking her phone out and swiping across the screen before placing it at her ear. "Straight to voicemail. Mum never has her phone off." The panic in Devon's voice is evident straight away.

"Of course I tried to call her. What do you think I am, stupid?"

I hold my tongue because that is exactly what I want to call the man for coming here thinking this would be where she is.

"I'm sure it's nothing to worry about and that she'll be back soon. I'll tell her to call you if I see her." Devon sounds unconvinced to me, but it's enough to fool Benny. Maybe he doesn't know her after all.

"Make sure you do." He grumbles his order at her. "You know, Devon, I'm very disappointed to find you shacked up with this lowlife," he says as he crosses the threshold back to the outside world.

Dev and I follow closely behind to shut the door after the unwanted guest leaves, and Devon slides her arm around my back in a show of defiance.

"My life, my rules. I do what I want, and I do who I want. You don't have to like it." With that she slams the door in Benny's face, leaving a smirk on mine.

"As much as watching you stand up to that man was a turn on of epic proportion, do you think it was a good idea to poke the beast right now?" I pull her towards me and hold her tight to my chest until her shoulders start to shake. I lean my head away from her so I can see her face. "What's the matter, baby?" I wipe my thumbs under both her eyes to rid her of the big fat tears that are falling over her cheekbones.

"Benny was right: there is something wrong. My mother never ever turns off her phone when she is in the house, let alone when she is out of the house. I just feel it in my bones, Owen. Something isn't right." Panic is written all over her face.

"Doesn't Saxon have eyes on her as well?"

Her eyes shine with hope at my declaration.

Not wasting a single second, I take my own phone from the pocket of my shorts and wait for Saxon to answer.

"Hey, Owen, what's up?" Sax cheerily answers the phones.

"We've just had Benny here ranting over Sandra going missing and thinking she was here. Did you not have eyes on her?" I can feel Devon's eyes boring into me as she waits for information. I hear Sax blow out a big breath.

"I'm already on the road, so I'll be there in two minutes." He hangs up before I have a chance to reply. I pull the phone away from my ear looking at it in disbelief.

"What did he say?" Devon asks carefully.

"He is on his way. He said he would be here any second."

A gentle tap on the front door makes us both jump. This time Dev answers it.

"Hey Saxon, good to see you," she says almost too calm considering she was crying just two minutes ago.

"Hi, guys. Listen, I didn't want to talk on the phone as you never know what tricks Benny has up his sleeve. I also can't say much on the subject, but I can tell you that your mum is safe." Sax turns to Devon as he looks into her eyes, making sure she can see his honesty and his apology over the stress it has caused her.

"Where is she? Can I see her?"

"Unfortunately, no. Your mum is in a safe house away from here, and more importantly away from Benny."

Devon starts pacing the room as she takes all this new information in.

"Saxon is there something we should know?" I ask, wanting to know as much as possible.

"Just keep your wits about you. Don't be alone; stay together. I'll have a man on you twenty-four-seven from now on. If you get called to fight, take Devon somewhere safe like Isaak and Remme's where there is already one of my guys there." He turns to Dev again as I zone out thinking about all this new information. I vaguely hear him asking Devon if she is okay to carry on staying here with me for the time being. Her answer is instant, and it makes me smile on the inside that she doesn't hesitate to say yes. However, she will need to go home and get more stuff—all of it if I have my way.

"Well, I shall leave you to it, but please don't worry, Devon. She is safe and I have one of my best men assigned to her."

"Come on, I will drive you over to your place to pick up more stuff," I tell her as I grab a shirt from the laundry pile and my keys.

CHAPTER 31
DEVON

I'm traipsing around my place trying to grab everything I need to pack, trying not to forget anything I may need for the foreseeable future. It's harder than you think, even with Owen sitting on the bed putting everything I throw at him in the case neatly.

"How much stuff do you think I need to bring over?" I shout from the bathroom where I grab my favourite fresh bottles of shampoo and conditioner and all my other toiletries before throwing them in my wash bag as I'm running out over at Owen's. As much as I like smelling like Owen, I need to start using my own products. My hair now has a mind of it's own. It's out of control.

"I don't know. As much as you want," I hear him shout, but as I walk back in he mumbles, "Bring it all."

I saunter over to him and sit on his lap placing the washbag in the case and wrapping my arm around his neck. He wraps his own tightly around my lower back, resting his palm on my hip, the other hand on my thigh.

"Do you really want that?" I query, sounding unsure. On the inside, though, I'm alive with anticipation and excitement that won't settle down. My stomach does somersaults as I wait to find out if it was a real question or just the heat of the moment.

I mean, this is Owen I'm talking about here.

I prepare myself for the let-down—for it all to be a dream—but yet again, Owen finds a way to surprise me.

"Yeah of course I mean it, I.—"

"You know, because if you didn't... Wait. What?"

"I said, yes. I meant it, Dev. Where have you been all this time? You have been staying with me for the past couple of weeks now. Yeah, you have some of your clothes there now but I'm getting a taste of what it would be like to have you twenty four seven. I have to say I kinda like it. Cuddling up with you at night before we sleep is my new favourite position in bed," he closes his eyes and heaves a big sigh. "However, waking up next to you is my favourite part of the day. So what do you say baby? Wanna go to bed with me every night just to wake up the next morning with me wrapped around you for the rest of our lives?"

I swear the squeals that leave my lips aren't human. I launch myself at him, making him fall backwards onto the bed with such force he rolls us to our sides still clinging onto each other for dear life.

"Is that your way of saying yes?" He laughs through his words. It feels like it's been so long since I last heard him laugh so care free.

"Yes...yes...yes. I want to fall asleep in your arms each night and see your handsome face every morning. I want all of that with you, Owen, because I have fallen so hard for you. So much so, I now know that I love you."

There I said it. I said the dreaded L word.

I watch him in silence as he takes in what I've just declared so openly. I start to panic that I've said it too soon, and my heart sinks as I worry he doesn't feel the same.

A huge smile breaks out across his face. "You love me?" He rolls us so he's hovering above me, leans down and smashes his lips to mine in a bruising kiss. "You know it's a good job you love me because I love you, too," he admits with his face barely an inch from mine.

I close the gap between us and we make out like teenagers for what feels like hours before we finally come up for air.

"We'd better get a move on: there's a lot to pack up. We might as well fill the car up as we are already here."

We spend the next couple of hours laughing and joking as we sort out what will be staying, what's going to charity shops and what will be coming with me—which won't be a lot, as Owen is adamant that I spend some of the money he earnt fighting for Benny to get new bedroom furniture for both our clothes. Until then, Owen is going to make space in his current closet space for me to put some of my stuff there in there now. The only piece of furniture coming with me is my dressing table. Not only will it go nicely in his—our—room, but it was the first thing I bought for myself when I moved out of the family home. Plus, I need somewhere to do my makeup.

Owen pulls open the top drawer of the only item we haven't cleared yet.

"Hey, these undies better be coming with us."

I turn to see him holding up my favourite, navy silk knickers with a smirk on his face.

"Just pack 'em, will you. We're gonna be here all day at this rate."

With a satisfied smile, he empties the entire contents into a case in one swift move.

"Hey, what's all this about?" Owen huffs out, "Was I not good enough?"

Looking back to Owen, he's standing there waving my vibrator around. Fuck I forgot that was in there.

"I...it was before you." I offer in way of explanation, dropping my face to the floor feeling a little embarrassed. He is on me in a flash lifting my face up to meet his.

"Don't go shy baby. I happen to think it's incredibly hot. You know this is coming with us right, we can have some fun with this." He smirks at me and I cant stop the smile from creeping up my own face.

We spent the rest of the day sorting stuff out until we were too tired and hungry to do anymore.

"Shall we order food to pick up on the way home?" Just as the words leave my mouth, my tummy growls its approval. When there's no reply from him, my eyes naturally seek him out. "What's wrong? You look like I just slapped your granny."

A big brooding smile lights up his features. "Nothing. It's just you said 'home', and I kinda liked it." He shrugs his shoulders like it's nothing, but I know this is a big move on his part, and I can't help but fall that little bit more in love with him.

"You're a sappy sod, you know that?" I laugh.

We settle on Indian for tea: butter chicken for me and balti for Owen with rice, a naan, poppadoms, salad and raita. We even stop off for a couple bottles of wine and a few cans of beer to celebrate my official moving in.

The rest of the car ride is filled with an electric static, the excitement of what we're doing together filling the air around us.

We pull up outside Owen's... Our home.

Jesus, this is gonna take some getting used to.

We take the food inside, choosing to eat before we tackle getting my cases inside, and while I get it ready, Owen runs off upstairs, returning a few seconds later.

"So, I have something you might need." Owen holds up a small set of keys with an old 'Elite Fitness' key chain attached to them. "Not that you will be needing them yet, but when all this shit with Benny is over and you get fed up with my company twenty-four seven—"

I raise my finger to his lips and hush him. "Don't spoil our evening with that man's name. Let us live in blissful ignorance for the rest of the day, please." I remove my finger and replace it with a gentle kiss. "Thank you." I take the keys from his fingers and motion for him to sit to eat.

"Don't get used to all this takeout food we have been eating over the past couple of weeks by the way. I normally eat very healthy and I love to cook. I just haven't been all that arsed or in the right mood I guess." I tell him as we start to spoon some food on to our plates.

"Oh, fuck my life! She's laying down the law on day one. Is it too late to revoke the invitation to move in with me?" he says in his cheeky-chappy kind of way that I love so much. I give him a swift nudge with my elbow.

"Oi, you wouldn't dare." I poke my bottom lip out and give him my best puppy dog eyes.

"Oh no, no, no. Don't give me that look; it won't work with me," he says confidently, so I go a step further by placing my head on his shoulder, looking up at him and pout my lip out a bit more.

His arm slides around my back. "I may regret telling you this but, I can cook, too. It's just been easier to order takeout lately, like you say, it's been a trying couple of weeks" Owen looks me square in the eye. "Thank you by the way," he says with all humour from his voice replaced with a serious tone.

"What for? I haven't done anything," I say, confused.

"For making me happy, for simply being you and for moving in with me. But mainly for showing me how to love and be loved."

I smile goofily at him as a tear escapes down to my chin. "I love you, too, ya big teddy bear. Now, let's eat and get the car emptied as I have a surprise for you after." I purposely don't look over at him as I shovel the spicy goodness into my mouth and hum my appreciation.

"Well, I like the sounds of that," Owen says around a huge mouthful of food.

We finish our meals in a comfortable silence, the only sound being the occasional clatter of metal hitting crockery. I stand and go to swill the dishes and load the dishwasher as Owen's phone starts ringing from somewhere and he leaves to go hunt it down.

Once I'm done, I take the chance to grab my handbag and head upstairs, knowing he will come find me soon enough so I don't have long. Pulling my navy knickers and matching bra from my bag, where I secretly stashed them, I quickly change into them. I spray myself with a touch of perfume and head over to the closet where his 'toy box' is kept, placing it at the foot of the bed. I lay myself seductively on the bedspread just in time to see Owen appear in the open doorway.

Unadulterated lust burns in his eyes as he spots the box and then what I'm wearing. He knows as well as I do that neither of us will be getting much sleep tonight.

CHAPTER 32
OWEN

I stroll into the gym with a fully satisfied grin on my face and my girl on my arm, feeling like King Kong. Jemma had opened up this morning, so Devon and I had a lie in before sharing a hot and very steamy shower. It's been a week since she moved in with me, and it's going well.

We don't really see each other at work all that much, considering we are in the same building, but I'm either with clients or in the office working on the books. So later in the day, when I see she's sitting beside the reception desk with no one waiting to be checked in or needing help, I pad my way over to her. The moment she spots me moving in her direction, she brushes a stray piece of hair behind her ear and bites her bottom lip like she can read my mind.

Not one for wasting time, I wrap her up in my arms, causing her to stand with me, and slam my lips against hers before dragging that bottom lip I love so much into my mouth, biting down on it firmly but not harshly.

She lets slip a soft moan, which is exactly the reaction I'd wanted.

"I missed you," she whispers into my mouth, her eyes still closed shut.

"Good, because I've missed you, too." I rub my dick against her leg, "So has he," I joke, placing a long bruising kiss on her lips again.

She eventually breaks free from my hold, but I sense her reluctance.

"Well, you'll just have to wait until you get home for that, Mister. You can go all night. I, on the other hand, need time to recover from ones extremely talented man-handling."

My eyes must hit my hairline at her openness in work. She's normally pretty shy about talking like this.

"My God, I've corrupted you," I say with a small laugh.

"I'd say, but in a really, really good way, right?" She smirks up at me. She knows exactly what she's doing to me, but it works both ways.

I lean down slowly and hover my mouth just below her ear and whisper with as much husk as I can for where we are to get her undivided attention. "Babe, if you think what we've done together sexually is me corrupting you, then you're in for a shock. That's nothing compared to what I have planned for you." I hear her sharp intake of breath just as Isaak decides to show his face.

"Fucking hell, can you put my sister down. It's too fucking early for that shit."

I look over to him at the sound of his voice, but he doesn't stop, just keeps on walking with his head down in the opposite direction.

Isaak has avoided me, Devon and the gym since he found everything out and had me pinned to the wall. It's no shock that he doesn't stop for small talk now. I know Isaak, sometimes it's best to let him work his shit out alone and let him come to you when he's ready. He heads straight up the stairs to no doubt see his wife and let her know he's here, before he heads back down to the gym area.

"Well at least he is here. It's a step in the right direction. Maybe you can go talk to him now that he has broken the ice," Devon says with hope.

"Yeah...maybe." I place another kiss to her head and let her go just as Isaak comes back down to the gym.

"Hey, Isaak. Can I have a word?" I jog over to his side, not really giving him the chance to say no.

He huffs out a huge sigh as if it's a pain for him to be in close proximity, making me wonder if he's gonna tell me to go fuck myself.

"I need a sparring partner," he grumbles, like he used to when we were kids.

"So that's how you wanna do this?" I know exactly what Isaak is thinking and what he's planning on doing, so I let him have his way if it'll help him. He doesn't grace me with a response, so instead I follow him as he walks over to the guys who are waiting to tape up our hands.

Once we are all gloved up and in the ring, I get ready for the hard hits that are bound to come in my direction.

"Come on, let me have it," I say through my gum shield as I bounce around, bobbing and weaving to warm up. That is, until Isaak stops moving and looks me dead in the eyes, sternly.

"Look, I'm only going to say this once, so listen real good. What we talk about now, in this ring, goes no fucking further. You understand me?"

I give a nod and smile, knowing we are going to be okay, and let him carry on.

"I'm sorry about the way I reacted. I was angry at you, shit, at everyone. I still am. I had just been told that my best friend, my brother, had been keeping secrets from me. It's not like they were little white lies either, man. You literally sold your soul to the fucking devil himself—a man I despise with every fibre in me. It's a fucking lot to take in, mate."

I notice him taking a step towards me. What I don't see is the right hook that he swings at me with so much force, I only just manage to duck out of the way. The glove creates a G-force draft across my face, not giving me a chance to regain my balance. The next swing comes at me fast and hard, connecting with my cheekbone. Then another and another and so on.

I try explaining to him why I did what I did, over and over again, but all the time I'm having to dodge his fists that seem hell bent on causing pain— to hurt me, to hurt himself but mainly to cause pain to the one person that he wants to hurt but can't. Benny. I know that's who he's seeing when he's throwing his punches my way. So, if this is the only way for Isaak to get rid of his demons and frustrations, then I'll gladly be that punch bag for him. Not only that, but I guess I deserve some of what he's dishing out, too.

"If I hadn't put myself forward to take your place, Benny would have forced your dad to make you do it. Benny had your dad by the balls, and Gavin knew it. Your dad was trying to protect you and the career you had worked so hard for. I knew I had to do something," I try explaining to him again, but Isaak throws a combo that lands in my ribs and I stumble back on my feet. He just stands there with a satisfied smirk on his face, not even slightly out of breath.

"It's not just that, Owen. Yeah, that pissed me off, but you're now dating my sister—a sister I only just fucking found out I had; a sister I never knew I wanted but also never had the chance to know. We missed out on the all the brother / sister stuff, you know? A big brother is meant to protect their little sister throughout her life. It was cruelly snatched away from us. Devon was deprived of a big brother to tease and wind up—to follow around. Fuck, I've even missed out on having someone looking up to me. I would have loved that Owen. I guess to be a cock block…" He pauses to take a breath and chuckle to himself. "You know, all the stuff siblings are meant to do. We won't ever get that back, and let's not even get started on the fact our dad died not having known his only daughter. He would have loved a daughter, you know. He would have loved her. Besides my mum, I'm all Devon has. It's down to me to protect her now, Owen. She is my blood." He drops his head and hands in defeat, takes a deep breath and blows it out heavily. "You know I'm not one to talk about playing the field, but I've changed; I hope you have, too."

"I didn't intend to go after your sister. When we started getting serious, none of us knew anything. I had no clue she was even supposedly Benny's daughter, but then she turned up at one of the fights and it all turned to shit." I rub at my still stinging ribs from Isaak's punch. As I do, I find myself looking over to Devon who is talking with Remme and Charlotte but whose eyes are firmly on me.

I feel Isaak as he comes to my side, but I don't break the connection I have with her. "She's special, Isaak. What you see when you look at Remme is how I see your sister," I explain honestly.

He doesn't move or say anything for a short amount of time, and I know it's because he's looking at Remme like she's his whole Goddamn world.

He finally breaks the silence. "Don't break her heart, Owen. Regardless of the fact that the girl is my sister, she has always been a good friend."

I turn to look at him, shocked at what I'm hearing. "Is that you giving us your blessing?" I ask him, unable to form any other words right now.

"I'm saying hurt her and it won't just be your fucking ribs you'll have to rub better." Isaak changes his stance, giving me a stare down worthy of any boxing match he is in.

"Brother, I love her. There is no chance of me ever intentionally hurting her. One day, I'm gonna marry her if she'll say yes." I go for honesty. I don't know where it comes from or why, but I'm not even scared of the truth I reveal to him before I even convince myself of it.

"Well, fuck me. I never thought I'd see the day either of us would settle down, get married and have kids of our own, although I'd say it was about time we both grew the fuck up," he says ending on a laugh.

Isaak stretches out his arm and, matching his action, I bump our gloved fists—his in surrender and mine in gratitude.

"I guess so," I tell him with not much thought about it.

"I'm sorry it took so long for me to see sense. I am truly happy for both of you." Isaak smiles, and I know we will be okay. Our friendship intact, we head over to our ladies, leaving all the soppy stuff behind us in the ring.

CHAPTER 33
DEVON

"**F**or God's sake, they're at it again," Remme says sarcastically from the side of me. Her head is turned in the direction of the ring where Owen and Isaak are sparring, so I only just make out what it was she is actually saying.

"Boys will be boys," Charlotte adds as she joins us too.

"You do know what is really happening in that ring don't you?" Remme asks when she turns back our way, causing me to raise my eyebrows.

"I have no idea. Looks like they're training to me." I look from the girls back over to the mat where the two sweaty, beefy men are having at it. That is until Isaak lands a good one to Owen's ribs. Owen isn't even trying to fight back which is weird. They both turn and cast their eyes our way, which makes me blush and spurs Remme to blow Isaak an over the top kiss.

I roll my eyes but smile at their antics anyway, like I always find myself doing. Words are exchanged between them but from here I can't make out what. It seems intense that's for sure.

"You can be so clueless sometimes, Devon, it's almost cute."

I whip my head at Charlotte, wondering if I should be insulted by her comment or not.

"Relax, Dev, she's just winding you up because she's jealous that no one looks at her the way Owen and Isaak look at us."

Charl sticks her tongue out playfully at the pair of us as we start laughing.

"Anyway, I was going to say that Isaak is giving Owen the 'big brother' talk, or should I say beat down," Remme finally finishes.

It takes me a couple of seconds to realise what they are getting at, and when I do, it all clicks into place and I feel my eyes bulging out their sockets. "Oh God. Poor Owen."

"They'll be fine. They're just working things out the only way they know how," Remme tells us both on a shrug. "How are you and Owen doing, anyway?"

"I see what you did there, but to answer your question, we're doing really well. As you know, I moved in with him last week. I'm really happy under the circumstances. I think Owen is, too, or at least I hope he is." For some reason, I find myself doubting what I've just said, which is stupid because Owen wouldn't have asked me to move in with him if he wasn't serious about us. I thank God the girls choose that moment to agree with me.

Owen and Isaak make their way over to us. Isaak wraps Remme up in his big sweaty frame, while Owen comes up behind me, placing his palms flat on the counter, effectively caging me in. He smothers his face in my neck leaving wet kisses in his wake, making me squirm in my now damp knickers.

"If I'm needed, tell them to give me five. I'm just going jump in the shower, real quick." Owen's breath hits the exposed skin on my neck causing goosebumps to break out. I nod to show I've acknowledged what he's said. He kisses me roughly and winks with a low growl before he's off towards the showers with Isaak leading the way.

"That man has got it bad for you, Devon. It's clear for all to see." Charlotte soothes me by rubbing my arm that's closest to her.

When I do lift my eyes from Owens retreating arse to hers, she's not even looking at me. In fact, she's staring away from me completely.

I look from Remme and back to Charlotte again when nothing else is said. Something or someone has clearly gained her undivided attention, and when I lean back on my chair and glance behind Rem's back, all is revealed.

"I'd say someone has it bad for Saxon."

This gets her attention and has her spinning back around in her seat and almost falling off the damn thing. "What? Who?" Her cheeks flush yet she seeks the man in question.

Here's me thinking I had the case of the green-eyed monster only a few days ago. Jesus, I've got nothing on this girl sitting next to me.

"And you call Devon clueless. Charl, the way you eye fuck that man is obvious to absolutely everyone except the one person you want to notice," Remme jokes, but her face soon turns sober when Charlotte drops her head in her hands letting out an over exaggerated and depressed sign.

"I feel so stupid. There's just something about him that I feel connected to. It's hard to explain. Not that it matters: he's always too busy watching everyone else to even look in my direction, let alone really notice me." She throws her head forward and slaps her hand against her forehead. "Great. Now I've said it out loud, it makes me sound like a right cow. I know why he's so busy, he's trying his best to keep everyone safe and—"

"Charl…" Her name goes unheard as she carries on talking. "Charlotte, will you shut your rambling and let me speak, woman!" Remme says with a raised voice.

"Sorry." Charlotte eventually shuts her mouth long enough for Remme to get a word in edgeways.

"I understand what you mean about him being busy all the time, but what I know about Saxon is that he takes his work very seriously. Regardless of that, if you want his attention, focus yours on someone else instead of him."

I can see a slight little smirk forming on Remme's face.

"What do you mean?"

"You never heard the saying, treat 'em mean keep 'em keen?"

Charlotte nods.

"I thought as much. So, turn your attention to someone else in our circle and see how he reacts. You will soon know how he feels about you."

"You mean lead him along?" Charlotte asks.

"Well, you aren't exactly leading him along if he's not making a move, are you? You'll just be showing him what he's missing if he were to pay attention." Remme elaborates further.

I get what she's telling Charlotte to do, and in a way, I hope it works for her, but in all honesty, I can see it taking a turn for the worst.

I try telling her it's a bad idea, but it falls on deaf ears. That's when I can see her really considering going through with this. "You sure you really want to do this?" I ask Charl.

"It's as good a plan as any right now. So yes, I do." with that said I know I have to be good friend and support her choices right now. Even if I do still think a bad idea.

After very little persuasion from Remme, Charlotte makes her mind up and begins planning in her head. We change the subject from men to baby talk and Remme's cravings, to Charlotte getting broody and thankfully ending the conversation on the safer subject of Remme getting everything sorted for when she starts her maternity leave in a couple of months.

Not long after Isaak and Owen head to the showers, Charlotte and Remme head back up the stairs to work. I'm actually glad they've both gone as I think the conversation was going to steer down a very dark path and I really don't want to see any of my friends getting hurt.

God I hope she knows what she's doing, because I sure as hell don't.

CHAPTER 34
OWEN

Nothing beats a nice cold shower after a workout in the ring with Isaak, but now I have bigger fish that need frying.

I head towards my office with Isaak on my tail. I need to find out if Saxon knows anything new or if he's come up with some form of a plan to get Benny out of our lives for good. Fuck, even half a plan would do me. At least it would be a step in the right direction and give me something to go on and to look forward to.

"Hey, Sax. Anymore grand ideas yet?" I ask sarcastically with a hint of humour as I walk through the door. Thankfully, the girls have all dispersed and are back doing their work, especially Devon, who is currently having a conversation with a nightmare of a gym member—they always have something to moan about, and unlucky for Devon she always gets the woman's wrath, just like she is doing now. I hope she'll be caught up in that for the next ten minutes at least, so she won't be able to listen in or watch the interaction like I know she will if not occupied.

"Oh, he thinks he's a comedian." He lays a hand over his torso and pretends to laugh. "On a much more serious note, if you must know, I have a plan in the pipeline, so to speak. I've just got to nip out in the next half hour to get some last-minute details ironed out, and then I'll fill you guys both in." He grabs his phone from the desk just as it alerts him to an incoming text.

"Sounds like a plan. Thanks, mate," Isaak speaks, confirming he did indeed follow me inside.

I turn to face him just in time to catch him giving Saxon a small nod of his head in thanks. In the process, Devon catches my eye as she stands up abruptly from the reception desk. Her head snaps my way and then back towards the door.

What the fuck has her looking like she's seen a fucking ghost?

I follow her line of sight as I spot her paste a smile on her face out the corner of my eye.

I stand stock still. "What the fuck does he want now?" I mutter under my breath.

"What's up Owen?" Saxon asks, coming to stand beside me, but I can't for the life in me form any words to answer him right now. I'm too busy watching Benny, of all people, interacting with Devon, who—God bless her—is trying her best to be natural. To the untrained eye, she is doing a great job, but I see the subtle shift in her demeanour just as I feel Isaak's body looming closer behind me. If I thought I was tense at the sight of Benny, it's nothing compared to how Isaak is feeling at seeing him here.

"What the fuck does he want?" he grits through his teeth.

"I don't know, but we're about to find out. Come on." I lead the way out of the office and over to the racket they are starting to make now in mid argument with each other.

"...give a fuck about her. I know you have her hiding somewhere. Just drop the act and stop playing Little Miss Innocent with me," he spits out at Devon.

"What act? If I knew where Mum was, do you honestly think I would lie about it just to spite you? I'm not stupid enough to do that, especially where you're concerned."

I see the moment Benny goes to lean forward over the desk, so I spring into action and make my presence known, regardless of whether he was looking for me or not.

"She has no clue where Sandra is. She's not lying to you, Benny." Neither am I. Saxon never actually told us where she was, just that she's safe. I'm guessing that because of times like this, so we can't blurt it out by accident or on purpose. Plus, it's safer this way, for Sandra.

"Ah... Owen. Just the man I came to see," Benny says with a smarmy smirk.

"Yeah, what do you want that a phone call couldn't solve, Benny?" I wrap my arm protectively around Devon as Isaak changes his stance from trying to keep his cool, to getting ready to knock Benny's block off in two seconds flat as soon as he gets the chance. I wouldn't stop him either.

"I have a few acquaintances to entertain at the weekend. You know the ones with the very deep pockets?" He looks at me like I might give a shit.

"Good for you, but what does that have to do with me?" I'm seriously not in the mood for this fucking bullshit today.

"You're the main event Saturday night," he answers quickly, with a sly smirk on his aging face, knowing I have no wiggle room and can't say no.

"What if he says no to this fight?" Isaak asks him, but I already know what the answer to that will be.

"Owen knows what's good for him. He knows what's on the line, don't you, Owen?"

My grip tightens on Devon and I look to Isaak, panicking when I see the realisation of what Benny is really insinuating all of Isaak's face.

"In fact, why don't you bring Isaak along with you, Owen? Show him what he's truly been missing out on. You never know, Isaak, you might like it. You know what, Owen, why not bring the whole damn family?" Benny laughs as he turns on his heels and walks away. He stops just short of the door and turns again. "Nine o'clock, usual place, and don't be late." He pushes his way through the door and is gone, leaving Isaak with questions for me to answer.

"What the fuck was he talking about, Owen? It better not be what I think it's going to be either," he grumbles.

"I don't think that's your main problem at the minute, Isaak." Saxons voice booms out from somewhere. I look around our little circle as he steps into view.

"What's on your mind, Saxon?" I ask.

"Benny has something up his sleeve, boys, and I don't fucking like it." He has a serious look on his face, which tells me his brain is working overtime, so I know he smells something funny. "Does he usually come to the gym to see you and make his demands? On top of that, he's inviting Isaak? He knows why you did it in the first place. He always thinks Isaak's in the dark about the deal you made with him in the first place, is he not? It all seems odd and very out of character for Benny, Owen."

I see what he is saying, but I can't think what Benny's angle is. "Please tell me you have a plan now because I'm not sure how much more of this shit I can take. The last surprise I had from Benny came in the shape of Alexander fucking Jenkins, so fuck knows what he will have waiting for me on Saturday." I admit to them all.

Devon squeezes me, letting me feel her comfort, silently telling me she's still there for me.

"Owen, like I said before, I have things on the go and things to set in motion. I tell you what you need to know and keep hold of what you don't. All I will say is that when I say the time is right, you better be ready because we will only get one chance at the element of surprise. If we fuck this up, not only will we lose the upper hand but we lose any chance of taking him down once and for all."

I hear Saxon loud and fucking clear!

CHAPTER 35
DEVON

I haven't been able to think straight for the past five days. Just seeing Benny at the gym, one of the places myself and the girls used to feel safe, made the hairs on the back of my neck stand up. Add that to the extremely cryptic words he exchanged with Owen, let's just say it didn't sit well with me. The fact I felt Owen tense up in my arms didn't comfort me in the slightest, yet I found myself doing just that to him.

As soon as Benny left the gym, everyone seemed to carry on somewhat normally whilst I stood there, wondering what the fuck happens next. Saxon is hell bent on keeping the plan all to himself until the moment each person needs to know what part they play. Like yesterday, for example, the other girls and I were all told not to make plans for this afternoon—that we are not to go anywhere until Saxon's guys come to pick us up. That's it. That all the information we have been given.

I've tried my best to fight my case, telling them that I am going to the fight—that I have a right to be there if I want to be.

Saxon has been pretty straight forward with me, telling me it isn't a good idea and that I will be safer staying away—that I will only be a distraction for Owen. That alone had me resting my case.

Owen hasn't been the same all week: he has either been working or stressing out. The only time I've seen him calm and sated is when he is sleeping. Even that has been limited to the odd hour here and there. I know that because I have been just as bad.

We are both exhausted.

He keeps saying Benny is up to something, he can feel it, and that whatever it is, he thinks it's going to be huge.

Standing in the kitchen, I watch Owen wear the floor tiles away beneath his feet as we wait for me to be picked up by one of Saxon's men.

Remme, Logan, Charlotte and I are all being put together for safety reasons. The deep feeling of dread in the pit of my stomach has me wanting to hold Owen close before he goes off to the unknown, doing God knows what.

Owen must sense my uneasiness. "Come here, baby."

I walk straight over to him without hesitation. "It will be okay, Dev. I promise. I may not know what he has up his sleeve—and that makes me nervous, too—but I do know I will fight hell and high water to get back to you in one piece." His vow eases me a little. Just knowing he is going to literally fight for us and our future makes me feel a little giddy inside.

"I love you, Owen, more than anything in the world right now." I speak into his chest as we embrace. His hand glides through my hair while the other rubs lazy circles on my back. We hold each other tight like it might be the last time we touch each other, yet at the same time, hoping it's not.

His lips come to meet mine tenderly. The moment is so intimate that if we had the time, I'm sure it would lead to us making sweet love. Just as we are enjoying a rare, quiet still moment together, there is a knock on the door, alerting us that Saxon's men are here to pick me up. Our time is limited and Owen places one last lingering kiss to my forehead before he breaks away from me to let them in.

"Are you ready to go, Devon?" Jason's voice asks me softly.

I look to Owen and back to Jason, ready to change my mind and demand I go with them.

"She's ready." Owen answers for me, with an authority I have never heard him use with me before.

A lone tear slips, I can feel the track it's leaving as it rolls down my cheek and I grab my handbag and my keys. I head out to the car with a guy I have seen with Saxon before. I have no clue what his name is. We have never spoken to one another.

"Hello, Miss Carter. How are you?" I remind myself that my bad mood is not this man's fault and that I should be polite back.

"Hi, it's Devon. There is no need for the formalities." I smile at him, but I'm sure he can see it's forced.

He opens the car door for me like some sort of chauffeur without uttering another word.

Thanking him, I climb in just as Jason comes out the house, followed by Owen. He opens the back door while Jason gets in, taking hold of my face and giving me a searing hot kiss before whispering in my ear, "Forever and always, baby."

I close my eyes for a second then whisper his words back to him. "Forever and always, Owen." I pull away and he closes the door, stuffing his hands in his pockets as Jase pulls away from the curb.

We eventually arrive at some random house after picking up Remme and Logan. I presume it's one of Saxon's safe houses he uses for work purposes. Rem is fussing over Logan as he cries for his daddy, trying to wipe his face with a wet wipe. I jump out of the car and run round to her as she gets out.

"Come to Auntie Dev, Logan?" I ask and put my arms out for him. Logan leans away from Remme towards me with open arms, with a tear-streaked face and a snotty nose. It couldn't have felt more comforting if he tried. Rem mouths over her thanks to me.

At thirteen weeks pregnant and with morning sickness that is kicking her arse, she is totally washed out. I can only imagine it makes dealing with a crying baby so much harder than usual. Not that she would ever complain. That girl is Wonder Woman in disguise.

Jason and the man I now know as Daryl lead us into the house where we find Saxon and Charlotte already there with another one of Saxon's men, again someone I don't really know.

Saxon immediately stands and comes to take Logan from me. "Hey, buddy. How's my favourite little man today?" He coos at a now calmer Logan. It's funny how all these big burly men turn soft as soon as a baby is close by.

Saxon turns to face us girls and introduces us properly to Daryl and Gary. He explains that both men will be stationed outside the house, one at the front and one at the back. We are not to leave the property until Saxon and Jason come to get us. Saxon hands Logan back to me after kissing his forehead. I take him back and grab the baby bag.

"Would you like me to go change him, Rem? I think he's full from the journey." I look over to Remme to see if she acknowledged me. She offers me a small smile and nods, mouthing another thank you.

I need some time to gather my thoughts and rid myself of the rising panic I can't stop feeling in the pit of my stomach.

Once he's changed, I take a sleepy Logan back to his mummy and notice Saxon and Jase have now gone.

"I think someone is a little tired, Rem," I say rocking the little boy in my arms.

Rem holds her arms out to take him, but I stop her.

"No it's okay. I'll take him upstairs and settle him. I don't mind."

The grateful look in her own tired eyes is all I need to know that I'm doing the right thing. I place Logan on the bed while I get comfy on it, too. Once I'm on my side and cradling Logan, it's not long before he is fast asleep.

The next thing I know, I'm at Benny's warehouse...

Benny has one of his goons pinning me up to the wall and I'm gagged. I try to fight them off but I'm just not strong enough. I look around in panic, trying to find the others, but all I see are faceless people milling around the outside of the dreaded cage. The only faces that start to unblur are Owen's and Benny's. I struggle with all my might again, when Owen turns and spots me. I don't get to shout for him as the goon back hands me across my face, trying to keep me quiet and under control. I don't miss Owen's face as it turns murderous. He struggles with the cage door, no one in a hurry to unlock it. Instead, the men dressed in black just stand by and laugh at Owen's useless attempts at getting out. That is until he mounts the wall of the cage and climbs over. My heart is pounding in my chest as I watch Owen's every move. He makes his way through the crowd and over to me. He's only a few long, purposeful strides away from getting to me, when out of nowhere a thunderous bang has me shutting my eyes firmly and cowering into myself for some sort of protection.

The warehouse is eerily silent, and I can't take it any longer. Something is wrong, I just know it. I open my eyes slowly, instantly trying to locate Owen. When my eyes lock on him, I watch as he falls to his knees. The look of sheer shock and fear takes over the angry expression he had just moments ago. He clutches at his stomach, and it's then I notice blood pouring from between his fingers. I try to scream for him, but all that comes out is a muffled screech. Benny's evil laugh booms out, sounding like something from a crappy thriller movie. My vision blurs with hot wet tears as I fear for Owen's life, and there is zero chance of me doing anything to help him because I can't get to him.

Another loud and sharp bang has me jumping out of my skin, and my eyes flying open as more fear licks its way over my body, the noise from downstairs waking Logan, too

It was a dream.

I rub the sleep from my eyes, thinking I might still be dreaming, but that train of thought soon stops when I hear Remme scream hauntedly and another loud thump.

What the hell?

I hear footsteps come bounding up the stairs. My heart rate picking up speed as I start to panic. I try my best to quieten Logan in my arms as I hop from one foot to the other nervously. Not only do I need to protect myself, I have a small child relying on me to keep him safe too.

The door opens, and a figure dressed in black with a matching black facemask comes into the room pointing a gun my way.

Where the fuck is Daryl and Gary?

"Get downstairs now, and do it quietly. And shut the fucking kid up, too."

I do as I'm told, hushing the scared little man in my arms and shielding him from view with my body as much as possible. If I can help it, I'll try my absolute best to make sure he hardly sees any of this.

What awaits me when I get to the bottom of stairs hurts my fucking heart never mind the burning tears in my eyes. Charlotte and Remme are on their knees, gagged and their hands zip tied behind them. The look of panic on Remme's face when she sees me and her baby guts me to the bone. There are three other men all holding guns at my family.

"Please, what do you want?" I ask, keeping Logan clutched tightly into me. Thankfully he has quietened down now there is no banging.

"We're all going for a ride. Benny requests your company." His menacing voice leaves no room to bargain. I guess I will be there after all. I just never thought it would be under these circumstances. I would never have wanted any of my family in danger.

I try to keep the men calm so no one gets hurt, unintentionally or not— not on my watch anyway.

"Why is my father doing this? Surely, if my father wants me, a simple phone call would suffice." I don't get an answer, just a menacing look from the man behind the mask. His eyes tell me not to question his judgement.

"Alright, alright, but please untie my friends. One of them is pregnant." I plead with him, but it falls on deaf ears. "Okay, we'll make no fuss and go with you. Please, just untie them. They have nothing to do with any of this. Let them go, please." I swallow the biggest lump in my throat as I wait for something...anything.

"No one is being untied till we get there, understand?" he grunts in answer.

"You have fucking guns...I mean, please. You have guns pointing—" I'm cut off when a scorching pain rips through my cheek, followed by Remme's motherly murmurs for the safety of her son. I fight to stay balanced with Logan in my arms.

"Quiet or you'll be zipped up, too. Right now, them being tied up is the only thing keeping that baby safe with you. You keep that kid quiet or you get tied up and I'll shut him up." He waves his gun at me as he talks, making it known exactly what he means.

Remme tries to cry out.

I close my eyes for a second before I look up at the masked man and agree.

Once he knows we were all compliant in some way, he ushers us out, grabbing the changing bag on the way out. I look around for Gary or Daryl and find one of them in a heap, out cold and zip tied behind a bush out of view from the street. I can't even tell if they are still alive.

We're pushed into the back of a plain van which plunges into pitch black darkness once the doors are shut. Luckily, Logan has nodded back off in my arms because he would have screamed the place down with how dark it is.

In what feels like no time at all, we come to a stop and the doors are swung open. Remme and Charlotte are both un-gagged and the ties are taken off. Remme automatically makes a play to get her baby but is stopped in her tracks.

"Where the fuck do you think you're going, lady?" the man asks.

I notice all the men have taken their masks off.

Kyle fucking Baxter, Benny's right-hand man and his band of merry fucking men, stand before me, guns still being waved about.

"I just wanted to cuddle my son." Remme points towards me and Logan.

"Fine, take your boy, but no funny business."

I hand Logan over to Remme's ever awaiting hands, and no sooner has she got him, I'm being pushed towards the back doors of the warehouse. I'm thrown through the door to the ground at Benny's feet followed by Charlotte while Remme is spared, thankfully.

"Well, well. Decided to join us after all, I see," Benny smoothly says.

Like we had a choice in the matter.

He nods his head to Kyle who grabs me by my clothes and pins me to the wall.

"Take them out the back until I call you."

All that comes to mind, is how my dream is coming true and Owen is going to die.

CHAPTER 36
OWEN

"**S**eriously, Sax. I've gotta be at the warehouse in twenty fucking minutes. Now is not the time to take a detour and pop into work," I spit at Saxon with a little bit more rage than I intended.

"Will you relax? You should know by now that everything I do has a reason behind it."

I look from Sax, to Isaak and why the hell not throw Jase in there for good measure. They're all just smirking at me, or giving me sideways glances, so I just toss myself back in the car seat and release a huff out under my breath.

"If you must know, there's someone I want you all to meet. As my office is still off the radar, I thought we'd do it here," Saxon explains further just as we pull up outside of the locked and guarded gates leading to his work office space.

"Fucking hell, Sax. This place is tighter than Fort Knox." Isaak speaks in wonderment, breaking the brief and short silence that was filling the car.

We all pile out, myself and Isaak looking around us like deer in headlights.

"If it wasn't, I wouldn't be able to do my job or keep my men safe." The way he says it with so much ease yet just as much meaning, floors me. I'm seeing a completely different side to Saxon. This is exactly the guy I need to help me break free from Benny. I'm grateful to have him and his team on my side. "This way, guys. Stay close or you'll get lost. Don't fancy one of my men shooting either of you by mistake."

I just about hear Saxon and Jase laughing hysterically together, yet somehow, I don't think he's joking around.

Without a second thought, I follow closely behind the pair of hyenas with Isaak hot on my heels as we make our way inside the building. On the outside, it looks like an old, rundown factory building with no signs to say what type of business is inside the dilapidated walls. In fact, from the outside, you would think there's no life inside the building at all.

Through the doors is a sleek modern foyer with a huge wrap around desk.

"Good afternoon, Mr Evans. Here are a few messages and the files that you asked for." A woman behind the desk hands him a piece of paper and two thin-looking files. "Also, there is a Miss Lawrence here to see you—said you knew she was coming. I sat her in the comfortable waiting room with a coffee." She beams at us all with a smile and Saxon thanks her, leading us away.

I nudge Jason in the arm to get his attention. "Hey Sax, shame all your staff don't look as good as her."

Saxon and Jason laugh it up, taking it for the joke it is intended, and Isaak slaps me upside the head.

"Remember you're sleeping with my sister, you stupid fucker."

I chuckle playfully at his big brother protectiveness.

"Don't you worry yourself, Isaak. Your sister is the only woman in my life, and trust me, with what she does to me…well I don't have to look elsewhere." I rub the sore spot on my head as we carried on moving. "I mean the sex—"

"Dude." Isaak holds a hand up in front of me. "Don't fucking go there or this fight tonight will be the least of your fucking worries, trust me."

I love winding him up.

Saxon opens the next door we come to and we all walk inside to find a woman slouched in a huge armchair.

"Jess, good to see you again." Saxon shakes her hand as she rises to her booted feet.

"Owen, Isaak, this is chief inspector Jessica Lawrence. Jess and I have been coming together with ideas for a plan of attack to bring Benny Brookes down once and for all," Saxon says confidently. This is clearly his comfort zone. The chief shakes mine and Isaak's hands.

"Hello. Good to finally meet you both," the chief says with a nod. "Owen, do you understand the arrangement between yourself and the police?"

I shake my head. "I understand bits, but that's it. Saxon has been very tight lipped about his plan, only telling us what we need to know when we need to know it for safety reasons." I want to be clear on everything before I go in there but she better talk fast I'm running out of time here.

"Yeah, I'm sorry about that. I'm sure you understand that we couldn't risk you slipping up and saying something to give him any kind of inkling we were on to him. "I nod my head in understanding before she carries on. "Benny has been a bit of a mastermind when it comes to his businesses and its locations. We know most, if not all, the buildings he owns aren't in his name but in an alias. This is why we're struggling to pin anything on him. Every time we think we're getting close, we find ourselves right back where we started: with nothing. Which is why we are going to be lenient with you as you are our only hope of closing in on him. In exchange for immunity, you are going to lead us to him, tonight. You'll also be required to give a statement once it's over, simply detailing everything you know, and be available for any follow up questions if and when needed. It's all been agreed to and signed off so there is no going back on our end." She looks me in the eye giving me the reassurance I need, yet it does nothing to make me feel better about the situation. I'll be known as a snitch regardless if word gets around about this.

"Great. From one bad deal to another," I grumble.

"This is the best outcome for you, Owen. You've been fighting illegally, and willingly might I add, without a fighter's licence, and I presume never at a proper venue. I know you've been forced into this, but if you had come to the police with this earlier, it wouldn't have got this far." She raises her eyebrow at me knowing she is spot on.

"Yes, I know. I just want this over with. For good," I say sincerely.

"Okay, let's get the show on the road, shall we?"

After being told to basically do what I have already been doing and follow Benny's orders, we are finally back on the road to the warehouse.

The chief had said to keep Saxon close or in view at all times if possible. He would be the key to knowing when to move and what to do. I feel sick to my stomach with dread.

The whole drive, I'm quietly trying to psych myself up for the fight I know is going to happen—doesn't matter what the plan is. In order to get the case to stick on Benny, I'm going to have to do this one last time. It's just the unknown that I don't like, the one thing Benny gets off on, keeping people in the dark as much as he can.

This can't go wrong, I have far too much to lose now, more than I did a few months ago, that's for sure. This time I have someone waiting at home for me. I will do everything I can to get back to Devon in one piece, just like I promised her I would.

Fuck me, if that doesn't make my adrenaline pump that little bit faster, I don't know what will.

Before I know it, Saxon is putting the car into a parking spot. I get out, my legs feeling like fucking lead, heavy and stiff, and my gut feeling like it could drop out of my arse at any moment.

I don't know what the fuck is going on, but I've never felt like this before a fight. Ever.

I know Benny has something planned; I just wish I fucking knew what.

I stand by the entrance, trying to remember how to breathe.

We almost immediately walk straight into the man himself.

"Ah, Owen. You're here. Follow me."

We all exchange looks at one another, not sure where we're heading or why. Benny pushes open a door and we all follow him into a narrow and now overcrowded hallway, spotting some of his goons at the other end of it.

Benny eventually stops and ushers us through another door closing it behind us. "Only three members of the Owen Slater fan club want to come see you fight?" The sneer in his tone doesn't go unnoticed by any of us."

"I didn't want your daughter to have to witness me fighting again." I force myself to reason with him.

"Come on, Owen, I think we both know that whore's daughter is not mine, so don't insult my intelligence anymore."

I look from Saxon, to Isaak then quickly divert them back to Benny.

"Who the fuck do you think you are calling my mother a whore?" Isaak snaps at him, pouncing forwards, fists clenched ready to knock Benny flat on his arse. Sax and Jase make a grab for Isaak's arms to hold him back.

"Really, Isaak? The reason your mother is with me is because of the love she had for you and for your father." Benny sneers in Isaak's face.

"What are you talking about? She left him for you. You're meant to love her not stand there calling her a whore," he gripes disbelievingly.

Benny on the other hand looks ready to blow a gasket at any moment. "I do love her. I love her more than any other could love a person. But then I found out that she was still going to see your dad, using you as an excuse for her visits," Benny angrily growls. "Gavin always had the best of everything, always what I wanted—what I deserved. Sandra chose him when we were kids. I thought she had finally chosen me. I guess not. I told her she wouldn't be going back to see any of you if she knew what was good for her. Then she found out she was pregnant, and I thought I was going to finally have the family I always wanted—a child I could finally call my own. Only thing was the dates never quite matched up. When I looked into it more, you could imagine my surprise when I found Devon's full birth certificate with a letter attached to it. Funny I had never seen it before because that bitch had taken Devon and registered without me that angered me but I hadn't thought much of it at the time. I am a busy man after all. Now I know why. Named under the father was a Brookes, only it was Gavin Brookes. So yeah. Whore seems about right to me."

Benny has hit well below the belt, and I can't blame Isaak for wanting to kill him. The fact he's now admitting this, after all these years, means Isaak is finally getting some answers, even though the timing sucks. Maybe that's part of Benny's plan: to get inside Isaak's head.

"You're a piece of fucking work. You broke up my family just because she didn't pick you when you were kids? Then you threaten her and my dad to stay away from each other. On top of all that, you stop my dad from getting to know his own daughter and me knowing about my sister. Twenty-two years I've been living a lie, and it's because of you. You really are a sick mother fucker." Isaak pulls himself free from the hold Saxon and Jason still have on him.

"Oh, I'm sure you will get over it. It's not like you didn't know her at all now is it? How long have you known, Isaak?" Benny pushes.

Isaak looks at me. I just nod. There is no point hiding what he already knows.

"Now, if the dramatics are all cleared up, how about we get down to some real business. Remember I said I had people coming with deep pockets? Well, they are here, and they are expecting a fight of epic proportions. Owen, tonight you have a great opponent. In fact, as much as it pains me to say, he's one of the best," he says smugly.

"Oh yeah? Who've you got for me, Mike Tyson?" I chuckle out, and the bastard laughs it up, too.

"Funny, though you're not too far off the mark." He turns to Isaak and smiles sadistically. "I have it on great authority that the cash that is being put down on this fight is huge. Put it this way, I could retire as soon as the night is through. If they lose that money to me, we will all be quids in," he says, aiming his words at Isaak.

"What's that got to do with me?" Isaak questions suspiciously.

"It has everything to do with you, Isaak, because you're the one fighting Owen. They will put all their money on you, Isaak—no offence Owen— while mine will go on Owen. You are going to throw the fight so Owen wins, making me a very rich man in the process."

The man has lost his fucking mind. There is no fucking way we will fight each other, let alone for him.

"Fuck you, Benny. Did you really think we would fight each other?" I spit through my teeth at his insanely ridiculous way of thinking. I can't believe this man. I knew he had no scruples, but he is taking the piss now.

"Forget it, Benny. It's not happening." Isaak stands tall knuckles getting whiter by the second.

"It's funny you say that. I thought you might have a problem with it, so I took precautions to make sure this happened. I have something that will most definitely change both of your minds."

Benny gets his phone out and puts it to his ear, the whole time no one makes a move, just watching for any sort of clue as to what game Benny is playing.

"Bring them in, Kyle." He hangs up and pockets the phone again, turns and waits.

We all look in the same direction, waiting for the door to open. As soon as it does, my heart rate picks up speed, rapidly, and I almost sink to my knees. The girls come into view with guns pointing their way. I feel instantly sick again. That's not the worst of it. Remme is clinging onto a terrified looking Logan, which does make Isaak hit the ground with an almighty thud as his knees connect with concrete.

This is all my fault. I've put my entire family in danger all because I couldn't face letting anyone down.

"Does that make your decision any easier, fellas?"

I can't bring myself to look away from the girls, but I know by the smug sound in his voice, he's sporting the biggest smirk known to man.

I want to charge at him and take him out once and for all, but I'll be put to the ground before I even reach him by one of the many goons surrounding him.

He's got us both by the balls, and he knows it.

Isaak and I look at each other. We know we have to do this to save our family. There's no other way out of this mess—nothing more we can possibly do. I glance back over to the girls, finally locking eyes with Devon, telling her with just a single look that what I'm about to do—what we're about to do—is the right thing.

CHAPTER 37
DEVON

We are taken into a dingy, dirty, low lit room—obviously one Benny doesn't use often, if ever—but at least here we don't have guns pointing at us intimidatingly.

Kyle takes great pleasure in letting us know that there's no way out—that we can try to escape, but it would be no use because we would be locked in. If that isn't enough, he and his goons are going to be on the other side of the door.

As soon as the rusty, grim looking door is slammed firmly shut behind them, leaving us alone, I run to check on Logan first then Remme and Charlotte.

"Oh, my god. Are you both okay?" I look them over from head to toe, one at a time, making sure they are not hurt in any way. I notice Remme is in a world of her own right now.

Logan starts to grumble, my guess he is sensing his mummy's worries and how she's not quite herself. I take Logan from her clad iron grasp, grabbing the changing bag at the same time. I leave her to gather her thoughts whilst

I sort Logan out and try to calm him back down. I manage to put him in a fresh nappy and find a food tub with some homemade concoction inside. I just hope he will eat it cold.

Taking a spoonful of food, I feed the little man on my lap the best I can in the light that we have, thanking my lucky stars that the time I've spent getting to know my nephew has paid off. He's now happily playing with some of the teething toys from his baby bag.

Remme starts to pace. "What the hell is Benny playing at? He's done a lot of questionable things since I've come to know of him, but kidnap? I didn't think even he would stoop this low." She rubs her head like it pains her to think.

"I don't know what use we are to him," Charlotte adds.

"We are just pawns in Benny's game. I don't know what game that is, but I know Benny. This is how he likes to play. If he's gone to all this effort to have us brought here, he wants us here for a reason." For someone in this kind of situation, I speak quite calmly. "We just have to stay as calm as possible, okay? Especially you, Rem," I tell them with all the confidence I can find in me. On the inside, though, I feel sick that the man who has been my father for the past twenty-two years has just had me and my family kidnapped, smacked around and now chucked into a filthy, locked room. "Saxon will have a plan, and the longer we're in this room the safer we all are," I say, more for my benefit than anyone else's.

"How can you possibly say that? They don't even know we're here," Charl grumbles as she throws her shaky hands up in the air.

"Right now they don't, but do you think we were bought here just to be kept hidden in this room?" I look between them, the pair of them shaking their heads limply. "No. I bet everything I own on the fact that we'll be used as a bargaining tool." I'm highly confident about this and hope I'm right.

I must have satisfied their curious minds for a while as they don't ask any more questions. There would be no point: it's all just one big guessing game from here on out.

To pass the time, and to keep everyone's minds off the fact we're trapped behind a steel door, I gather them all together and we all sit close, huddled up and playing with Logan until we hear a phone ring outside the door, causing us all to pause.

Kyle's booming voice sounds through, just enough for us to make out his words.

"You got it, boss. We'll be right there."

We know our time's up, and that we're heading somewhere else. Then the lock on the door clatters followed by the door swinging open on an ear piercing screech.

"Time to go," Kyle says gruffly with a slimy smirk across his face.

We make our way back towards the main room of the warehouse, Charlotte up front, Remme and Logan next and then me last with Kyle sticking his gun into my side sharply as we walk. I can't fight this feeling anymore. The sense of dread as we walk through the door is something unexplainable.

We come to a stop a few doors from the old factory floor. Kyle opens the door wide, and the sight that greets me is something I could never explain. The haunted eyes of Owen staring back at me causes my entire being to shake uncontrollably, fear gripping every single part of me.

Then I witness the heartache of Isaak as his eyes find his whole world walking next to me as he assesses the full situation which brings him to his knees. Even Saxon looks like he is drilling holes into Charlotte right now.

Owen silently communicates with me with his eyes alone. I know exactly what he's trying to tell me without hesitation. I don't know if I should be pleased about what he's saying or scared of the unknown. He's asking my permission for something, I'm not sure what, but at the same time he's telling me he is sorry. The sorrow and defeated look on him doesn't sit well with me, and it's breaking my heart. So much so I have to look away.

My eyes flick to Isaak again, and I see the same look in his eyes only they are aimed at Remme and their son.

"Oh shit," I whisper to myself, but Remme and Charlotte somehow manage to hear me over everyone's deep breathing and pained grunts. "I think I've just figured out what's going on and why we're here." I feel Remme tense up as she grabs my hand with her free one whilst she continues to hold Logan tightly in her other arm.

"Oh no, I think I'm getting it, too," Remme whispers back with dread lacing her voice. Then we hear it—confirmation from Owen solidifies what we're hearing.

This nightmare we're in is only just beginning.

"Okay, you've got our attention. You've given us no other choice; we'll do what you want."

I don't need to look at Isaak to know that he agrees with Owen.

"We will fight each other. For them, not you." Owen tips his head in our direction as if he needed to clarify.

"I want your word: not a hair on their heads gets harmed," I hear Isaak say and Owen mumble his agreement.

"Say it!" Isaak's voice booms and echoes off the brick walls, making myself and Remme jump. Logan, too, lets out a slight whimper and Charlotte a gasp.

"God, I can't watch this," Remme cries, tears falling down her face as she tries to soothe and settle Logan back down again.

If I didn't feel like I'm holding everyone up at the minute, I think I would cry myself, but a big part of me doesn't want to show Benny a single sign of weakness. I get the feeling that if I do, Benny will have more leverage to use against the guys then he already has. I don't want that—not at all.

"Settle yourself down, Isaak, lad." Benny has the nerve to look smug, not even bothered by the fact Isaak and Owen, shit even Saxon and Jason, all look like they want a piece of him. "I thought that might have persuaded you both. Funny what the power of family can achieve. No harm will come to them if everyone behaves themselves, it all goes as planned and I get my money by the end of it." Benny walks up close and personal first to Isaak and then Owen, looking them both deeply in the eye, as if to warn them of no funny business. "You have half an hour to get ready and warmed up. Make it look real, too. I don't want no half-arsed shit. These are not the type of guys you can fool easily. They are the big leagues."

I watch as Saxon turns and appears to mumble something to Jason, but he doesn't even flinch.

"Fine, but just know Benny, when this is all over, I'll make sure you get what's coming to you. For Owen, and most definitely for this," Isaak grits out.

Benny just laughs him off like what he's just heard is an extremely funny joke. He's not fazed in the slightest.

"I wanna check the girls. Just to make sure you have been treating my friends with the respect they deserve," Saxon demands, and I'm hoping beyond all hope that Benny agrees. I need him to tell me there's a plan and that he can stop all this.

Benny is destroying the family that I've been lucky enough in my life to find. I don't want to lose it. If this goes ahead, it's not just fighter against boxer, it's brother against brother. They have been through so much together. They've only just come back together after finding out who I am. Now this. Will they survive it? I honestly have no idea, but it's not going to be easy—not for any of us.

Benny's movement catches my curiosity as he speaks to one of his men closely, too close to make out what was said. It doesn't help the fact I'm busy consoling a hormonal Remme and now a very upset and unsettled child.

He walks out, taking Owen and Isaak with him, but not before giving Kyle a nod as Saxon and Jason approach us. Jason stands close enough to Kyle to give him a death stare. Saxon starts with Charl as she's the closest to him, making sure she is okay and giving her a quick hug. He moves on to Rem and Logan, double checking then triple checking with them both, which is very much understandable. When he's one hundred percent sure they're both unharmed, he gives them both a tender peck on their heads.

He comes to me, pulling me into a tight hug whispering in my ear a fast cryptic message. "I need you to stay the strong one, for them and me. Take Logan from Remme, and stay low. I have a plan. You will know what to do when the time comes." He grabs me tighter for a brief moment before pulling away again. "Are you okay? Did they hurt any of you?" he grits out through clenched teeth. He is facing me but it's a warning to the goons to keep their hands to themselves.

I nod and answer anyway. "Yeah we're all fine. Just a little roughed up from all the pulling and pushing around, but nothing to hurt us physically."

He gives my face a once over, pausing when he sees my lip and cheek. "I'm alright, Saxon, I promise. It probably looks worse than it feels."

He looks at the bruises that are no doubt forming before he huffs a huge puff of air and gives me a stern nod of the head and a soft, sad smile.

"It can be our little secret for now, as Owen would lose his shit if he was close enough to have seen this. That's the last thing I need him to do right now."

Kyle announces that their time with us is up, but before Saxon stands to his full height, he whispers in my ear again.

"Trust me, this will be over soon enough. Just sit tight and stay strong for me and the guys." With that said he's gone again and the comfort he's just instilled in me grows strong.

CHAPTER 38
OWEN

Having been escorted out from one of the side rooms, Isaak and I follow Benny out into the main centre of the warehouse. I vaguely remember Saxon talking to the girls. I'm on autopilot and in a daze, like I am every time I get ready for a fight, only this time it's different and in more than one way.

I'm fighting Isaak.

My brother.

On top of that major detail, the love of my life is only a few feet away, being pulled along by one of Benny's goons, the rest of my family with her. Whether they are blood or not doesn't matter: they are and will always be my family.

When the metal cage—the bane of my existence—comes into view, I walk ahead of Benny towards the back to get changed with Isaak hot on my heels. I pass Isaak some shorts and tape for his hands. Luckily, I always pack spare clothes and gear in my gym bag. I just never thought it would be for this reason.

Benny announces his presence to the men in expensive suits, who have more money than they need. This is their sick and twisted way of spending it.

"Owen, hold up," I hear Isaak call after me. We have been through some shit together growing up, but right now he isn't the man I want to talk to.

"How can you be so fucking calm, Isaak? Your pregnant wife and son are out there, not to mention your sister and their best fucking friend."

To his credit, he doesn't try to stop my rant: he just lets me get it off my chest. His calm exterior is from years of boxing. I never needed to learn that part of the training; I wished to God I paid attention now.

Isaak places a hand on my shoulder in a soothing gesture.

"Those people over there are the only reason I'm acting so calm, Owen. On the inside, I'm fucking raging, but showing that rage will get us pair nowhere and only make the girls panic. I also know that Saxon and Jase have everything in hand. They will be sorting a new plan out as we speak." He placates me. I know he's right, but this nervous energy is racing through me at a hundred miles an hour.

As if he senses this in me, and on cue, Saxon walks over to us followed closely by Jason.

"What the fuck, Sax? You said they were safe. You said your men had them securely covered. You also said they would come to no harm and wouldn't be involved with any of this shit." I can't control the rage that is fuelling my anger right now, and all that anger is being spat in Saxon's direction.

"I don't know what the fuck has gone on. Jase can't get a hold of Daryl or Gary, but I can assure you that it will be dealt with just as soon as this issue is sorted first." I can tell from the look on his face he isn't happy about what's happened either. Saxon was with me the whole time so I know the girls being here is not entirely his fault.

"Tell me you have a new plan man?" I fire my question at Saxon, but my eyes bounce between him and Jason, not caring who exactly answers me as long as the answer is yes.

"Owen, you need to chill the fuck out." He says it like it's any ordinary fight.

"What the fuck is wrong with you all? I will calm the fuck down when my family are all back with us, safe, unharmed and miles away from Benny and his fucking men!" I say through gritted teeth so only the three of them can hear me but so they know just how pissed off I really am. "Now do you have a revised fucking plan or not?" I wait, getting more and more annoyed with every passing second.

"I'm working on it, Owen, but what I need from you two is a real fight— at least real enough to make it convincing. I don't want Benny to know you're both holding back on your punches, so you both need to take one for the team."

"Jase will keep his eyes on the girls. I've spoken to them. Apart from being shaken up, which is expected, they're okay." He looks to Isaak with pride in his eyes. "You have one very brave little boy, Isaak. He is doing good, everything considered."

It was just what I needed to hear and some of the tension washes off me. "Can't you get this all stopped before the fight? I don't want to fight my brother. The whole reason I'm here in the first place is so he didn't have to be. He could lose his career over this, Sax," I plead with him. I don't want everything I have gone through, everything I've done to get myself in this situation, to be in vain—for him to lose the one thing he has been passionate about since I have known the big fucker.

"I'm going to do my best. I have to find a secure place to call Jess first as now we know the girls and Logan are here its changes the game. She can hear us, but she can't talk back to me, so for now, I want you to go out there like you're gunning for each other. Put on a show for the greedy bastards waiting, and let me deal with the rest, okay? Don't worry though Jess and the rest of the cops are close by and ready to roll when they have what they need to take the fucker down." He looks me dead in the eyes, and I believe every word he's telling me. If he can get us out of this beforehand, I know for a fact he most definitely will.

"Okay. On that note, where in this dive is secure enough to make that call?"

"Your best bet is the room back there. We sometimes use it as a piss can." I point to the door at the far end of the room.

"Nice." Saxon's face says it all.

I take a few deep breaths, change and begin the warmup with Isaak, just like we would if we were at the gym getting ready to spar and train. Maybe I should just try and look at this fight as that: just another day in the gym, sparring with Isaak albeit harder and more intense than usual.

Yeah, keep telling yourself that, Owen. See how that works out for you.

This small corner—hidden behind one of the main walls, out of view from the cage and peering eyes—is a lonely place when you're sitting here with only your thoughts before and after a fight. Tonight, all my thoughts are of Devon, the love of my life, wishing she didn't have to see her brother and boyfriend going however many rounds it takes before we get out of there. My thoughts waver to earlier today, before she left, and how good she felt in my arms. I wish I could hold her like that now; I just know she would calm me instantly. I need to feel that connection with her—I need to be out there where I can see her and know she can see me, too.

"Isaak, let's go. It's time."

He gives me a stern nod of his head. He has been just as quiet as me. It's not that surprising really. I've seen Isaak prepare for war in the ring so many times before now; it's like there's no other living soul around him. No one dares talk to him, and he rarely speaks to anyone.

We round the corner to the main part of the warehouse. Just before the cage comes into view, we give each other the same look, the one that says, 'Whatever happens in the cage, stays in the cage. Always brothers no matter what.' We carry on walking, our faces turning to stone. Not giving anything away.

Heading towards the cage, I see Benny with his big wigs straight ahead. The girls are nowhere to be seen. Isaak's shoulder crashes with mine, as he barges his way past me, not even making eye contact. Getting into role.

The action doesn't go unnoticed by Benny and his cash cows. Benny's lips curve up ever so slightly as he makes his way over to me, just as Saxon comes up next to me.

"Looks like Isaak is ready to go. Remember what I said, Owen: make it look convincing. That way, you save the girls from any unnecessary harm," Benny tells me harshly.

"Where are the girls, Benny?" I ask, looking around for them. By the way Saxon's head is turning like an owl, I can tell he's looking for them, too, but like me, he comes up with nothing.

"They are coming. You didn't think I would let them miss what is going to be the fight of the year. With a celeb like Isaak fighting in my arena, well, I can't lose." He grabs his phone and laughs into it as he mumbles something to the person on the other end before hanging up swiftly.

My fists turn white with impatience. Sax shifts next to me, just enough to remind me what I have to do.

"Your wish is my command."

Benny points behind my back, smirking yet again, and I turn around just in time to see Devon roughly pushed to the ground behind the huge crowd that has built up.

"Son of a bitch. You can't let them treat—" I'm stopped in my tracks when a firm hand grabs at my arm. Saxon. He knows I was about to fucking lose it.

"Now, Owen. You will get them back when I get my fight. They are my insurance policy to make sure you and The Bruiser over there play your part. Don't let me down. You're about to make me a very wealthy man. If this goes tits up, Owen, you can say goodbye to the whore you claimed as your girlfriend. In fact, you can say goodbye to them all. I will kill each and every one of them agonizingly slowly and make you and your so-called brother watch," Benny sneers my way.

"Now it's your turn to listen to me. You leave them alone. Your problem is with me, not them. I will fight for you, Benny, but so help me God, if you touch them, I will come after you just as fucking fearless as you have made me. Take my word for it." I'm almost up in his face, but I walk past at the last second and make my way over to Isaak at the cage door.

CHAPTER 39

DEVON

I can't stand this any longer: the feeling of being so helpless and defenceless, knowing I'm the main reason the people I love are going through this nightmare and there's nothing I can do about it.

Yeah, okay, Owen kinda already got himself into this situation with Benny, but if I didn't know him or hadn't fallen in love with him, there's a high possibility that none of us would be here. Benny's interest would have remained with Owen and making his dirty money. A lot of issues have come to light the last hour or so, that's for sure.

The man I've thought is my father for so long, the man I always find myself seeking approval from, is nothing but a careless monster, who will stop at nothing to get what he wants—regardless of the consequences or who he may hurt in the end.

Finding out he's not my biological father was the best news I, my mum and even this family I now call my own could have received. It will make bringing him down so much more enjoyable and pain free, and it will happen—whether it's me who does it, Saxon's unknown plan or someone else, it doesn't matter. Benny is going down tonight, and there is nothing he or his many goons in black can do about it.

Now, I just need to form my own plan silently in my head whilst everyone's attention and focus is on Owen and Isaak as they walk inside the cage. The high pitch squeal of the gate sealing shut and the thud of my heavy beating heart will forever haunt me, but I need find my strength from somewhere.

Saxon's words of wisdom ring in my ear, on repeat, rattling my brain as if Sax is saying them over and over again to me.

"You need to be the strong one and keep them safe..."

I snap my head in the direction of Remme, Charlotte and my beautiful nephew Logan, blinking slowly and eventually lifting my heavy eyelids. They shield and protect each other the best they can but they're who I need to be strong for.

I cast my eyes upon the ring just as Isaak lands a sweet jab to Owen's jaw. That's where I find my strength: in Owen, the love of my life and in my big, unapologetic brother Isaak.

The room erupts with cheers and boos as they take in the action from the cage.

Off in the far corner, I can see everyone making their final bets on who'll win the fight, the whole time Benny's slimy, smug face beams for the whole world and his dog to see.

I look back over to the intimidating circle. Isaak and Owen both have seen better days. From what I can make out through all the chaos, there's blood covering the tape wrapped around their hands and blood marking their faces. I don't know if its actual cuts or just transferred from the tape, but seeing the punches Isaak is delivering to Owen, and the hard high, through-the-air kicks Owen is landing on Isaak, I'd go with the former.

Lucky for me, I've missed most of what has happened. They're hurting one another so cruelly and mercilessly, and it has got to be tearing them to shreds on the inside. God knows what Remme is going through watching all this in her shocked and hormonal state.

"Don't worry. They're both going to be okay." I quietly mouth the encouraging words her way, following them up with a tight smile in the hopes it will ease some of the stress and agony she is facing. She only nods her head timidly at me.

At least she's understood what I've said.

I go to take a step towards Benny when Kyle roughly grabs me from behind by my hair, forcing me to the ground.

"Not so fast, bitch. Where the fuck do you think you're going?" he grunts at me.

My hip hits the concrete causing me to hiss in pain, but I quickly cover it up, not wanting to give Kyle any satisfaction from his actions. I sit myself up and cradle my side discreetly. "I just wanted to talk to Benny, that's all," I eventually say through gritted teeth. I'm really starting to dislike this man—more than Benny, and that's fucking saying something.

"Not a chance." He laughs and walks off to the side again to resume his position from which he guards us.

I eventually see an opening to communicate with Benny, so I go for it. Fuck the consequence.

"Why are you doing this, Benny?" I find myself asking before I can stop the words from slipping out.

He turns on the balls of his feet, slowly and precisely until he is facing me. I'm still on the floor and he stands above me, something I bet he's loving—probably getting a cheap thrill from it as well.

God, he is a complete stranger, and he makes me sick to the stomach.

"To get the things you want in life, Devon, you need to be ruthless," He states simply.

"Haven't you already taken enough? You're ruining lives in order to make yours... What, Benny? You think money can buy you everything in life, but with every penny you make, you're losing the people around you. Soon enough, you'll have no one left. Is that what you want?" I don't know why I care enough to ask him this, and a part of me knows he doesn't really care what he gives up as long as he gets his money.

"I've been losing things all my life, Devon. Always been second best. Well, not anymore. After this fight, I'll have more money than I will ever need." He shrugs like that answers everything.

"Money can't buy you happiness, Benny," I state truthfully.

"Maybe not, but happiness isn't what I'm looking for." With that, he turns his back on me and slides up close and personal with Kyle who's standing on my right, always on guard.

"Keep them quiet Kyle, by any means necessary. I don't want them drawing attention away from the main event now, do I," I hear Benny order before they both laugh calculatedly.

I don't know what's gotten into me, but now I've started, I can't seem to control my inner thoughts or questions. Me being me, I've never been able to stop when I get ahead of myself. I just have to open my mouth and continue baiting the beasts.

"Benny is making all the money, but what do you get out of this little arrangement, Kyle? Besides being Benny's dog body and star pupil."

"That's none of your business. If you don't want that pretty little face of yours getting more improvements, I suggest you stop while you're ahead," he states as he gets closer to me.

I can hear Remme and Charlotte asking me what I'm doing. Have I gone mad?

Fuck, I guess you could say I have. Clearly, I don't know what's good for me anymore as I decide to poke the already angry bear's back.

"Oh, I get it. You please the boss and he gives you rewards for such good behaviour. No judgement here, Kyle."

I know I've hit a nerve when Kyle swings his body around to face me and his evil glare locks with mine.

"What the fuck you just say?" he spits as he strides with purpose over to me. When he reaches me, he bends at the waist and gets up close and personal with my face. "I dare you to repeat it, now." His breath coats my skin as the menace in his voice hits my ears, causing me to recoil.

You may think this gets me to keep my mouth firmly shut, but it doesn't.

I like the fact I've gotten under his skin—that he's not the one fully in control—and for that short-lived, split second, I feel good about myself, like I am achieving something.

I don't know what that is, especially under the circumstances, but I smile wide and bright up at him.

I feel the sting on my cheek and upper lip as my neck whips to the side, followed by my body landing flat against the cold grimy ground. I'm in shock, and it's the only reaction I have as I lie cradling the side of my face. I didn't see it coming but I sure as shit felt it. When I remove my hand, there's blood in my palm. I wipe my lip again with the back of my hand and sure enough, that's where it's coming from. The prick has split my lip open.

I hear the sound of someone scuffling next to me, catching a glance of Charlotte through the strands of my hair that have fallen loose from their confinements.

She tries to come over to check on me, but she's swiftly and roughly pushed back to her position by the wall. She lets out a whimper of pain as her body, too, gets slammed to the ground. Jason comes into view with a fire in his eyes and anger in his features.

"Not another step, hero." Kyle's smarmy voice curdles my blood.

Jason does as he's instructed, perhaps he knows it would be better for everyone's sake to not piss Kyle off anymore than he already is, but the look on Jason's face tells me all he wants to do is kill the bastard standing in his way right now.

"Keep your fucking hands to yourself, then we won't have a problem." Jase fires back at Kyle.

Remme sensibly just looks on at us with sadness in her eyes, not knowing what to do whilst she continues to shield Logan from it all. The look I give her tells her to stay put and stay safe. She gets on the floor next to Charlotte.

Whilst Kyle seems more interested in Jase than with me, I scurry over to where the girls are sitting on the floor. Logan reaches his arms out to me and leans across the short gap between us. I put my hands out for him when Kyle takes a few steps away from where we are being huddled.

The crowd starts to boo and hiss, dragging my attention from the altercation between Jason and Kyle to the cage, but for the life of me I can't see what's going on from my position down here. So instead, I cuddle Logan into me and send up a silent prayer that both my brother and boyfriend are okay. I think staying down here out of sight may be best, none of us actually want to watch our loved ones beat the shit out of each other.

Something is happening over there that's for sure.

The warehouse erupts into chaos, and whatever it is, doesn't sit well with Benny.

For the first time in my twenty-two years of living, he looks scared. The well put together Benny looks around, seemingly unsure of himself and completely uncomfortable. That is, until he spots me watching him.

He marches my way with purpose, leaving me fearing for my life and the life of the little boy who I hold dear in my arms.

I vow right here that I will protect this little man with everything I have. I keep him tight to my chest, prepared to give my life before they touch a single hair on his head.

That is a promise I will not be breaking.

CHAPTER 40
OWEN

I've lost count of how many rounds I've gone with Isaak. By the way he's looking at me, I know he's had just about enough of this. *Fucking ditto.*

I thought I had it bad from my fight with Alex, but this is worse. Isaak most definitely hasn't held back with his punches. Then again, I've not been holding them back myself—not because I intentionally want to cause Isaak damage, or win the damn fight like Benny wants me to. I'm putting it down to the fact that all my built-up rage and frustrations have finally found a release. I've obviously needed to let it out, and unfortunately, Isaak is in the firing line. It's like Benny has planned it this way, knowing how we would react.

I've apologised so many times to Isaak after landing a jab to his face or ribs, anywhere. The first couple of punches I threw, I did so blind because I had to close my eyes, just so I didn't see my brother standing in front of me.

My right eye has finally given up on me. It's swelling up from the countless times Isaak has clipped it. Each pounding jab he's landed on it, has made the split grow so now it's completely closed on me and the blood just keeps leaking from the wound. It leaves me totally defenceless on my right side having no vision. On top of that, I'm sporting a busted lip on both sides.

As for Isaak, he clutches his left rib, trying to make it go unnoticed to anyone that he's suffering, but I see it. The fact I felt his rib crack as my foot impaled in his side, I know it's broken.

Isaak is a trained boxer that's something no one can ever take away from him. What he doesn't know, is that for the last nine years I've been locked in this cage and left to learn how to defend myself in more creative ways. I don't just use my fists: I've learnt to fight dirty along the way, not by choice but for survival. I've learnt to use my feet, legs, elbows, knees and know where to aim to inflict maximum discomfort.

The fact this has shocked Isaak hasn't go unnoticed, but it is the crippling hurt on his face that has broken me. I see what he sees: the fact I've lied to him about something else. Being able to fight this way wasn't a choice, it was what I needed to do in order to get through every single fight Benny had me taking part in. There is undeniable hurt and mistrust in his expression. Let's just say I am more determined to get my revenge on Benny for causing all this in the first place.

This is the turning point in the fight between us, this is the point we both know we were taking our every frustration out on one another, no longer holding back any punches or any kicks.

For the people watching, they are getting exactly what they came for: a good old fashioned fight between two decent, yet completely different fighters. One disciplined; one unhinged—both putting on a show nevertheless.

Our expressions mirror each other's. He's in as much pain as me. He can't deny the beast created in himself from being here has done to him— that it's here for all to see and it's me who's caused it all. He doesn't want to do this just as much as I don't, but knowing we have no choice in the matter, we're getting the job done the only way we know how.

The pain in my chest at what I'm having to do outweighs any of the physical pain inflicted on me. I deserve everything Isaak is giving me and more. If it weren't for the choices I've made in life, we wouldn't be here now, and the girls would certainly be safe instead of shaking with fear at what could potentially go wrong.

Like it could get any worse than it already is.

No matter how much I try to fight my inner demons, it won't change the outcome: I'd still find myself where I am because I would do every single fight again if it meant Isaak had the life he has.

All that matters now is finding a way to get this over with and get the people that matter to me most home and safe.

My muscles ache and no doubt have already started to bruise, turning black and blue like a damn road map. I can feel the burn in my arms and legs more than I've ever felt before, and the fact Isaak is sweating buckets just as much as me, tells me I'm pushing him further than he's ever gone before—more than either of us have needed to. We've both dug deep for this fight.

This is the one fight I never thought I would find myself in, yet here I am.

All of a sudden, the feeling of anger turns to a split second of panic, like I'm having some kind of out of body experience. It's unexplainable, and I don't know why or how, but something deep inside of me is telling me that it has everything to do with Devon—like she's in some kind of trouble and needs help desperately.

Acting on that feeling alone, and the fact Isaak is giving me a breather, I glance in the direction I know the girls were placed when they entered the main warehouse.

What I witness makes me murderous. It lights a fire in my blood, and I let it fucking burn. I let it burn through my veins and take over my entire body as my rage becomes uncontrollable.

Kyle lays his hands on Devon, and no one stops him. Devon scurries away as Jason makes a move towards her, but there're two other guys standing guard with Kyle meaning there's no way Jason can take them down easily without causing people to notice.

I'm shaking, not with fear but with an undeniable violent anger that is surging through me. My fists clench at my sides, so tight that my nails dig into the palms of my hand.

Isaak must sense my unease and follows my line of view. Whether he sees what I've seen, I don't know, but he's at my side in seconds.

"Owen... What do you wanna do? If you want to stop this, then I'm with you, but now may be the only chance you get." Isaak's voice breaks through the clouds of my thoughts.

I quickly take everything in, from the endless crowd of blurred, obscured faces and black suits outside of the cage to the location of every person who means something to me in this God forsaken warehouse.

Benny and his friends look over at us, no doubt wondering why we have stopped the show. One particularly pissed-off-looking, but smartly dressed city slicker turns to Benny, mouthing what seemed to be angry obscenities from my vantage point.

Not that I actually give a fuck.

Benny deserves everything he gets and a whole lot more. I don't give a shit who gives it to him as long as someone does.

I turn back to Isaak, ready to give the okay, when the plan Saxon has devised with the police hits me square in the eyes. If I fuck their plan up, Benny could walk away with clean hands. I can't watch him getting off scot free, not now. We've come too far.

Spinning around, I find Saxon. To anyone else, the fucker looks crazy right now talking to himself, but I know different. He slightly narrows his eyes and gives me a stern nod of his head, letting me know I have the okay to get my family back. I go to give Isaak the okay, too, but he's no longer by my side.

"The cage door is locked, and they won't open it."

I turn towards Isaaks voice. "We're gonna have to go over." I shout, already placing the toe of my shoe in the small holes of the cages fencing. Isaak is hot on my heels, and only a second after me, his feet hit the concrete on the outside of the locked cage.

Two heavy, booted shoes come into our view. We both look up from where we've landed in sync as they stop directly in front of us.

Standing tall with fists clenched tight and knuckles turning white, we prepare ourselves to fight through the long line of bodies currently in our way to getting to the girls. Isaak only has to look at me for the message to get across. I know exactly what he wants me to do. We'd done it plenty of times when we were younger out on the town.

I go to step forwards, making the goon think it's me he has to be worried about, watching on as Isaak's fist connects with the man's jaw so hard he's knocked clean to the ground without any more issues.

Looking back towards Benny, I catch him barging past everyone as he tries to make his escape, but when he turns in the opposite direction from one of the fire exits and journeys towards Devon and the others, fear licks its way up my spine. I have a disturbing feeling something is about to transpire, but I have no clue what and so can't stop it from happening. All I can do is get over to them and do my best to contain whatever occurs.

"Oi, where the fuck do you think you're going? I've got forty-five grand down on you. Get back in that cage and finish what was started," some prick says to Isaak as he tries to push him back towards the now open cage door.

Isaak loses it with him. "Finish this, dickhead."

The guy hits the ground from a single jab delivered by Isaak. I try to pull Isaak free from the man as he continues to rain punches down on his face. Just as I pull him back and we start moving again, a fist skims past my face and a jittery looking wannabe gulps hard. My focus now on him, he tries his luck again, actually landing a pathetic jab to my nose, catching me off guard. I notice a fight or flight expression taking over his features and it's all I need to snap back into action, flattening the guy to the ground, my fist pounding into his face. Only when I'm sure he won't be getting up any time soon do I stop.

Taking a look around me, I see the rest of Benny's men have taken a step back—smart men—leaving the two beaten on the ground.

"You may wanna have a think about the man you're backing, as he's ripping you all off." The look of confusion on every person's face is laughable, and if I weren't so worried about Dev, the girls and Logan I'd be hysterical. "The fight was rigged from the start. Benny knew you would all put heavy money down on a professional boxer to win. Benny, however, was backing me—the guy you'd think never stood a chance against the pro, no matter how much I've already fought for Benny." I'm breathing heavily and I just want to get to my girl. I don't know why I never thought about any of this when I first walked in here. I guess when you think back on events there are things you always wish you had said or done. This is one of them moments for me. I shake my head at their blindness to the stunt that Benny almost pulled off.

"Now if you don't mind, we have more important things we need to deal with," Isaak adds for good measure.

Thankfully, one by one, the bodies start to clear, making a path for us to walk through.

Looks like they've made their minds up.

As we get to a clearing, I search for Devon but am distracted by a high-pitched scream above the din of the room, and following the endless ringing in my car, I find who the scream belongs to.

Remme...

CHAPTER 41
DEVON

"Please, Benny. You don't need to do this," Isaak pleads. Benny is using not only me as a human shield but Logan, too. My vision is blurred by tears and I can't fully see the whole situation, but when I feel the cold, hard edge of something on the back of my head, I cry harder, clinging onto Logan tighter. I can't even pass Remme her son back if I want to. She's not within reach to grab him off me, and the thought of just letting him go terrifies me in case he gets caught in the middle of something.

"Come any closer and I'll shoot. That goes for you too, Owen."

That confirms everything for me: I have a gun pressed to my head, a small child embraced in my arms and no way of getting loose of Benny's unyielding grasp.

"You don't wanna do this, Benny. She's your daughter, maybe not by blood but you bought her up as your own. You made her the woman she is today." Owen tries to reason with him, but if anything, it riles him up more.

"You really think I'm that stupid? I've known a lot longer than you have that she was my overachieving brother's flesh and blood. I've just been playing along. Your right though, I have been bringing her up as mine but the older she got the more like my brother she got. I hated it, I hated her." Benny snarls back at them as he presses the barrel of the gun into my head again.

I'm not going to lie, hearing Benny say all that about me stung, but I try my best not to make a noise, partly in case I turn Benny's attention and anger towards me, but mainly because of the fact I've got Logan, who's starting to become unsettled. He doesn't understand why he can see his daddy, why he is holding his arms for him but he's not coming to get him.

Isaak sees the attention that Logan wants from him, and the helplessness radiating off him causes my heart to shatter in tiny little fragments. I turn Logan's head into my chest and try to comfort him the best I can under Benny's hold so Isaak doesn't have to watch the tears rolling down his son's face any longer.

"Do you realise what you've done? The pair of you have ruined everything. Tonight, I was finally going to have my millions. What you see here, this was only the beginning. I was scaling up. Instead of having one underground fight club, I would have had dozens all over the country— possibly even America."

I watch in shock, mirroring Isaak and Owen who are standing frozen with just as much surprise on their faces as me. Benny had plans none of us had even taken into consideration.

"I guess I can kiss goodbye to that happening any time soon. Thanks to you two." He removes the gun from my head and points in their direction, flicking it between them. The arm he has around me grips me tighter.

"Just let Devon and my boy go; we can talk about it then, yeah?" Isaak pleads again, taking a step towards us.

"Don't take another step. Stop trying to play the hero, Isaak. You really are your father's son. He wanted to be the hero; look where that got him." Benny's sadistic laugh fills my ears.

"What's that supposed to mean?" Isaak questions, taken back by what Benny has just insinuated.

"Gavin was getting too involved in Sandra's life again, getting too close to her, and when I found out he was backing out of his side of the deal, well,

I snapped. I couldn't let him tell the police what I was up to. He had to go. It was around the time your mother found out she was pregnant with Devon. At first, I thought my luck had finally begun to change, but then I started working out dates and the change in Gavin. It was all making sense. They had a plan to send me away and run off together, so I did the only thing I knew would work: I eliminated the threat. I had to get the timing just right so I didn't rouse suspicion but it was worth it in the end even if I did have to wait years to get it," Benny admits.

It's like he knows he's running on borrowed time so he's getting one last 'fuck you' out there.

"So you're telling me you had my father murdered just so my mother wouldn't leave you and you could carry on with this charade?" Isaak roars from deep within his chest. This is breaking me as much as it's him, the only difference is, I never knew our father; he did.

"Yeah, pretty much. In my line of work, you have to make tough choices. Your father wouldn't stop, he was persistent. He would have found a way to take me down and take everyone away from me. I couldn't let that happen. So, I waited, and I waited, finally getting rid of him altogether." Benny shrugs it off, like it's nothing.

Pushing my hair out of the way, I get a full glimpse at the sight in front of me. Owen is completely gutted by the situation; Isaak... He looks like he's getting ready to commit murder himself.

"You fucking bastard. You took everything from me. First you take my mother from me when I was just a fucking child, then you take my father from me, for your own selfish reasons. Then you mess my brother's life up for the best part of nine years all because you couldn't get your own way."

Benny hasn't noticed Isaak moving towards us, with every declaration that's unfolding, he's looking in all different directions. Benny is clearly distracted. Either that, or he's gotten so used to having other people doing his dirty work for him. The fact we've got an audience now doesn't escape Benny's attention, though, as Isaak carries on.

"As if that wasn't enough, you kept the fact that Devon was my sister from me. You stole not only my childhood, but Devon's and Owen's, too." Isaak clarifies to everyone in the warehouse just what Benny is really capable of and what he takes from people without a care in the world.

His deep voice echoes off the walls. "I really fucking hope you get what's coming to you. You deserve nothing but to rot in your own filth for all the pain you've caused my family alone," Isaak grits out with a tight-lipped snarl.

"I couldn't care less what you think of me, Isaak. As for you, Owen. You owe me a lot of money after the stunt you've pulled tonight." He aims the gun at Owen now, giving me a little wiggle room.

"I owe you Jack shit, Benny. If anything, you owe me. I stopped taking money from my fights along fucking time ago," Owen spits at Benny.

"You... You… The pair of you have ruined me. This will not be the last you hear of me. I'll get my own back, just wait and see. You'll be looking over your shoulders for the rest of your miserable lives," Benny tells them, clearly irritated by the whole thing. "What's the matter, neither of you have anything else to say?" Benny's words don't come out quite as confidently as he usually sounds, and his uneasiness is making me nervous.

Movement at my side catches my attention. My eyes land on Saxon. He appears to be talking to someone in the shadows, but I can't see who it is. He must also grab the attention of Isaak and Owen, unbeknown to Benny. He gives them a stern nod of his head, like they know something I don't. He then shocks me even more as he reaches behind his back and pulls a gun out in front of him, flips the safety off and points it up in the air.

For a split second, I wonder how the fuck he managed to get his hands on a gun, but I suppose there's still a lot I don't know about Saxon.

I don't miss the brief exchange between Owen and Isaak, words are said, but I can't work them out. Isaak takes Owen's matching blood-stained hand in his and grips it tight.

Whatever is happening, happens quickly, and I have a suspicious feeling this is the moment Saxon was preparing me for. His words 'when you need to know, you will,' ring loud and clear in my mind.

Benny must sense a change in the atmosphere because his hands start to shake as he continuously moves the gun from me, to Owen then on to Isaak.

For the longest time no body says anything.

Within a matter of seconds, all hell breaks loose, then the echo of a gunshot rings true through the air, bouncing off the concrete walls and eventually hitting my ears.

The fire exit doors belonging to the warehouse are swung open. We're bombarded with more people as police take charge, everyone ducking and diving out the way, not knowing who fired the gun or where it came from. Everyone runs around in different directions, making their own demands. There are policemen in black vests heading towards us—I hope they're on our side and not Benny's payroll. After everything he's declared tonight, having police in his pocket wouldn't surprise me in the slightest.

Saxon's and Jason's fast-paced reactions kick in beside me, doing what they're good at, starting with the two guys that were helping Kyle out.

God, I hope Remme and Charlotte are alright.

"Looks like you're not leaving this building unless it's in a pair of handcuffs, Uncle Benny," Isaak shouts across at us, a small smirk in place.

"If that's the case, then you won't be making it out of here at all," Benny counterpunches. His grip on me loosens slightly, giving me enough room to squeeze free. My feet hit the ground, the blood not quite reaching my toes, and on shaky legs I grip hold of Logan and run the best I can over to where Saxon is with the girls.

No sooner have I reunited my crying nephew with his nervous wreck of a mother, does another two rounds of shots get fired.

I whip my body around in the direction I've come from. All I see is Isaak's heavy body hitting the ground with an almighty, defendant thud.

He's not moving.

He doesn't try to get up.

He's built like a brick shit house, why is he not getting up?

Tears fall freely down my cheeks as I take in the scene before me, Remme's deafening, endless screams of horror and Owen bolting off towards Benny.

I can't take my eyes off Isaak, my brother, as he lies there lifeless, a puddle of crimson drowning him.

I send a pray to the guy upstairs, asking him not to take my brother away from me. Away from his family.

For once I hope he heard me.

CHAPTER 42
SAXON

I knew walking into the warehouse with this plan was a long shot and no doubt risky. Then having to deviate from the original plan didn't help the matter. I saw the flaws in both, but didn't have the heart to tell Isaak or Owen. But these people who I've gotten close to, who have become more like family than just a close circle of friends, needed my help. I was willing to try anything.

When all their lives were at stake at the hand of a greedy and somewhat disturbed human being who would shoot his own nephew, I knew it was up to me to keep them all safe and get them out of this nightmare in one piece and alive.

Isaak getting shot was never part of my plan. It wasn't part of any plan. Seeing his lifeless body lying there breaks something in me, but as much as it hurts to see, I still have a job to finish and I have to stay as calm as possible. I have to not look at this as my family now, but as the job. I have to shut off and deal with my emotions later when this is over.

There will be no more blood spilled under my watchful eye that's for sure. The police are all over the shop arresting people left, right and centre.

Remme's continuous outraged screams of dread and sorrow ringing loud and clear; Logan's earth-shattering crying; Devon's tear-streaked face; and Charlotte's completely shaken up body, dithering in my arms are more than I can take, but are enough to push me back into action.

"Jase, help me get the girls out front out of harm's way." I rush out. I know the girls won't be the polices first priority, not in this type of situation. So that's why I take it upon myself to get them all to safety.

He nods and follows my instructions, peeling Charlotte out of my arms and passing her over to a police officer who chooses that moment to help.

She starts to panic.

"Charlotte, look at me."

She does, instantly.

"I promise you will be safe, but we need to get moving, okay?"

One look and a couple of words from me, she goes with a little more ease. When I know the police officer is almost out of the warehouse safely, I make a dive for Devon, just in time to stop her from going after Owen.

The dumb fucker is going after Benny, isn't he.

"Devon, I need to get you out of here."

She attempts to hit my arm, trying to break free of my hold, shouting about how she needs to help Owen. It's in vain as Jason lends a hand, practically dragging her out over his shoulder, kicking and screaming.

Last are Remme and Logan. The look of pure devastation and the total loss in her eyes is soul destroying—one I will never forget. No matter how much good I do in the world, it will never make up for what I let happen tonight.

Leaving Isaak behind as the paramedics poke and prod at him, trying with everything to resuscitate him, is going to be painful for her, but she needs to do it—for herself and for her son.

"Remme, I'm just going to take Logan from your arms, but I promise he won't leave my side."

She whips her head and locks eyes with me, panicked at the loss of her son's touch.

"Look, he's here—he's safe in my arms—but he'll be safer if we can get him out of there. Can you help me do that?"

She doesn't say anything, but I can see her contemplating what to do for the best. I know she doesn't want to leave Isaak by himself, but somehow, she knows that getting herself and Logan out safe is what Isaak would want.

"I don't think I can leave him behind on his own, Saxon. What if he's asking for me?"

I don't have the heart to tell her that I doubt he's asking for anything, but right at that moment, the paramedics start dragging his body on to a stretcher and out of the warehouse. I take that as a sign to get her moving, even if it means I have to lie to her—something else I will never forgive myself for.

Only when she sees he's being moved out does she nod for me.

That's all I need. I grab her under the arm and lift her, securing her tightly in my arm as I do the same with Logan, tucking his head into my chest. I manage to get them outside where the ambulances, police cars and raid vans are all scattered around. Blue and red lights flash blindingly, lighting up the sky like Blackpool Illuminations.

For the first time since walking into the warehouse tonight, I really take in my surroundings—not like I'm surveying the place or scoping the place out, but really taking everything in. The area is in chaos. Not one person is standing around doing nothing. Everyone is doing what they should be.

I pass Logan over to Charlotte as Devon is being attended to in the back of an ambulance.

"Remme, you go with Isaak," I call over the hustle and bustle just as I see them loading Isaak's stretcher into the back. She goes to take Logan from Charl, but that's the last place any child should be.

"Logan will be safe with Charlotte and Devon, I promise. You need to focus on Isaak. Now go before they leave without you."

I call Jase over from talking to a police officer. "Make sure Remme gets in the back of that ambulance with Isaak."

He nods and takes Remme by the arm, leading her to the van. They make it there just in time before the doors slam shut.

"Is he...going to be..." Devon stutters as she makes herself known. God bless her soul, she can't even comprehend what has just happened.

"I'm not going to lie. From what I've seen and the amount of blood he's lost, it's... It's not looking good. You might wanna start preparing yourselves for the worst. Take care of Logan for Remme."

With that, I walk away, not liking the way they're looking at me. I can't cope with the fact it's me that's causing them more pain, but I can't keep up the pretence. It will only hurt more in the end the longer I try to sugar-coat it—myself included.

I over hear on a near by cops radio that they can't find the suspect, another replies that they haven't found the informant that went after him either. That makes up my mind, I set off looking for Owen in the madness that's still going on inside the building. Most of the guys in suits have either been arrested or managed to slip away. I see some of Benny's men getting cuffed, but I can't see Kyle or the other two goons around anywhere, which doesn't sit right with me.

Where the fuck is Owen?

I rush down dark smelling corridors looking and listening as I stick my head in each room I pass. I find myself in another huge room its windows at the far end of the room letting the only light into it.

I just so happen to see movement in the shadows over by one of the fire exits. Off in a dark corner is scuffling and moans of pain. I head in that direction with caution, not to startle whoever it is. As I approach, I hear a voice that is filled with so much venom and disgust that it can only be one person.

Owen...

"You mother fucker!" Owen's voice bellows, followed by more groans of pain. "You've killed him!"

The sound of bone crunching hits my ears, but he doesn't stop.

"You selfish bastard. This is all your fault. I never should have made that deal with you."

I'm now within reach and can see Owen has Benny underneath him, raining down punch after punch on the evil prick's face, but if I let Owen carry on, he will kill him. That's the last thing I want, and I know for a fact Isaak wouldn't want him going to prison for murder.

"Owen, you need to stop." I voice my opinion softly but precisely. I don't recognise the man looking back at me. His eyes are completely black, and he's got more blood on him than he did when he was in the cage with Isaak. I don't even know if he's seeing me.

"Mate, if you carry on, you will kill him." I motion down at Benny's limp body. He's still with it, but he's taken one hell of a beating from Owen. I need Owen to see sense. I know what I say next will snap him out of it. "Do you think Isaak will want this—for you to go down like this? Because I don't. In fact, I'm almost certain he would want you to take care of his wife and children."

Something in him changes instantly. The dark cloud in his eyes softens, and he looks down at his hands and Benny a few times before jumping back up to his feet.

Just as he does, a police officer I've seen on jobs before approaches us. He sees the scene unfolding, getting ready to call it in on his radio, but I hold my hand up to stop him and he freezes.

"You didn't see this. You found Benny like this. You hear me?" I order with as much authority as I can muster. Thankfully, he nods his head in understanding.

Jason chooses that moment to show his face again. He takes one look at Owen and then Benny knowing exactly what went down.

"Take Owen outside for a breather; I'll be out in a second."

"Sure thing, Sax." Jase grabs Owen by the elbow and leads him back outside.

I get Benny to his feet and move him to a spot where he can sit down and a paramedic can look over him. His face is a state, but I've seen much worse. He's lucky I found him when I did: any longer under the assault of Owen and he wouldn't be awake right now.

"Who are you?" Benny hisses out through the pain of moving his jaw just as Jessica and another police officer join us.

"Benny Brookes, you're under arrest for illegal dealings, fraud and murder. You do not have to say anything, but it may harm your defence if you do not mention when questioned something which you later rely on in court. Anything you do say may be given in evidence," Jessica cautions Benny, who hasn't taken his swollen eyes off me.

When he doesn't acknowledge her, or what's been said, she looks at me and then back again.

I just shrug her silent questioning off as I don't know Benny's angle myself.

"You still haven't answered me...Saxon, is it?" he asks, sarcastically.

"The name is Saxon, yeah," I tell him, crossing my arms in front of me.

He squints up at me through his heavy eyes. "The bodyguard, right?"

"Yes, among other things. Why are you so interested in me, Benny? It's not like it'll make a difference now."

Benny wipes some blood that's leaking from a wound behind his head, "Just humour me."

"Not that it's any of your business what I do for a living, but as you can tell I'm more than just a bodyguard. I'm the best at what I do, but more importantly than that, I'm one of Isaak's oldest friends, and you've just made it to the very top of my list of enemies, Benny." I grit my teeth and tense my jaw, fighting the urge to land a swift uppercut to his already delicate jaw, but I hold back. Maybe that's what he wants.

"You fooled me. Not many people have had the pleasure of doing that. I thought you was a nobody a low rent security for Isaak. I underestimated you." he laughs the best he can under discomfort.

"The pleasure was all mine, believe me." With that I turn and walk away, Jessica following close behind.

She finally catches up to me as Benny throws me some parting words. "You're on my radar now, Saxon. I hope you enjoy playing games as much as me." He laughs, loud and hysterically.

I don't stop and most definitely don't give him the satisfaction of an answer.

"See you soon, my friend," Benny adds as I carry on walking.

Finally getting some much needed air, I exit the warehouse with Jessica by my side.

"Should we be worried by what Benny's just said?" Jessica asks, and I don't miss the concern in her voice.

"I wouldn't worry about it: it was just words. Plus, I can take care of myself," I tell her, giving her some reassurance.

"It's not you I'm worried about."

I don't know where it comes from, but I find myself laughing, and it doesn't take long for Jess to join in.

"Haha, funny. Whilst I have you, can you let the officer watching Sandra at the safe house know she's free to leave now. She also deserves to know about Isaak."

"Of course. I'll get the officer to drive her to the hospital. Listen, I've got another job you might be interested in. After the work you've done with us over the last few weeks, I think you would be suited for it." She stops walking as we reach Charlotte and Devon sitting on the step of an ambulance.

"I still have a lot to sort out after the events of tonight. I'll have to look at things at work to see if I have the time to spare, so I'm sure if I—"

Jessica cuts off my rambling when her hand touches my shoulder.

"I don't mean right away, Sax. Just have a think about what I said and let me know when you're ready. Okay? Just don't take too long." She offers me a small, sweet smile and gets back to business.

Charlotte walks to me, giving me a weird look. "What was that all about?" she asks, glancing back and forth between me and Jess.

"Nothing, just work." I shrug genuinely.

"Hhmm, okay. Anyway, I just wanted to say thank you, for...you know. Back inside the warehouse. I was having some kind of out of body experience and, well, I just wanted to tell you that I appreciate everything you did for me, for everyone."

I turn my head fully in her direction, about to tell her that she doesn't need to say anything, but as I do, the unthinkable happens.

Her lips brush mine. It's brief and messy, and it isn't meant to happen.

"Omg, I'm so sorry. I was just going to kiss your cheek, but then you turned and..." She blushes and drops her eyes to the floor in embarrassment.

If it weren't for the situation we're in, I'd say it was cute and flattering. "Devon and I are heading to the hospital with Logan so they can have a better look at Dev's face. Just thought I'd let you know so you know what's what." She still hasn't looked back up from the ground.

"Thanks for letting me know. I'll get Jase to follow you there with Owen." With a petite nod of her head, she's walking away from me.

What the hell was that all about?

I spot Jase leaning against a metal fence with Owen. Walking over, I don't say a word to Owen. I can't. He looks like he's having an internal battle with himself.

I have a quick conversation with Jase, unbeknown to Owen. I doubt he hears a damn thing I'm saying. I hand Jase my car keys as I still have a ton of shit that needs sorting and I'll have to head to my office at some point tonight to grab the files I have that I forgot to give Jess earlier on, the police will need all the information—like this night couldn't get any fucking worse. Then again, anything beats going to hospital and seeing everyone look at me with disappointment. I don't think I will ever feel better about how this all ended. I was meant to protect these people not let one of them get shot. No amount of thank you's would make me feel any better. Jessica was strict on the fact that they needed solid evidence of a crime that would put him behind bars a long fucking time, only then would they come in unless something else happened before hand.

Isaak put his trust in me, and I failed him.

I feel like I failed them all.

How I'll ever look them in the face the same way again, I'll never know.

I don't think I can. It'll just remind me of the one time I epically failed at my job. I told Benny I was the best at what I do but I'm not sure I am any more. I know doubt is normal after failure like this, I just hope I can bounce back. My livelihood is at risk otherwise.

CHAPTER 43

OWEN

I'm perched up against a metal fence on the cold floor outside the warehouse when Jason comes to sit next to me. He hands me my phone and places my gym bag on the ground in front of us. Apparently, he had to ask the chief inspector if it was okay for me to have it. As it isn't evidence, and I have already given Saxon copies of all the text messages between myself and Benny beforehand, Jessica has decided it's alright to hand them back. I look at my phone blankly, wondering what the fuck I may need it for. Everyone I need to contact is either in the back of an ambulance just outside this building, or already on their way to the hospital.

Jase sits with me in the quiet I've created around myself, letting me work through my own thoughts and feelings.

There's not much to work out. All I feel is numb.

Seeing Isaak laying down like that, was as if he'd given up. The way the girls reacted to it was like they had already given up too.

Do I give up myself?

Isaak is my brother I can't give up on him that easy. If it was the other way around he'd be fighting teeth and nail for me.

I know I should get to the hospital and be there for Isaak and Remme, and Devon too, but I can't seem to move now the adrenaline is gone from the fight and the guns. Isaak is in the best place with best people looking after him. I'd only make matters worse if I showed my face too soon. After all, this is entirely my fault.

This whole night has gone by in a blur, and I'm left with everything that has happened playing on repeat in my mind—from the moment we arrived at Saxon's office to the moment Benny took Devon and little Logan hostage with a gun to their heads. It all runs through my mind at a speed so fast, I barely have a chance to remember any key moments. The memories from when the first shot went off it, however, have all slowed down. As I sit here, I can see every single event that occurred happening again, only this time in slow motion: the way Isaak's shocked and scared eyes locked onto his wife's equally terrified eyes; the high-pitched scream that left the back of Remme's throat; Devon and Charlotte's own cries that were almost a match for Remmes; the rush of people coming from every direction behind us. Then I remember the gurgling sound that came from Isaak as his body thumped to the ground. His head gravitating to the side, the blood oozing from the corner of his mouth as he began to choke, coughing for that much needed air to enter his lungs.

Two gunshot wounds: one in the shoulder and the other in his lower abdominals.

What haunts me the most is the memory of his cold, dying eyes as he stared up at me—full of nothingness.

I was brought to my knees. I'd just sat there, frozen to the spot next to him, not knowing of a single thing to do. I also remember not being sure of anything going on around me apart from the gurgling noise coming from Isaak, the way it demanded my attention. His mouth had been moving like he was trying to say something but was struggling to get any words out.

"What is it Isaak?" I frantically ask.
"Take...care..." He starts to cough and splutter up more blood from

the back of his throat. "Them...me." He suddenly stops and starts to cough again, choking on the thick, red fluid in his mouth. His body convulses, shaking and lifting from the ground.

Then there's nothing.

The silence had been deafening. I vaguely remember looking around in a panic as the paramedics came running towards us, getting up from the ground, shouting in their direction for someone to fucking help him.

For someone to help my brother.

Feeling nothing but an all-consuming rage, there had been only one thing on my mind.

Revenge.

Benny, where the fuck is Benny?

I'd wanted him to feel every bit of pain he had caused not only me, but Isaak and his family and Devon. I can just remember my feet moving of their own accord, taking me in the opposite direction of Isaak.

One step...two steps...

I was in a full sprint.

Everything after that is a blur—only a few flashes of what I was doing coming back to me, which leads me back to where I am now, sitting outside the warehouse, watching the fresh blood dripping from my knuckles in smug satisfaction.

I got a few good digs in for Isaak, but it will never be enough.

"Did it make you feel better?" Jason asks from next to me.

"Damn fucking right it did. I have waited so long to get out from under that man's grasp. It's bittersweet, though. I did it for Isaak, not me."

"You think you broke it?" He raises a brow at me and starts inspecting my hand for damage.

"Maybe. If so, it was fucking worth it," I grunt out. "Do you think he will be okay? Isaak I mean, he didn't look good did he?"

Before Jason gets the answer Saxon rocks up, dangling his keys in front of Jason's face. I can hear the mumble of their voices, but it's all just background noise to me. Only at the mention of Devon's name do my ears perk up.

"Devon and Charlotte are on their way to hospital in an ambulance. Why don't you take Tyson, here, and get him checked out, too?"

Jason chuckles like a girl as he takes the keys from Saxon's grasp.

"Ha-fucking-ha," I mock as I rise up from my perch on the cold concrete.

Leaving Saxon to finish up whatever he needs to, we eventually climb into the car and Jase puts the pedal to the floor.

"This is the worst day of my life," I utter, gazing mindlessly out of the window and more to myself than Jason.

He must take it as a sign that I'm now ready to talk again. "Benny will get what he deserves," he says with a sternness I have never heard from him before.

I don't say anything back. There is no need to because he's right: Benny will get exactly what he deserves.

I flex my hand to stretch it out then ball it back up into a tight fist, loving the pain, knowing that it's from hitting the smug bastard in the face.

Before long, we are pulling up at the hospital at the same time Devon, Charlotte and Logan are being unloaded from the ambulance.

I head straight over to a crying Devon and swaddle her up in my big arms. Her beautiful face is starting to bloom with horrible shades of pink, purple and black.

"I'm sorry, baby. There was nothing I could do to stop it. If I could have taken those bullets instead of him, I would have. I tried to stop all of this from happening," I confess to her truthfully.

"Then I would be crying over you and not my brother. I know you would have died to protect him, Owen, but there was nothing you could have done. This is not your fault."

I know she's right, but it hurts so much. All those years ago, I did what I did to protect Isaak and his career, and it was all for nothing. He's ended up getting catapulted into this life anyway.

I failed my brother.

"Shall we head on inside? I think you all need to be checked out," Jase says from the door of the A&E department.

We get checked in along with Logan and Charlotte and head in further to one of the waiting rooms for out-patients. We're not waiting long when they call Devon's name. I make it known I'm heading in with her and thankfully the nurse agrees to see me at the same time.

"Jason, can you stay with Logan and Charlotte? I don't want her to be on her own right now, and I don't think Logan should be in there," I ask my friend, and once he agrees we head through.

The nurse insists on checking me over first as my injuries were are far worse than Devon's, but at my protest she finally gives in. A few minutes later, Devon is given the all-clear. She has a cut on her lip, but luckily it doesn't need stitches. She has some swelling and bruising on her cheekbone and under her nose, but thankfully no broken bones or damage to her eyes.

As for me, I end up having one eyebrow glued and the other needing twelve stitches. I have a black eye, which is completely shut due to the swelling. It's going to take a few days maybe even weeks for that to go down, but the eye should open up sooner than that. My hands are pretty banged up, too. Once the nurse has cleaned them up, it's clear they're not as bad as they first looked—nothing that won't heal in time—and again, thankfully, I've not damaged the tendons or broken a single bone in either hand.

Forty minutes later, we follow the nurse out of the cubical we are in, and she leads us to the one room I fear the most: the friends and family waiting room.

I walk in behind Dev to find Charlotte and Jase now with Remme. Mother and son now reunited, she cradles her sleeping baby, sniffling into a tissue.

Devon heads straight over to her, and I once again follow behind. I bend down and place a kiss on her head, taking Logan from her reluctant grasp so she can talk and cry as much as she wants.

"Any news?" I ask, not able to wait a second longer.

"He's still in surgery. The doctor said he is in bad shape, Owen—that we may need to prepare ourselves."

My heart sinks to the soles of my feet.

"I can't lose him, Owen. I just can't."

Devon embraces her as she sobs uncontrollably. Charlotte gets out of her seat and runs straight to Remme's.

"He's a fighter, Rem. He will pull through this. I just know he will," I say, trying to give her something to cling to, even if it's false hope. I choose that moment to take a step back with Logan sleeping soundly in my arms and let the girls console each other, using the time to fill Jason in on the details of Devon's wounds as well as my own.

We sit in the room for what feels like hours, and Remme's cries finally subside, as she quite literally cries herself to sleep. One of the nurses kindly wheels in a crib with a blanket, baby food and nappies from the maternity ward so we can change Logan and put him back down to sleep. She also informs us that the media are camped out the hospital having heard the news about Isaak. I guess it was only a matter of time. I will have to call his management team.

Devon curls herself up on my lap and holds me tighter than ever before. I know what she is getting at: I don't want to let her go, either.

I sit in silence, looking from one family member to the next wondering how our lives have come to this. The last time I was in a hospital was when Remme got pushed down the stairs at the gym. It seems to be one bad thing after another. I know my life choices haven't helped in the journey here, but surely we deserve a bit of good news—surely our luck has to turn around for the better at some point.

I'd do just about anything if I knew it would help Isaak survive.

Absolutely anything.

Like I think it will help, I start to silently pray and hope that just one person up there can fucking hear me.

Like my prayers have been answered, the door opens and a tired-looking doctor in scrubs walks in.

Please be good news.

"Mrs Brookes?"

Charlotte gives Remme a tender nudge to wake her. She sits with a startled look, and when she spots the doc, she's on her feet in seconds.

"Would you like to go somewhere a little more private?" the doctor asks her.

Well, that doesn't sound like good news.

Please say no. I can't wait one more painful second.

"No, we're all Isaak's family. They deserve to know just as much as me. You can speak freely. How is my husband?"

EPILOGUE
OWEN

A few months later...

I watch as Devon says her goodbyes to the last of the gym users. They pass her by the door with the keys in her hand ready to lock up for the day. Owning a gym means we sometimes work until late, so all the city workers can stop by to wind down after work. Remmes physio appointments finish at five pm, so they have all left, too. Isaak is more family orientated these days.

After a near death experience and surgery to remove the bullets and stop the bleeding, Isaak chose to leave behind professional boxing—as a fighter anyway. He's retired from the profession and now owns the building next door that we have had attached to the side of the gym with a connecting slide-open door. He teaches self-defence classes there now and sometimes hires out the other large rooms for yoga, zumba and other fitness classes. He still trains in here and does the odd boxing class in the ring, but I think that's just his way of not fully letting go of the second love of his life—second to his wife and two beautiful kids.

Remme gave birth to a healthy baby girl, Gracie-Lou Brookes, making their family complete, for now. They're more in love now than they were at the start of their relationship—if that's even possible.

They both have managers and spend more quality family time together, doing things that families should be doing.

Charlotte still works as Remme's receptionist but has also taken the role of manager for her so she can have more time off work and not worry about anything. It's become a big family affair around here, but I wouldn't have it any other way.

Devon and Isaak have spent time getting to know each other as brother and sister since he's been well enough to. Now they are closer than they were before, only Isaak has taken the role of 'protective brother' a step too far, but I'm eternally grateful they have that close bond with one another.

After such a difficult time for everyone, things are starting to settle down for the better.

Benny's murder trial started a few weeks ago—after so much media attention around this, the trial was pushed back. More evidence was found, witnesses on Benny's end kept changing. It was like Benny was trying to buy himself more time to get out of this untethered and found not guilty. The fact that he has been charged with murder,

kidnapping, illegal underground fighting, possession of a firearm with no licence and the intent to harm, he would be one lucky fucking sod if the judge didn't lower the gavel and sentence him to life without parole. Benny must know it looks bad for him, and so he should. He needs to pay the price for all the misery he's caused people.

If I'd had it my way, and if Saxon hadn't stopped me, I would have killed him where he lay when I had the chance. But then I wouldn't be here now, and I'd be the one behind bars awaiting trail and not Benny.

"Hey, where did you go without me?"

My head snaps up to Dev, who stands directly in front of me, smiling brightly like her world starts and ends with me. My world starts and ends with her, too, and I just can't see that changing anytime soon, if ever. She has changed my life for the better with her presence alone.

"Just thinking, baby." Reaching out for her, I pull her close. She clasps my hands around her back and wraps her arms around my neck like she has so many times before.

Balancing on her tiptoes, she places her soft lips to mine. I moan into her mouth as she presses herself into me.

"If you want this self-defence class to happen, you need to stop rubbing up against me, right now, you little minx." She is so sexy and carefree, and I couldn't love her anymore if I tried. "Come on you." I drag her to the defence mats and we begin our training.

It's not long before we are both sweaty and tired. Devon steps aside to take a breather and I watch a bead of sweat run down her neck over her collar bone, then down her perfect cleavage.

I lick my lips and make my move, almost predatory like.

I grab her waist, lifting her feet slightly off the floor and lay her down with me hovering over her.

"Owen," she giggles. "What are you doing?"

I'm so turned on by her, all I wanna do is sink myself into her.

I pin her arms above her head, securing them with one hand as I bring the other hand down her arm and stroke the side of her neck. "I love you, Devon Brookes," I tell her honestly and truthfully and yeah she did change her name back to her birth name. She wanted to honour Gavin and Isaak by becoming a Brookes again, but I want it to be something else entirely.

"I love you, too, Owen."

I know her words are true. I'm forever hers.

"Marry me, Devon." As proposals go, it's weak and unplanned.

The look of shock on her face is almost too cute. "What did you just say?" Her brows rise in confusion.

I repeat myself clearly so she knows just how serious I am.

"I said, marry me." I throw her a beaming smile.

"Owen, this is not the time for jokes."

Now it's me who's confused. "What makes you think this is a joke? We have been together for a while now, Dev, and we have been through a hell of a lot in that time. We've gained a new family member, we've got your mum from Benny's grasp, we have even uncovered truth and lies. Now it's time for us. You have changed me from my playboy ways, making me a one-woman man, and I couldn't be happier. I never saw you coming. You completely and utterly knocked me sideways. I couldn't imagine my life without you in it, and I don't have to because I'm never letting you go. I love you so much, Devon. I don't have a fancy ring because, well, I didn't expect to be doing this, but I will ask one last time. Will you marry me? Will you become my wife forever and always?"

THE END...

SAXON'S STORY COMING SOON.

OWEN'S PLAYLIST

Genuine – Pony

Another Level – Freak me

Omarion – Oh

Mario - Let Me Love You

Usher – Burn

Usher – Got It Bad

Ellie Goulding – Burn

Usher – Caught up

Christina Aguilera – Fighter

Ja Rule ft Ashanti – Always On Time (Explicit)

One Republic ft Timberland – Apologize

Annie-Marie – Birthday (Explicit)

N-Dubz ft Mr Hudson – Playing With Fire

N-Dubz – No Regrets

Kygo – Freedom

ABOUT THE AUTHOR

K J Ellis was born in Staffordshire, Stoke-On-Trent in the UK.

She's twenty-nine years old and lives with her partner of fifteen years, Adam, and their four year old son, Logy Bear.

She's a bubbly, out-going person who's always up for a laugh.

She is an avid reader and loves a good MC or Mafia book.

Besides the love for her family, she has an obscenely and pretty unhealthy addiction to Nike trainers—so much so, she has a wardrobe just for shoes.

She asks you not to judge her.

(Doesn't help matters that she works in a shoe shop.)

She entered the book world around six years ago as a reader, then had a hand in swag making and blogging for authors before having the courage to write a book herself.

Seeing the love that the book community has to offer only pushed her more, prompting her to finally release her debut book, Isaak, in the world for you all to read.

OTHER BOOKS KJ

Isaak
The Counterpunch Series (Book 1)

Mr And Mrs Brookes
A Counterpunch Novella (Book 1.5)

Love Ever after
A Dandelion Anthology

COMING SOON

Saxon
The Counterpunch Series (Book 3)

Jason
The Counterpunch Series (Book 4)

No Matter The Weather
(Standalone)

AUTHOR'S SOCIAL LINKS

Author Group
facebook.com/groups/299056614378189/

Amazon
amazon.co.uk/K-J-Ellis/e/B08LDR91XY

Author page
facebook.com/KJ-Ellis-Author-104813721422926/

Goodreads
goodreads.com/authorkjellis

Instagram
instagram.com/kjellisauthor

Printed in Great Britain
by Amazon

76601574R00160